Borland's Sorrow

Also by Philip A. Fortnam

Walking Greenbush

Borland's Sorrow

Philip A. Fortnam

BORLAND'S SORROW

iUniverse books may be ordered through booksellers or by contacting:

iUniverse
1663 Liberty Drive
Bloomington, IN 47403
www.iuniverse.com
1-800-Authors (1-800-288-4677)

Because of the dynamic nature of the Internet, any web addresses or links contained in this book may have changed since publication and may no longer be valid. The views expressed in this work are solely those of the author and do not necessarily reflect the views of the publisher, and the publisher hereby disclaims any responsibility for them.

Any people depicted in stock imagery provided by Thinkstock are models, and such images are being used for illustrative purposes only. Certain stock imagery © Thinkstock.

ISBN: 978-1-5320-0663-0 (sc)
ISBN: 978-1-5320-0662-3 (e)

Library of Congress Control Number: 2016918739

Print information available on the last page.

iUniverse rev. date: 12/19/2016

For Annie

Love does not consist in gazing at each other,
but in looking outward together in the same direction.

—Antoine de Saint-Exupéry

Contents

Duty
2003–5

Love
2009–10

Home
October 2010

Acknowledgments

This novel would not be much of a story without the help of many people, in particular Sergeant First Class Marc Harris, who served with the 1058th Transportation Unit of the Massachusetts National Guard. SFC Harris met with me, provided information about the unit, put me in touch with members of the ten-five-eight, and patiently responded to all my pesky e-mails requesting information.

Also very much appreciated is Sergeant Kate Cross, also a member of the 1058th, who took time to meet with me and reply to my e-mails with a wealth of information about her role with the unit.

Thanks also to Staff Sergeant Paul Cross, Master Sergeant Jim Smith, and First Sergeant Bill Chiano, all of whom are current or former members of the 1058th, for letting me interview them and for providing detail about their experiences with the unit as both drilling Guardsmen and members of the unit who deployed to Iraq in 2003 with the 1058th.

The characters in this book are not based on the experience of any particular member or members of the 1058th, but these soldiers talked with me about their experiences, providing me with details that I wrapped around the main character.

I am also indebted to Kelli Ramirez and Romy Nelson, coworkers of mine at the Central Arizona Project; June Lopez, teacher at Mountain View Elementary School, Phoenix; Chi Duong, DO; Colonel (and brother-in-law) Vincent Torza, USA; MCC Elisandro (Alex) Diaz, US Navy Reserve Component Combat Camera Group Pacific, who let me interview him about his experience in Baghdad; Sergeant Carol Munoz, Arizona Army National Guard; Glenn Emmanuel at Central Arizona Project, for his GIS skills; Rick Kaneen, for his in-depth knowledge about World War I; retired Massachusetts National Guard

Brigadier General, and Director of Massachusetts National Guard Museum, Leonid Kondratiuk; Benjamin Hernandez, emergency department paramedic, Paradise Valley Hospital, for explaining the immediate treatment that would be required for a wound like the one the character Keith sustained; and my brother Michael for photos of Fort Revere.

In addition to the people mentioned above, I offer many thanks to the first readers for their editing, honest feedback, and suggestions: Amy Stirrup, Bill Lax, Dan Fortnam, MCC (Ret.) Jane West, CDR John Ferrari, Norm Bizon, Susan Lanzillo, Suki Edwards, Terri Sue Rossi, Anne Torza, Catherine Sardinha, Dave Skill, Vicky Campo, and Bob Stanton.

October 2010

Deployment × 2
Operation Iraqi Freedom
Camp Arifjan, Kuwait

"How is this deployment different from the 2003 one?" asked Corporal Christine Hamblin as she and Staff Sergeant Keith Morris sat in a Humvee waiting for the convoy leader to roll.

"Well, we're still driving trucks, but what we're hauling is different. You know the 1058th is set up as a light–medium truck company, and that's what we deployed as in 2003. It was crazy. The logistics chain was barely in place, the rules of engagement kept changing, and how we operated was always changing because of the way the enemy worked against us. This time, things are a lot calmer. All the various doctrines and procedures have been established. It's still dangerous and we can't get lax, but overall it's way less chaotic and nowhere near as wild as it was the on the first deployment."

"I still don't understand why we didn't deploy as the ten-five-eight this time."

"The 1058th will still get recognized for the deployment, but the army needed a whole equipment transportation system to haul all the big stuff out of Iraq. So we merged with two other companies, the 1166th and the 1060th, to temporarily create the 1166th Combat HET Company."

"Why aren't we using our flag?"

"We are. And wherever we go, we are the ten-five-eight, but administratively we are operating as the 1166th, because the 1166th was the only Massachusetts Guard transportation company that hasn't had an overseas deployment. Now they will get recognized as having an overseas deployment."

Keith saw the lead vehicle move and simultaneously heard Sergeant First Class Desmond Jarvis's voice crackle on the radio, ordering the convoy to roll.

"Here we go," said Hamblin as she put the vehicle in gear.

"This is most likely our second-to-last mission," said Keith.

"Second to last? I thought this was it," Christine responded.

"Yeah, I thought so too, but as we were finishing inventory and pass-down last night, we discovered we still need to recover the truck that broke down last month near Karbala."

"I thought Smitty handled that."

"So did I, but he didn't. Now that he and just about everyone else in the unit redeployed and are back in Hingham already, it's on us to wrap things up."

"Really? Do we really need to retrieve it, or is this more army bullshit?"

"It's both," said Keith. "Does it really matter that we account for it? No, this is a paperwork drill. But that's what the LT wants. We're pulling everything out of Iraq, and that means we take as much of our stuff as we can.

"Besides, you've complained about being bored just sitting around. Doing this civil action team resupply run gets you out of your CHU for the next couple of days. Plus, we're out of here and back home in a couple of weeks."

"Whatever." Christine shrugged and looked out the window as they passed the exit control point. "Can we relax the body armor? This stuff is not cut for women."

"Yeah. Let's get a few miles down road, and then we'll loosen it."

While they waited for the convoy to pass so they could fall in place as the rear guard, Keith noted that the convoy consisted of four Humvee gun trucks and six HEMTT A4 trucks with containers—a standard convoy configuration.

Keith and the remaining 1058th soldiers were based at Camp Arifjan in Kuwait. They spent most of their time on the road hauling equipment from Iraq to airfields or seaports in Kuwait for shipment to

Afghanistan or stateside. Throughout the deployment, the premission intel briefs indicated less and less enemy activity, and fewer locations and holdouts, as the months progressed. Unlike his first deployment, when mortars and the sounds of weapons being fired were a daily occurrence, this entire deployment had been void of enemy contact, for which he was glad.

He tensed up every time he went outside the wire. Everyone did. However, for Keith, each convoy inflamed memories of the IED he came up against during his first convoy on his first deployment in 2003. Unaware, he touched the scars on his neck and cinched his body armor tighter. He glanced out his door window and then looked over to Hamblin's window. He looked right past her. As he refocused his eyes to the inside of the vehicle, he saw that she was looking at him. He pulled his hand away from his scarred neck.

Keith studied the GPS unit in his vehicle. They had a few hundred miles to cover to complete their mission. First, they were to deliver supplies to an army civil action team that was putting the finishing touches on a school in Zubayr, Iraq, that received reconstruction funding. They were to drop shipping containers in Zubayr, travel north past Baghdad, and terminate at Camp Speicher. There they would spend the night, pick up three shipping containers, and deliver them to the Port of Shuaiba in Kuwait. On their return, Keith, Desmond, Christine, and two dozen other soldiers would make one last sweep from Speicher to Camp Arifjan, retrieving the disabled truck en route.

"Sergeant?" Hamblin asked.

"Yeah?" he replied, grateful for the break in the tedium of a flat road and utterly unremarkable terrain. He and Hamblin worked and traveled well together. He felt she had matured throughout their nine months of deployment. In spite of their senior vs. subordinate roles and working across the gender line, they had far-reaching conversations during the monotonous drives in the mind-numbing landscape of Iraq.

"What do you think of the repeal of Don't Ask, Don't Tell?" she asked.

"I don't think it's a big deal. The politicians are making it much more of an issue than it really is."

"What do you mean?"

"There are a couple of gay guys in the unit that I'm aware of, and there are plenty of lesbians in the military. They're here and doing the job. I think most of them would like the policy to fade away without all the fanfare."

"So, it doesn't bother you?"

"Are you trying to tell me something, Hamblin?"

"No. I like men. But I'm bored, and you and I usually have interesting talks when we're working together. In this case, I'm wondering how you think things are going to change."

"Little will change, 'cause the military is not a nightclub. We're in the service to do a job, not to meet our next one-night stand or lifelong partner. But that happens too."

"Yeah, that's what I think. So it doesn't bother you?" she asked again.

"Did you ever meet Sergeant Major Bluefield?"

"No. Who's he?"

"He was our command sergeant major. He is gay, but you'd never know it by his voice or demeanor."

"How do you know he is gay?"

"He told several of us a couple of years after we got home from our first deployment. We had a summertime weekend drill at Camp Edwards. It was training for squad leaders and some of the senior enlisted—all guys. We set up a tent on an unused range, ran to the exchange, and bought some beer. That evening, we just kinda shot the shit while sitting around the fire, and he just said it."

"That simply?"

"Almost. There was a lot of bullshit flying. Everyone was exaggerating their intelligence or strength and how many women they'd slept with and how tough of a warrior they were and so on. Everyone was smoking a cigar and had a buzz going. It was a good time, just kicking back, lots of laughs. Someone said something about a guy in the unit who was being thrown out because he was gay. He and another guy had been caught in the act. The sergeant major said he couldn't stand those fags. Then he said he was gay but that he hated those effeminate-sounding and -looking queers being in the military."

"No shit. That must have been awkward."

"Yeah, that's an understatement. But after the initial shock, he said a couple more things that put the group back at ease."

"Like what?"

"He said he knew what everyone was thinking and that he hated the barracks showers as much as everyone else. Someone made a comment about how much easier it must be to get sex from a gay partner than a wife, and Bluefield said, 'Oh no. It is easy to get laid early on in the relationship, but just like a hetero couple, someone starts feeling used and unappreciated.' He said it was no different from what his straight friends at his civilian job would say about their wives. Then someone started asking him about deviant sex things, and he got angry. He said he was appalled when he read about the Catholic priests molesting boys, and he stated that kiddie porn was horrible. His values were no different from yours or mine. Everyone started bragging about sex and this and that, like they were asserting their straightness. At one point, the conversation drifted around to white women and black men, and someone asked Bluefield if black guys were hung better. He replied, 'Only in the minds of white women.' Everyone laughed, and then Sergeant Mouldy—"

"You're kidding. Sergeant Mouldy?" Hamblin said, interrupting.

"Yeah, no kidding, that was his name. Black guy. He was an ugly shrimp of a soldier. He was smart but not a very good leader. He told us not to let the secret out, as the big-dick myth was all he had going for him. After that little discourse, the group relaxed, and it's not been an issue for me since."

"Guys. You're weird. You actually talk about that kind of stuff?"

"Oh, come on. Women talk about that kind of stuff on a whole different level. Females use a different language that conveys a lot that's unspoken, and they use innuendo and implications more than a specific description."

"True. But I can tell you—sometimes it gets embarrassingly detailed."

"To be honest, a gay guy like the sergeant major doesn't bother me at all. He's as masculine as a guy should be. But the effeminate ones, yeah, I don't like being around them. They're creepy, hypersensitive, and not a good image for the army."

5

"They're good people."

"Yes, I'm sure they are."

Keith and Hamblin had run the course of that conversation. The tedium of the road returned.

"What are you going to do with all your GI Bill money when you get back home?" Keith asked.

"Buy myself a new car. A Mustang, red and fast," Hamblin replied.

"I don't think you can use the GI Bill to purchase a stud magnet."

"I know. I was talking about all the money I made here: hazardous duty pay, separation pay, and a few other pay categories that I don't even know about. Plus, it's all tax-free."

"It is a chunk of change we get for living in this shithole."

"For an E4, I did all right."

"I just found out I made first class. Too bad we're here for only two more weeks. Making E7 pay for a couple of months would be a nice chunk of change," said Keith. He thought about his statement for a moment and then added, "No, it wouldn't be worth it. The sooner we're done here, the better."

"Really! Congratulations! When do you pin it on?"

"Don't know. The LT told me this morning. He said he'll get me a copy of the message when we get back."

"I'm very happy for you. Are you going to be able to stay with the unit?"

"I don't think so. No open spots for an E7, but I'm not going anywhere for at least a year."

"Well, if you leave, I'm going with you."

"Uh, um, thank you."

"I won't be the only one either."

"Really?"

"Oh, come on, Sergeant First Class Morris," said Christine.

"I haven't advanced yet," Keith interrupted.

"Oh, deal with it, Sergeant First Class. I'm glad I got to be the first one to say it, and I like saying it, so get used to it. And yes, there are lots of people who think you are a really good leader, because you take the time to teach and make sure people know their jobs. Like me."

"Thanks."

"I also want you to know that I was taking some prerequisite teaching courses at Bunker Hill before we deployed, and when we get back I will start the teaching certification program at Bridgewater State. I got an e-mail a few nights ago saying I was accepted into the program. They will insert me into the program after we get back and I'm ready to start."

"So you're going to be a teacher. Excellent. You'll be great."

"I'll be a teacher because of what you said about my showing Specialist Dearborn about driving the truck. What you said stayed with me, and I looked into teaching. I only told a few friends, but over the last year I've been volunteering in a classroom at Gavin Middle School in Dorchester."

"Really? How'd you like it?"

"I love it."

"Kids give you a hard time?"

"A little. Most of the time, though, they were great."

"Yeah, that's how they are, great most of the time and really annoying every so often. Middle schoolers can be tough. Good for you if you're connecting with them."

"What about you, Sergeant? What are you looking forward to when we get home?"

"My job, my dog, my life. I'm looking forward to sleeping in my own room. I'm looking forward to talking and not having to yell over the sound of a generator. I'm really looking forward to eating a greater variety of foods than what the DFAC offers. I'm looking forward to riding my bike and going for a run and not having to stay behind concertina wire."

"What about that woman who came to the farewell bash with you? You said she is someone you knew back in Arizona. Is she someone you're going back to?"

"Yeah, Allison. We dated, years ago, in high school. We reconnected when I went to visit my mother in Arizona last year. She was in Boston the week before we deployed. We went out to dinner and had a great time. We've swapped a lot of e-mails and phone calls while I've been here. I really hope something gets going, but I don't know what she is thinking. Her e-mails have been a little odd lately."

"How so?"

"It's hard to say. Maybe it's pressure at work. I don't know. I'm just looking forward to seeing her, and who knows. I hope something will get going."

"What you said makes me curious. What kinds of things do you like in a woman?" asked Christine.

"Oh, the usual, boobs, butt, hair, things like that."

"Yes, I'm sure. You and every other male in the world. But I know you better. I'm sure that's not all you like. You're not that superficial. So, really, what do you like?"

"Well, I like all the female parts a lot. I like someone who is informed, has energy, and can talk about something other than what the latest pathetic celebrity is up to. I like trim, but I understand weight is a complex thing for women. I don't want to hug a bag of bones, but trimmer is definitely better than heavier. But what I really like is smart. That's only dawned on me in the last couple of years. If I had to choose only one thing, it would be someone who is smart.

"What about you?" Keith asked. "Most of the female soldiers here talk about some guy back home or are hooking up with some guy here. And I know the young male soldiers are doing the same thing."

"It's not just the young single soldiers hooking up."

"Yeah, true. There's been lots of Article 134 actions here this time; that's a huge difference from the first deployment. I can remember hearing about only a couple of instances of adultery charges on the first deployment. Now, it seems like there's a couple a week. Anyway, what about you? If I remember correctly, there was some guy with you at the farewell."

"I had a pretty serious boyfriend when I graduated high school. He was at the farewell. He goes to UMass in Amherst. I went to visit him there a couple of times, but it was awkward. I joined the guard and then this deployment happened, and it just kinda faded away."

"That's too bad," Keith said, thinking he had to say something.

"No, it isn't. There are a couple of guys here who I gave my phone number to, but I told them to not ask me out while we're here. I promised myself I wasn't going to get all guy-crazy while I'm here. I see what the other girls are doing, and there's so much drama. I can't stand it. I want to get my degree and career going before I spend too much time thinking about some guy."

"I respect that."

"So, they say they'll look me up when we're back home. We'll see."

"Anyone from our unit?"

"No. But one guy is an officer. Can I date an active duty officer while I'm in the guard?"

"I don't know. That's one of those murky areas. By the rules, I think, probably not, but I'm sure it happens all the time. Just be careful who you tell. You never know what someone will react to."

The radio crackled. It was Sergeant Jarvis in the lead Humvee. "We've got a signal from a patrol ahead that there is a convoy heading our way. We'll rendezvous with them for any intel they can pass on. About two kilometers out. Keith, come forward, scout, and stop. Then cover the rest of us as we roll in. Copy?"

"Roger. Moving up," Keith replied.

Hamblin was driving. She stepped on the gas, saw a clear stretch of road, and moved out in front. She saw the wide spot in the road. "There it is."

"Yeah. Slow down," said Keith. The rest of the convoy had stopped, waiting for the all-clear. Keith stood up and wriggled into the gunner's seat. He cocked the .50-cal., and scanned the area. "All right, you know the procedure. Nice and easy."

Hamblin slowed the Humvee and drove past the spot, while Keith studied the terrain surrounding the stop. Christine turned onto the hardscrabble desert and circled the area. They tightened the circle with each orbit around the rest area, like it was a noose being set. They stopped a few times when one of them spotted something that looked out of place or unusual. Keith would inspect the object with binoculars, his heart pounding. Finally, they felt it was safe and radioed the 1058th/1166th drivers and the other approaching convoy to proceed.

The other convoy was the same size and configuration. The Humvees rolled in first, and then came the three HEMTT A4 trucks. Keith and Christine stayed with their truck, Keith sitting in the gun turret, Christine remaining at the wheel, keeping the engine running. There was no air-conditioning and they were not wearing body armor. The premission intel brief reported no enemy activity. It had been a year since an IED exploded in southern Iraq. Keith had told her that she could remove her armor. They watched as the soldiers dismounted, greeting each other. There was one female soldier with the other convoy.

"Even from here, that female seems like she's tough," said Christine.

"I was thinking the same thing," Keith replied.

"I don't like those women who think they have to be like a guy and act all tough," Christine said, as she watched her. "I'll bet she's one of those women who doesn't cut anyone any slack, particularly other female soldiers."

"So, like my being creeped out by effeminate males, you get weird around butch women?"

"Butch doesn't bother me. Meanness does."

"I always thought females had some kind of connection and watched out for each other," said Keith. "You know, a variation of the going to the bathroom together that happens in clubs and places like that. But then I've seen some female soldiers, officers and enlisted alike, just destroy another female 'cause she had a moment."

"Yeah, I've run into a couple of those. They're brutal. They view any kind of feminine quality as weakness."

"What about you? How do you think women in the army should be?"

"We should be ourselves. We shouldn't have to feel like we have to prove anything. I'm a girl, I've got boobs and long hair and everything else. I like being a girl."

Keith laughed. Hamblin had a good sense of humor and was not uptight. She never crossed into inappropriate or raunchy; she was just an easygoing soldier.

"I mean, why should I have to hide it if I like to cook, if I cry when I see something sad, or if I want to try to comfort someone if they're upset?" She stopped talking when Desmond called on the radio and told them to come in. They saw another Humvee move in their direction to be the lookout.

"Guess we get to see her up close and personal," said Keith.

Another gun truck rolled up and gestured for Keith and Christine to join the main group. When they got to the group, Keith stayed in the gun turret and Christine stepped out.

"Where the fuck is your body armor?" the female soldier bellowed.

Christine stopped and said, "We took it off."

"You're fucking kidding me. You're in a war and you decide to take off your body armor, the single biggest thing besides your weapon that will save your skinny ass."

"Master Sergeant," Keith interrupted. "I told her that she could relax the body armor."

"Well, then you're more stupid than this dumb cunt," the master sergeant yelled.

Master Sergeant Jarvis walked into the fray. "What the hell is going on, and who the fuck do you think you are being disrespectful to my soldiers?"

"What kind of convoy you running, Master?" she asked, staring at Desmond.

"The best one in Iraq. What's your problem?" Des snapped back.

"You let your soldiers outside the wire without wearing body armor, that's what's going on."

"When Intel reports that there is no threat, I let my squad leaders decide weapon condition and body armor."

Keith looked at one of the soldiers belonging to the yelling master sergeant's convoy. The soldier looked back and shook his head as if to say, *She's like this all the time.*

"Just give me a route brief and leave. I don't need your shit," said Master Sergeant Jarvis.

"Yeah, fine. I don't want to be around your unit when the shit hits the fan. We'll spend our time saving your ass, and that'll put my soldiers at risk. Your route is clear. Nothing unusual about the traffic or roadside activity."

She turned to speak to her soldiers, when the lookout gun truck started moving and a voice said over the radio, "Vehicle approaching, three o'clock."

They all turned to see an old car limp on its three good tires into the parking area. It did not stop moving; rather, it continued to thump its way toward the soldiers. Keith cocked the .50-cal. Other soldiers scrambled toward their vehicles, unslinging their M4s as they ran for a safe firing position with some kind of cover.

"Stop. Do not come any closer," yelled one of the soldiers in Arabic.

The car stopped. The lid of the trunk popped up and then settled back down. Keith could see it was a well-maintained older Hyundai, a gold-colored sedan. He could see, on the inside, tassels hanging from a cloth banner over the windshield colored with the red, white, black, and green of the Iraq flag. The driver-side door opened and a man stepped out. He wore the traditional white *thawb* and red keffiyeh. He extended his arms away from his body and stepped away from the car.

Keith could see other shapes in the car, but he couldn't tell if they were male or female or how many there were. He watched the man make a gesture toward the tire. The man stepped suddenly toward the rear door of the car.

"Stop!" another solder yelled, again in Arabic.

Keith released the safety and pointed the weapon at the car. He could hear a woman inside the Hyundai scream.

The man stopped and slowly formed his arms into a gesture as though he were holding a baby. Then he pointed toward the backseat of the car.

"Hold your fire," said Master Sergeant Jarvis.

Keith watched as a baby appeared in the rear door window of the car and was passed to the man. The baby was fussy and crying. The passenger door opened and a woman stepped out. The rear doors opened and another woman and a boy slowly stepped out. Keith felt the tension throughout his body. For the first time in years, he felt the beginnings of a migraine. He tried to figure out what was happening. The man, women, boy, and baby were probably a family, but al-Qaeda in Iraq was ruthless and sent mentally handicapped women and children with explosives attached to their bodies into areas where soldiers gathered in order to kill them. Every time there was the slightest movement from the vehicle, he moved the gun ever so slightly and held his finger on the trigger.

The boy spoke in incomplete sentences, "Food. Baby sick."

The boy and the older man spoke in Arabic. "Wheel broken; doctor," said the boy.

The father moved to the back of the car and opened the trunk. A cacophony of "Stop," "Don't," "Halt," "You're dead, Hajji" ensued. The man stopped. The women cried louder, and the boy froze.

"Someone, get on the radio and get a translator to tell us how to tell them to move away from the vehicle," said Jarvis. Five minutes later the translation came through. Once instructed, the family moved away from the vehicle.

"Keith," said Jarvis, "you and Hamblin armor up and go around and see what is in the trunk."

Seconds later, the pair donned their body armor and slowly rolled toward the car. They moved in a slow, wide arc toward the vehicle and stopped one hundred feet behind it.

"Easy does it," came Jarvis's voice over the radio.

Christine put a pair of binoculars to her eyes. Keith was in the turret, crouched as low he could go while still being able to have a clear view of the car. "What do you see?" he asked.

"I don't see anything. I can't get a solid look into the bottom of the trunk."

"Pass the glasses to me. Maybe I can get a better angle."

She passed the binoculars up.

"I can't get a clear view either," said Keith. "Take another arc around the car and close up the distance by half." When she completed the maneuver, he had a better view.

"Des," he called on the radio.

"What do you see, bud?"

"I think it's safe, but we won't know for sure unless we dismount and inspect."

"Yeah, that's what I thought you'd say. The female master sergeant says we should light it up with your .50-cal."

"No. I don't think so. I think it's a poor family. We destroy their car and they're fucked and forever hating Americans, if they don't already. We'll move in a little closer. My gut says there is no threat."

"Roger. I'll get the translator to tell them to get out of the car and step away," said Des. "Easy does it, you two."

13

"Yeah. No shit. I don't care for those things that go boom. Hamblin, you been listening to this?"

"Yes, Sergeant."

"You know what to do, just like we practiced."

"I'd rather be at a cookout."

"Me too."

She eased the vehicle forward and approached the car. Slowly the large, heavy tires crunched the gravel, adding to the tension and giving off an uneasy quality. She stopped the Humvee twenty feet from the car. Keith scanned the car again with the binoculars. Nothing. Hamblin opened the heavy door, cinched her body armor tighter, positioned the neck plates, turned the collar up as high as it would go, and lowered her head as deep as she could into the pocket she had created. The last thing she did was put on the ballistic eye protection as she stepped toward the car. Keith watched her as she moved slowly. If there was a bomb, she would die, no doubt. He did not want to witness that. He also knew that if there was a bomb, he stood a very good chance of being killed too. If he didn't end up dead, he knew that his organs, brain, and entire neurological system would be fried for the rest of his life. Memories of his misery with the headaches and PTSD he had from his previous deployment, and the thought of a lifetime of the headaches, entered his brain. He hoped if there was an explosion he would die. Then an image of Allison at the restaurant in Boston popped into his head. He refocused his attention on the vehicle.

Hamblin had reached the car. She slowly lifted the trunk lid and made a gesture indicating that everything was okay. Methodically she examined the rest of the car. She used a mirror on a pole to look under it. The Iraqi family shuffled as if they were bored. The soldiers were tense with concentration and dread. At last Hamblin gestured that it was all clear.

The soldiers relaxed their weapon conditions.

Desmond walked over to Keith and Christine and gestured for the family to return to their car. The father went to work on changing the tire.

"That baby looks like it's struggling," said Desmond.

"Yeah," agreed Christine. "I worked in a day care center for a while. I can tell that that baby is sick."

Desmond radioed for two members of the 1058th to bring water, Gatorade, and food for the family. As the pair walked toward the car, the other convoy started to roll away. The female leader stopped her convoy and said, "I'm not risking my soldiers any more while you try to save everyone."

"Thanks for the cover," said Keith.

"Keep your body armor on," she responded hostilely, adding a look of contempt at Keith and one of hatred at Christine, who watched the convoy disappear.

"Fucking bitch," said Des.

The car was operable again. The family was clearly appreciative of the food and water. The baby was asleep. The father gave Keith and Desmond the customary kiss on each cheek, offering each of them a handshake too. One of the women gave Christine a colorful scarf.

Hamblin admired the scarf.

"On my first deployment—and this one too—I've noticed that even though these people have very little, they are gracious," said Keith. "Makes me think we Americans could stand to be more gracious."

"You two okay? Ready to roll, or do you want to take a couple more minutes?" asked Sergeant Jarvis.

"I'm good," replied Christine.

"I got the traces of a headache. I'm going to see if I can walk it off," said Keith.

"You want me to get Doc?"

"No. I've learned some tricks that seem to help avoid them. I just need a couple of minutes, and then I'll know if it's gonna pass sooner rather than later."

"Okay. Keep the armor on."

"Rog."

"When we're rolling again you can decide whether to relax the body armor or not."

"You're not going to listen to Master Sergeant Bitch?" asked Christine.

"Fuck her. I'm still going to let the squad leaders make the call, but for now we're exposed, so the body armor is on. You can loosen it later if you want."

Keith walked as far from the road as possible. It was hot, the highway noise incessant, and his headache was teetering on awful. He turned his back to the noise, closed his eyes, and took several deep breaths. Allison had suggested he try pinching the web between his thumb and index finger to release endorphins. It seemed to help, or maybe it was thinking of her that helped. From his breast pocket, he pulled out a photo of him and Allison together and looked at it. It had been taken on the morning that he and the rest of the 1058th left home. Over the months of deployment, he had developed a light fantasy of being with Allison. It was an autumn walk in the park in Hingham. He'd dreamed it one night, and it had stayed with him. He rarely recalled dreaming and even less often remembered a dream. But the dream of taking a walk with Allison stayed with him. He nurtured it into a whole scenario that he rendered large and detailed, when he had the time.

It worked. Sensing that the headache had shifted, he knew it would fade soon.

He walked back to his vehicle and told Hamblin that she would be driving for the next couple of hours. He radioed Desmond and said he was ready to go.

Des assessed the convoy; everybody was in place. Keith and Christine were in the lead, the rest of the convoy behind them. The Iraqi family had finished the repairs and were back in their car and moving. They stopped alongside Keith and Christine and waved. Desmond watched Keith open the passenger door, speak to the family, and then wave as they moved forward and stopped at the edge of the highway to wait for a break in traffic.

Des thought Keith offered the right advice by discouraging the idea to light up the Iraqi family's car.

"Roll up to Morris and Hamblin," he told his driver. When he was alongside Keith, Des yelled over the engine noise, "You made the right decision, Keith. There was no need to destroy their vehicle."

Keith shrugged. "Yeah, there was no reason for that."

Over the radio, Des ordered the convoy to roll.

He watched Morris and Hamblin's vehicle roll forward and stop about five feet behind the Iraqi family's car.

Over the engine and highway noise, Des identified a unique sound from the unit's predeployment training at Fort Sill. It belonged to the blast of an RPG, which was now launching and ripping its way through the air. In the moment before the brutal air wave slammed into his body, Des saw a microbus across the road from the family car. A man lost control of the RPG launcher from the recoil, three other men were firing machine guns, and the grenade slammed into Keith's still-open door. He prayed the armor was strong enough and yelled Keith's name. During his incoherent gap in time, Des watched the Humvee explode. He saw a body fall from the vehicle. Another soldier materialized in the smoke, dust, and flames, and covered the fallen body.

Confusion settled on Des. His comprehension and then essential awareness failed.

WARNO

July 2009
Weymouth, Massachusetts

Keith returned to the living room and found Caisson, his sixty-pound chocolate lab, settled on the couch. The dog had been agitated all evening, pacing at the door to the backyard and flopping at Keith's feet while he watched the Red Sox game. Caisson was fidgety tonight like he was on the long, cold days of winter when Keith had to stay late at Weymouth's Academy Avenue Elementary School, where he, Mr. Morris to his students, taught fourth grade. The dog also behaved in a restless manner when Keith was going for a drill weekend or leaving for his annual training. His students called him Sergeant Morris when they knew he was leaving for a drill weekend.

"Caisson, get down. You know better," said Keith.

The dog lowered his head onto the cushions and tilted his impish eyes up at Keith, his tail thumping against the leather couch.

"All right, you win," said Keith as he sat down. Caisson maneuvered his head onto Keith's lap. Keith stroked the dog's head. He looked at the baseball game on TV and spoke as though Caisson understood. "The Sox are losing anyway. As soon as this inning is over, we may as well go to bed."

Keith turned the television off and walked toward the stairway leading up to the bedroom. Caisson slid off the couch and followed. They were at the foot of the stairs when the phone rang.

"Hello?"

"Sergeant Morris?"

"Speaking."

"It's Sergeant Jarvis."

Keith knew the voice at the first syllable. It belonged to Sergeant First Class Desmond Jarvis, one of the active duty staff at the Hingham armory. Keith knew him as Des, because they were best friends.

When Des called to go out for a beer or dinner or fishing, he'd ask for Keith. However, when Sergeant Jarvis asked for Sergeant Morris, that meant he was calling on official National Guard business. Usually, Des only called on guard business a few days before the drill weekend to brief Keith on the weekend's training evolutions. Drill was still three weekends away.

"Yeah, I figured," Keith replied. "As soon as your name came up on my caller ID, I took a wild guess and thought it might be you. What's up, Des?"

"I'm giving you a heads-up. The unit is being mobilized again. We've got about six months before we leave."

The line went quiet. Rumors about another mobilization had been capricious, ricocheting around the unit for months. Because he was friends with Des, Keith knew mobilization was imminent, but still, every day, waiting for the call revived random memories of the unit's first Operation Iraqi Freedom deployment in 2003, his encounter with a roadside bomb, and its consequences. Now, a tiny shiver shot through his body. He ran his fingers over the skin graft that patched the shrapnel scars.

"When?"

"After the New Year; no specific time line yet, but an advance party will leave first, and the rest of us will follow a couple of weeks later. It sounds like it's a long way off, but you know how it goes. We'll start ramping things up next drill weekend and get everybody ready to go."

"Well, at least we got more notice this time. Last time we had three days before we pulled out. It still amazes me that the planners didn't start thinking about needing lots of trucks until just before the invasion."

"Yeah, but that was 2003, and who knew Saddam would pussy out so easily? Besides, Rumsfeld and company wanted to fight a war on the cheap."

"Where we going?" Keith asked.

"Back to the sandbox, but with a stop at Fort Sill in Oklahoma for a couple of weeks of training first. We'll be based in Kuwait and run missions into Iraq. We're hauling all the big stuff out. With transit and training time, it'll be about a nine-month mob, not counting leave and whatever else comes up on the tail end."

"Well, at least it seems better there now. Less of us are getting killed or hurt, but the Iraqis seem to be blowing each up more often," Keith said.

"We did some good being there. Maybe the Iraqis can fix their own country now that Saddam is dead," said Des.

"I'm not convinced it was worth the price."

"Yeah," Des agreed. After a moment he continued. "The ten-five-eight was one of the first guard units in there, and now, with the president ordering a drawdown, we'll be one of the last guard units out of there too. Just last year we finally got our inventory of trucks back up to premobilization levels. For a transportation unit, we were really hurting for equipment for a couple of years. Good thing we didn't get any bad storms over the last two years."

"Yeah. Well, thanks for the WARNO," said Keith.

"Also, we're not going as the 1058th. We're being merged with 1133rd Heavy Lift Company for this mob."

"Why?"

"They don't have mob under their flag, so we're going under their flag, but the ten-five-eight will still get credit."

"Whatever."

"Oh, one more thing, Keith," Des continued. "You'll have a new soldier in your squad next drill weekend. Female."

"Oh, come on. Do you ever assign a new soldier to anyone else? You've dropped some real winners on me lately."

"You get the young soldiers who might need a little guidance and patience," replied Des.

"The young males are social retards," continued Keith. "It's like they never got away from video games long enough to ride a bike, climb a tree, or chase a girl. They don't even know how to talk to a girl—anything. And the females act like they don't even know what the word *no* means. The last female you dropped in my squad was screwing everybody in the unit. I don't know what she thought she was getting into when she enlisted, but she sure wasn't interested in doing her job, at all. I did ten months of paperwork on her to cover the six months she was with the unit. I don't want another one like that."

"Blah, blah, blah, you like getting the new soldiers and helping grow them," said Des.

"Yeah, I do."

"Yes, we've had some dopes assigned to the unit once in a while, but we've had some great soldiers too," said Des. "Some of them just require some extra guidance. With you being teacher and like a big brother to everybody, you get some of those soldiers. Think of them as your special-needs soldiers.

"You know as well as I do most of them turn out pretty good. Remember Private Rosales? Victor?" continued Des. "We turned him around. He avoided prison, went back to school, and was eventually selected to be a warrant officer. I think he's flying Apaches in Afghanistan now. Diaz too. She was a really good soldier, focused on her job, good at what she did, and loyal as could be to you. You've told me she watched out for you after you got hurt."

"Yeah, she was good. Tough. Didn't take crap from anyone. I still swap e-mails with her every once in a while," said Keith "There's really been only one guy who was a complete sack of shit, Corporal Stivdednek. Did you ever meet him?"

"Never met him. He was discharged before I got to the unit, but I've heard a lot about him. None of it good," said Des. "He was looking for a reason to kill somebody. Heard he tried to run over every Iraqi he saw."

"Yeah, but what he was really looking for was a reason to go on his own personal crusade. As far as he was concerned, they all were Muslim terrorists. He hinted to me one time that if they didn't accept Jesus as their Lord and Savior, then it was his duty to kill as many of them as possible. The army did the right thing when they sent him back to the States."

"The army did the right thing when they discharged him."

"Always makes me wonder how many of our own homegrown extremists are in the service."

"Anyway," Desmond said, redirecting the conversation, "this girl seems like she's got her head on straight. I haven't seen her service record yet, but I talked with the master sergeant at her old unit. He said she wants to do the right thing, but sometimes she doesn't always know what the right thing is. Too much growing up done online and in front of the television, is his opinion. She's, like, nineteen."

"Fine. What's her name? You got an e-mail address or phone number for her?"

"Private Christine Hamblin. I'll send you her e-mail address. You have any questions about the mob? Seems like we should have discussed it more."

"No. It'll be FUBAR from the word *go*, but one way or the other it'll all work out okay."

"Don't be pessimistic, Keith. The army has come a long way in how it brings National Guard units into active duty, how it prepares a guard unit, and how it plugs guardsmen into big army. They still need to figure out what to do with guard soldiers when they demob and have no military resources close by, but things are better than they were at the beginning of the war."

"Well, it has to be better than the last time. That was a charlie-foxtrot the whole way," said Keith, his tone signaling the end of the call.

"You want to go fishing this weekend? We'll take the boat off Scituate, near Minot Light. We've had success there."

"Can't. I'm heading to Arizona to see my mother for a couple of weeks," Keith replied.

"How's your mother going to take the news of you being mobilized?"

"Like all mothers, I suppose. She'll worry, but she'll be supportive too. I'll let her know when I see her. I'll call my father after I tell her."

"Do they get along?"

"For the most part. My father says they get along better apart than they ever did together."

"What's your mother say?"

"All she ever says about their relationship is that he was a good father. Anyway," said Keith, "school opens a couple of weeks after I get back. I got to go in and get ready for the school year. Now I get to factor in a mobilization and deployment in the middle of the year."

Keith added, "You should come with me to Arizona sometime. We'll go to the Grand Canyon and head over to Vegas or San Diego, or just stay in Arizona and do some hiking in the mountains."

"That would be a blast, but I doubt Savanna would be keen on my going to Vegas," said Des. "She thinks I'd act like I was a single soldier on leave."

"Savanna's cool."

"Yeah, I lucked out."

"You know, last weekend she tried to fix me up with one of her friends, again."

"Yeah, she always gets a report after one of your dates. Then I get to hear all about it. That's the price I pay for having you as a friend. Have you ever considered being a monk or a eunuch? By all accounts you're pathetic. I told her to stop playing matchmaker, but she never listens.

"Anyway," Des continued. "As much fun as it would be taking a road trip to Vegas, there is only so much a married guy can get away with. Winter camping in a tent with six feet of snow on the side of a mountain in Maine with you is fine, but drinking and gambling with strip clubs on every corner, plus being three thousand miles away, no, that won't happen. Hope you have a nice visit. When you get back, give me a call. See ya, bud."

"Okay. Hey, wait a minute. How many unit patches do you have in Supply?" Keith asked.

"I don't know for sure, but the last time I looked we had a pile. I'd guess we have fifty or so."

"Good. I'm going to swing by first thing tomorrow and grab a handful of them."

"Giving them to your students again?"

"Yup."

"I'll set them aside. They'll be here in my office. Oh, and I'm not driving a desk on this deployment. I'm going with you."

"Sheesh, talk about special-needs soldiers."

"Knew I could count on you for your support."

Keith hung up the phone, leaned back in his chair, and let out a long, slow breath. His right hand was sore from clutching the phone so tightly. He looked at his left hand and saw that it, too, was clenched into a fist. He shook his hands and fingers a couple of times to release the tension, took a deep breath, and released it slowly.

He stood to walk toward his bedroom. As he passed the bathroom, he saw his motion reflected in the mirror. He stopped, turned the light on, stepped in, and assessed himself for a moment. Having to maintain a weight and physical-readiness standard in order to stay in the guard made him content with his body.

He tilted his head up and studied the scars on his neck. The civilian plastic surgeon the army sent him to after the 1058th returned from its first deployment in 2004 did a good job. He ran his fingers over the jagged lines where the shrapnel tore through his neck. They were almost invisible, but the slightly off-color and irregularly mottled skin created by skin grafts were what people noticed. When he was introduced to someone or was just in the supermarket, glances and eye contact went to his neck first, next to his face, back to his neck, and then to his eyes. Even his fourth grade students noticed the disfigured skin. At first it bothered him and he tried to hide the scars. Eventually, however, as the inflamed and bitter skin calmed, he stopped trying to hide the wound.

Looking at his scars more closely than he had in years, he remembered his ambivalence when, a few months after the unit returned, his enlistment was expiring and a fellow teacher asked him if he was going to get out. He said no. Being in the guard was part of his life and he enjoyed it. But his peer persisted and asked if he wasn't afraid of getting deployed and hurt again. Keith replied no. He explained that the fact he had been injured at all was an unlikely twist of fate. His injury was mild compared to the horribly disfiguring burns and amputations that had happened to other soldiers. The rapid blood loss was what almost got him. In fact, the doc had cleared him to return to his unit and full duty three weeks from the day of his injury.

Plus, he'd added, since it had already happened once before, the chance of it happening again was incredibly remote. The conversation ended with the teacher resignedly saying he was crazy.

He refocused his gaze and reached for his toothbrush. As pleased as he was with his fitness level, he wondered if the climate, terrain, and dust would affect him more so on the impending deployment. On the first deployment it took time for everyone to adapt to Iraq's geography and climate; this time he would be six years older when he got back in country.

Behind the shorts and Red Sox T-shirt he wore, Keith was six feet tall, two hundred and ten pounds, and clearly in shape, but he was not bulging and muscle-bound. He was not the biggest or fastest or strongest guy in the unit, but he consistently passed the quarterly PT test in the top 25 percent. When he crossed over thirty years old, the PT standard became slightly more generous. He was given a couple more minutes to finish the run and needed to complete five fewer push-ups to pass. When he was running or doing push-ups around the young guys in the unit who were just off active duty or fresh from boot camp, he worked to stay competitive with them. Just two months earlier on a drill weekend at Camp Edwards, one of the young soldiers tried to give Keith a compliment and said he hoped to be in as good of shape when he was Keith's age. Keith nodded and acknowledged the praise, but most of the soldiers in the unit were now younger than he. Keith wondered when that had happened.

He finished getting ready for bed. Usually he fell asleep quickly. This night, however, he lay in bed with memories of the previous deployment and speculations as to what the upcoming mission might be like. He wasn't afraid, but he knew bad things happen on deployments. He once witnessed a gruesome accident involving two trucks that were, fortunately, not part of his unit. One of the soldiers was nearly cut in half. Memories of the Iraqi children he and the other soldiers befriended and taught at the civil affairs center they established on the base tried to enter his thoughts. But, as always, he refused those thoughts and deliberately concentrated on something else to redirect his brain.

His redirecting effort stopped on his and Des's deploying together.

He was pleased that Des was going. He and Des had a strong friendship that began almost immediately when Des transferred in a couple of years after the unit's 2003 deployment. They were the same rank then, and about the same age. Des had grown up in Weymouth and left when he enlisted. After years of transfers, deployments, and exercises, Des accepted a full-time position with the Ohio National Guard. After four years there, a spot for a full-time guardsman opened up with the Massachusetts Guard. He transferred from Ohio, bringing his wife and son, and ended up in Hingham.

On a drill weekend they kept it professional, but over the years, between drills and before Des's wife got pregnant with their second son, the three of them, plus child, explored New England, with Des as the tour guide. They went hiking in New Hampshire; took weekend trips to Cape Cod; explored Boston; and went to Red Sox and Patriots and Celtics games. Savanna started fixing Keith up with her single or soon to be single again female friends. When she got pregnant, she stopped drinking and Des grew into more of a homebody. Keith was the second child's godfather. He liked it that all three of Des's children called him Uncle Keith.

He thought about the rest of the soldiers in the unit and how they would react to the mobilization order. In his squad there were only three married soldiers. They would have a much harder time preparing for deployment than he. Life as single guy was uncomplicated, and deployment made it even less so. The most complicated thing he was going to have to do was to find someone to watch Caisson and check on the house periodically. Most likely, Savanna would offer to be the caretaker. On deployment, all he had to do was his job. Everything else was provided.

Unlike the previous deployment, he did not have a girlfriend this time. *Just as well,* he thought. *Deployment is tough on relationships.* The Dear John letter he received four weeks into his first deployment stung, even though it was not entirely unexpected.

In spite of Savanna's relentless efforts, he remained single. He had stories to tell, for sure, but sometimes his home felt empty. Even on his annual training with the unit, when the guys were talking or complaining about girlfriends or wives, he thought about having someone more permanent in his life. *It would be nice to have someone to think about during the deployment,* he thought.

Keith's heart leapt when Desmond first said the *mobilization* word. Moments after the initial wave of anxiety passed, his methodical and disciplined mind fell back into place. Lying in bed, though, he could still feel the residual adrenaline in his body.

He knew how it would go. Like the last time, it would all work out, one way or the other. Orders would be cut, canceled, rewritten, and modified. Eventually the paperwork would be correct and the orders executed. Some supplies would arrive promptly, and other stuff would not arrive at all. The unit would get too much of one type of gear and not enough of another. The officers and senior enlisted members would do their best to make sure everyone was physically and mentally ready to go and prepared for the possibility of grievous harm.

The soldiers would PT harder and more often on their own. They would think of the things that needed to be done before they left: finish painting the house, get the tires on the car replaced, make sure the snowblower is ready for winter, and hire some neighborhood kid to clear the driveway in the winter, mow the grass in the summer, and rake the leaves in the fall. Most of the married male soldiers would ask a friend to act as a handyman for their wife and family while they were away. The married female soldiers wanted to make sure everything at home would run as smoothly as possible. They would explain with intricate detail where things were in the house, like the boxes with the summer clothes. They would also elaborate on where to get the best deals on items like laundry soap and toilet paper. Most of the women were terrified that the overwhelming feeling of leaving their children and possibly never seeing them again would paralyze them the day they had to say good-bye.

Many of the soldiers would think of things they wanted to say to their spouse and children to reassure them. Many of the young soldiers would try to express a loving, caring sentiment to their current lover while showing the face of a hardened, duty-bound warrior. The older, married soldiers usually wouldn't say much. Some soldiers would actually write a letter, to be opened only if the worst happened. Many

Mobilization

Three days, that was it. Seventy-two hours to report to the armory, and even less time to get ready. There was little sleep that night. Keith's mind was racing, thinking of all the things he had to get done. It was almost overwhelming. He moved around his house and started to pack some clothes, but then he got distracted and went to check the expiration date on his car insurance policy. He found his policy, but halfway through reading it he went to check the oil tank for the furnace. *Do I need to get it topped off before I leave?* he wondered. He knew that he had to heat the house slightly in order to keep the pipes from freezing and bursting for the remainder of the winter, and maybe next winter too, depending on the length of the deployment.

Unable to decide where to begin or to concentrate long enough to complete any task, he stopped, sat down with a pad of paper, and started to make a list. The more he wrote, the more things he thought of. As he looked at the list, he saw what was important and needed to be attended to promptly, and concurrently identified those things that really did not matter. He looked over his list and realized the most important thing he felt he had to do was not on it.

Keith picked up the phone and called Sharon Wells, the principal at Academy Avenue Elementary School in Weymouth—where he taught fourth grade—and told her about the mobilization.

"You don't have to come to the school at all," she said, her voice slightly breaking. "We'll take care of everything."

"I appreciate that, but I've got to come in and talk to the kids.

They know something's up because of September 11. They know it's big, but they don't understand what it's all about," Keith replied. "If I disappear into all the war chatter they're hearing, it'll confuse them, and you know they'll grab at all kinds of inaccurate information to explain it to themselves. I want to come in and tell them what is going on and to say good-bye."

"Do you know where you're going?"

"No, not yet. Maybe Afghanistan. But with the buildup in the Gulf, I'm betting it's Iraq."

"We should do something for you. Maybe a little get-together in the lounge?"

"Sure. That'd be nice."

"Are you scared?"

"No, I wouldn't say I'm scared. Uneasy, but not scared. Right at the moment, though, I'm just scrambling to get my stuff together. The list I started just keeps growing. I'll be gone for at least a year, and I need to think about everything from underwear and uniforms to finding someone to cut the grass next summer to getting my mail forwarded to me in a place that I don't even know yet."

"Is there anything I can do to help?"

"Thanks, but no, not really. I'm trying to get the important things situated before I go. A few more days' notice would have been good, but there's nothing I can do about it. I'll get as much as I can in place and hope that the things I can't get to won't have much of an impact."

"If you want to give me a key to your house, I'll keep an eye on things, and when you get settled I can at least send you your mail."

"Thanks. That will be helpful."

There was a long pause. Keith could hear Sharon draw a couple of deep breaths before she spoke. "We can meet and you can give me an update on the class. I know most of your kids are doing okay, but what about Marie, Anna, Tony, and Ramon? Do you have any thoughts on what we should do with them?"

"Not yet. I've been thinking about those four ever since I got the word. I think Anna and Ramon will be okay, but Tony and Marie, boy, I don't know. If their routines get out of order, they might take the other two down with them. We'll come up with something."

"Okay. I'll get a substitute for tomorrow. Call me and let me know when you're going to come by," Sharon said.

"All right. Talk to you tomorrow."

When Keith hung up the phone, another wave of reflection swept over his thoughts of planning for deployment. He loved teaching and was going to miss his kids. Teaching was not his career choice coming out of high school; he stumbled into it after college when he needed some money and started substitute teaching.

He reached down to pet Caisson, but then he sat down on the floor next to the dog instead.

He knew it was the turmoil abruptly thrown into his life that made him consider the security and predictability of his life. In this wave of contemplation, he acknowledged and was grateful for the serendipity of his career. The kids were young enough to still be genuine, and old enough to be reading and writing on their own. They could start a conversation and turn it into a discussion. Every one of them liked math. Their personalities were defined, and their minds were still open to alternative views. They were, most days, fun, eager to learn, and enthusiastic about everything.

The first year Keith worked as a full-time teacher, he took the kids outside and off school property a couple of times. He knew it caused a stir about safety concerns with some of the parents. What if someone fell and scraped a knee and it got infected? Who would cover the costs? What was the school's liability? Several parents were fearful their child would suffer allergies or catch the flu. One mother felt her son was too frail to endure an extended period out of doors, so she refused to let him go outside with the class. The boy was miserable sitting in the other fourth grade class while all his friends were outside having a ball. His mother let him go the next time, but she insisted upon joining the outing, at which point she happily discovered that her son was indeed sturdy.

By Keith's second year of teaching, his excursions were known and admired throughout the school system. Every year since, at least once a month he would take the class outside and explore. Sometimes it was a walk on the nearby streets. Others times he held class at Libby Field or Legion Field. At least once each season they explored the swampy area near the playground. On each adventure, each student was to find something different. Back in class they talked about each item. If someone found an old bottle, it could launch a discussion about litter or antiques or how glass is made. The kids caught two or three frogs every year and brought them back to the classroom. They made a home for them in the classroom aquarium, and Keith led a spontaneous lesson about amphibians. Invariably, after a few days, the frogs were not looking too healthy, so the class took them back to the swamp and released them. Springtime flowers led to discussions on colors and smells and botany. The winter excursions usually led to prolonged snowball fights. The kids enjoyed it when Keith ordered them to attention, did a mock inspection, and called cadence while marching them outside for an adventure.

All his students were good kids. Most of them came from stable homes. Several had learning challenges and required extra attention. Three were in the accelerated learning program. The parents were always the real challenge. Every day the kids' behavior revealed clues about their home life. Keith could usually tell when a father had gotten a particular child ready for the school day. The hair was not brushed or combed well. Lunch was usually too much: sandwiches overpacked with lunch meat or peanut butter or whatever. When the parents were fighting, their child was withdrawn, aggressive, frightened, or sad in class. The students who read every night were generally ahead in class, and the ones who were raised by television were usually mediocre performers. The children thrived on each other, and that vibrancy pulled the lagging students up and pushed the already well-performing kids farther.

Keith felt fortunate, as over the years he'd had to make only a couple of calls to social workers to report suspected abuse. But now, with deployment imminent, he thought, it was not commonplace, but it certainly wasn't unheard of for a troubled child to pass through Academy Avenue Elementary School. Fortunately, the school system had good programs to help. However, it was very unusual for four children from such disparate backgrounds to be roughly at the same level of developmental delay and be in the same grade. They tested well for intelligence and lack of learning disabilities, but each one of them had faced misery and suffering at the hands of angry, drunk, or lazy adults. And they were his students.

Anna immigrated to the United States from Romania when she was two. Her father was quickly consumed into an Eastern European mob in Boston. A stable foster home led her to Weymouth, where a good family took her in and she began to grow. She needed routines. She had to know that the things she saw and did one day would be the same things she experienced the next day. Once her routines were satisfied, she could handle something new being added. Her second grade teacher had noticed that music soothed her, classical music in particular, and told Keith about the effect music had on Anna. Keith bought her an iPod and loaded it with classical music. When Anna was getting anxious, Keith allowed her to discreetly put on her earphones and listen for a minute. It helped.

Tony and Marie were siblings. One morning when they were in second grade, they witnessed their father kill their mother. A bachelor uncle who lived nearby took them in, got custody, and tried to keep a sense of familiarity going for the children. Their first attempt at fourth grade was pointless.

Keith was the only unmarried teacher at the school. He lived close to Tony and Marie. He was able to give them extra time after school, and occasionally went to their house for dinner and visits on the weekend. Sharon Wells cautioned him against getting too involved. He replied that he knew he was running the risk of complicated emotional connection with Tony and Marie, but he felt that their uncle, some terrific women in the neighborhood who had plenty of maternal drive to share, and he were the kids' best chance at putting the tragedy in a less toxic place.

Ramon, the last of his four extra-effort students, had had his back broken at the hands of his mother's abusive boyfriend. His first attempt at fourth grade revolved around his adapting to a wheelchair. On the weekends prior to the swamp adventures, Keith and several of the fathers of the children in his class went into the swamp and cleared and improved a path so Ramon's wheelchair would not sink in the muck. With a net, Ramon scooped up pollywogs and caught butterflies. On his sketchpad he drew unusually detailed drawings of the swamp. His drawings won a citywide art contest. His work was exhibited at the state capital. During his first attempt at fourth grade, Ramon failed every subject except art.

Two days before deployment, Keith put on his Class A uniform and went in to talk with his students. He first stopped outside his classroom and listened. There was muted chatter and the flush of a toilet. Two girls emerged from the bathroom, giggling on their way back to class. The faint smell of lemon-scented disinfectant lingered. The hallway was empty now. He put his hand on the doorknob to his classroom and, for the first time, simultaneously felt the coldness of the metal and its smoothness, except for one little nick on the inside of the handle he felt with his pinky. He shook off the wave and opened the door. The kids stopped their chatter when he walked into the classroom. For just a moment it was quiet, and then one of the boys said, "Cool." Then the excited chatter erupted.

Keith had brought ten chili-mac MREs (his favorite) and a photograph of himself standing in front of one of the unit's iconic five-ton drop-side 6×6 M923A2 cargo trucks to school. He set the items down and answered the students' questions.

"Do you have a gun?" asked the same boy who'd spoken earlier.

"No. I will get one later, and I will be very careful with it."

Several of the students raised their hands.

"Mr. Morris, what do those colored lines on your sleeve mean?" asked one of the girls.

"This one means I am a sergeant," Keith replied, pointing to the stripes on his arm. "These are medals I've earned," he said, pointing to the four rows of ribbons on his chest.

"Can I see?" someone else asked.

"Sure. Come on up here."

The kids swarmed him. A cacophony rose as they touched his medals, looked at his shiny polished shoes, put his hat on their heads, and bombarded him with more questions.

Mrs. Wells and several of the other teachers gathered in the doorway to his room. The substitute teacher seemed to fade away.

Keith walked over to Ramon and kneeled down so the boy could see all the military trimmings too.

"Are you going away?" Ramon asked when the din dimmed for a moment.

"Yes, I am."

"Are you coming back?"

"Yes, I am."

"Where are you going?" another one of the girls asked.

"I don't know yet."

"Get back in your seats for a minute. I want to talk to you, and then I've got a couple of things for you," said Keith. After they settled down, he continued. "So, you all know I'm a soldier, and you know what happened to our country on September Eleventh. I'm going to go and help our country find those horrible people who did that to us, and I'm going to work hard to make sure no one else ever does that to us again."

"Are you scared?"

He thought about giving the same evasive answer he had given Sharon when she asked the same question, but it would take more understanding and subtlety than his students had to understand the difference between scared and uneasy. He said, "Yes, I am, but I'm going to take a deep breath and think about what I have to do—and then I'm going to do it. I'll still be scared, but maybe a little less so. No matter what, though, I'll keep on doing what I have to do."

"Are you going to die?"

"No. There are thousands and thousands of soldiers, sailors, marines, airmen, coast guardsmen, and other people who want to make sure our country will never be attacked again, and very, very few of them get badly hurt."

One of his students said, "My daddy says people who go to war are bullies and just want to fight. He says people fight wars because they're greedy."

"Hmm." Keith was not expecting that statement. "He's right. There are some people who are bullies and who just want to fight. And some are greedy too. No one joins the military to get rich. I don't want to fight, and no one I know in the army wants to go to war, but until the bullies in the world stop trying to pick fights with us, our country has to have soldiers who will go and stop the bullies."

"When are you leaving?"

"This is my last day with you. I have to pack tonight and get things ready, and then I leave the day after tomorrow."

"What are you going to do?"

"I'm a truck driver. The other soldiers in my unit and I are going to make sure other soldiers have everything they need to do their jobs."

"When are you coming back?"

"I think I'll be back when you're all in the fifth grade."

"We'll have a big party when Mr. Morris gets back," Principal Wells said.

"That's right," Keith added. "For now, though, I have some army food you all can try. And I have a picture of me you can hang on the wall. Who wants to put it up?"

All the kids raised their hands.

"Okay, Anna. You pick a spot and I'll get the thumbtacks."

Anna carefully studied the room. She quietly got up from her desk and walked over to Keith. Once again, he studied her odd gait. Her arms did not swing as she moved, her shoulders stayed level, and her feet never left the ground; they slid alongside each other. She took the picture and placed it at the front of the row of the kids' self-portrait art projects that hung from the wall, circling the room. The drawings were in alphabetical order. Anna placed Keith's picture right next to her self-portrait.

"That is the perfect spot," said Mrs. Wells.

"I'm very happy you put my picture there, Anna," said Keith.

Anna settled back in her chair. She slid her earbuds in place and closed her eyes as "Ave Maria" softly played.

"Is Caisson going with you?" one of the boys asked.

"No. The only dogs there will be ones some soldiers use to do their job. One last thing," Keith added. "I brought a bunch of unit patches so I can give one to each of you." He explained the symbolism in the patch as he passed them out. Not one of the children forgot their patch at the end of the day.

"Now, let's try this army food. Who wants to help me?"

The kids swarmed him again, each one of them clamoring to be the one selected to help their teacher-soldier. Keith gave each one of the kids a task. They ate the MREs. Keith hugged each student, and all the teachers and support staff at the school, and promised to e-mail as often as he could. The entire student population and all staff gathered in front of the school and waved good-bye as Keith drove away.

The drive out of the school parking lot was difficult. Keith wished he could take a deep breath, but the lump in his throat made it very difficult. Plus, the sting in his eyes made it hard to drive. He turned out of the school property and stopped the car to catch his breath and rub his eyes.

The further he drove away from the school, the more he thought about his answer about being scared. Only a fool would not be worried about going to war. Deep in his heart, he wondered that if he came under attack and things went bad, would he be courageous or would he succumb, impotent in the face of fear?

Farewell

February 2003
Hingham

In the dead of the winter of 2003, the 1058th mobilized in support of Operation Enduring Freedom / Iraqi Freedom. The members were finally told they were heading to Iraq.

There was no time for long, tender good-byes. The armory buzzed with activity for seventy-two hours straight as soldiers processed orders, answered questions, issued gear, and otherwise prepped the unit members, their families, and the community for the unit's first mobilization since the first Gulf War in 1991. The last thing the unit did was to host a family meet and greet in the evening, hours before the convoy rolled out. Once the families left, that was it. The soldiers would be locked in the armory until the buses arrived in the morning to take them away.

Keith was not the only soldier there who had no local family or family who were unable to attend. A couple of friends of his and several teachers from school came to say good-bye and to wish him Godspeed, but for most of the evening he and the other single soldiers sat in the chairs, talked among themselves, and watched. One of them asked a question: "Why join the guard?"

When Keith answered, he said, "I'm not sure. I was always interested in the service, but I never felt real strong about joining. An old girlfriend's father told me stories of his time in the service, and he enjoyed it. All the vets I meet are really proud of the fact that they served. So a friend of mine in college was going to the recruiting office one day, and I went along. The rest is history. I had my degree, but I didn't have a job lined up, so I went back, signed up, and left for boot camp.

"I like my time in the guard. I get just enough of the military to enjoy it, and when I get tired of its dysfunction, I step back into teaching and all of its satisfaction and dysfunction. Now, six years in, I get it. I know what to take seriously and what is just army bullshit."

"I'd say heading to war in Iraq is serious," one soldier said.

"Yeah," Keith replied. "It sure is."

The group of soldiers fell quiet.

Throughout the evening Keith watched the families, in particular, the females.

Most of the wives or girlfriends of the young soldiers were openly worried. A few were distraught. In a couple of cases, their worry struck him as excessive. He wondered what was the cause of the extreme despair. Was the spouse emotionally unstable or profoundly worried and wearing her heart on her sleeve? In one case he thought there some histrionics on display. It appeared that this woman poured on the tears and wailing whenever a reporter was close by.

The males were mostly quiet and stayed close to their wives or girlfriends, who occasionally kissed or hugged their soldier.

The mature mothers were visibly uneasy yet still dignified. Most of the women were middle to lower middle class. They were working women, living life feeling overwhelmed most of the time, tired and devoted, proud and scared. There were a few wealthy women in the crowd too. They were as devoted, proud, and scared as all the other mothers. Rich and poor, educated and dropouts, the mothers empathized silently together, clinging to each other, acknowledging no supercilious or economic boundary. Their sons and daughters were going to war.

Keith's thoughts jumped to his Arizona upbringing in a nice big house. Every house in the neighborhood in Chandler was at least three thousand square feet. All the houses were in a horse-lot development, so each had at least a couple of acres, stables, and open space. His mother, Kathy, managed a branch office for a commercial insurance group. She'd wanted the horses. They had two. When he was young, the three of them rode together, but she rode less and less as work

43

took over her life. His father went along with her wish to own horses, but when she stopped riding and taking care of the horses, he sold them.

Keith was an only child, so he had stuff and trips and playdates, but he always wished for a sibling.

His father, Tom, was an aerospace engineer and worked at the Apache helicopter plant in Mesa. He was extremely fit and mostly serious, but Keith remembered him being lighthearted and playful too. They would play games of hide-and-go-seek in the house, and Keith would go on scavenger hunt adventures with his parents in the neighborhood. When it was just Tom and his son roughhousing, Keith laughed a lot.

His father took him fishing out at the Verde River and four-wheeling in the desert. He was busy with work and went on extended trips to different places in the country as each aircraft was extensively tested prior to its delivery to the army. He took Keith into work with him several times. There the boy met soldiers and pilots and other people who took their jobs very seriously. Gradually, around the house, Tom spent most of his time either avoiding his wife or growing sullen when she overreacted to what seemed to Keith to be insignificant things.

When Keith's mother was around, he tried to remember not to upset her. He would try his hardest not to spill anything or leave his shoes out in the living room. It confused him when he saw his friends spill drinks or food, or oats for the horses, and their mothers didn't seem to get upset. His father often said his mother worked hard and always felt overwhelmed, which was why, he explained, it seemed as though she was always tired or angry.

His mother hired housekeepers and usually fired them within weeks. The housekeepers often acted as a nanny for Keith. All of them were immigrants who barely spoke English. They came in and cleaned usually twice a week, making sure Keith was fed and not in trouble. He grew fond of one named Lupita.

Lupita lasted the longest, twelve weeks. Initially, she cleaned house. By the end of the first week, Kathy asked her if she would help her with Keith, picking him up after day care and taking care of him until she or Tom got home. Lupita had to leave by five o'clock so she could get home to take care of her own kids. The first week went as planned. Lupita took the bus and was dropped off as close as possible to the house, which left a two-mile walk from the bus stop. Once at the house, she lightly cleaned. Kathy had developed a specific cleaning protocol. One of the housekeepers once deviated from the rules and was fired on the spot. The deal was, Lupita was to arrive before two o'clock, clean for two hours, and use one of the family cars to pick up Keith no later than four thirty. Later, either Kathy or Tom would be home and drive Lupita to the bus stop.

Lupita was fun. She brought Mexican food and shared it with Keith. She taught him a few Spanish words and played with him at the park. If he still needed to do homework, she sat with him while he did it. He taught her some English words and a few sentences. At the park, she was energetic. They had footraces.

Tom met Lupita the first week. By the end of the second week, he was home every day to drive her to the bus stop. By the end of the third week, he and Keith would drive her to pick up her kids and return them all to her house in Phoenix.

During the twelfth week, the three of them were at the table having a snack when Kathy came in.

"Get out of my house," Kathy screamed.

Lupita may not have understood the words, but she knew what was said.

"No, stay," Tom said. He stretched his arm across Lupita as she moved to stand.

"You get out too. You and your Mexican slut."

"What are you talking about?"

"Don't play stupid." She tossed an eight-by-ten envelope onto the table.

Tom lifted the flap, peered into the envelope, and saw the image of him and Lupita kissing in his car at the end of a nearby road. Whoever took the photos must have had a big telephoto lens The next series of photos showed Lupita's head in his lap, and his pants were clearly unbuckled. He closed the flap. "Let's go, Lupe," he said, sighing. "I'll drive you home."

"Oh, fine. Why don't you see if you can get one more blow job on the drive?" Kathy said.

"Don't talk like that in front of Keith."

"Don't come back."

"I'm coming back to get some clothes."

"Take them now. I don't want to see your lying, cheating face ever again."

Tom nodded.

Kathy glared alternately at Tom and Lupita.

"Lupe, Keith, come with me," Tom said.

"Keith is not going anywhere with you," Kathy screamed. "Come on, Keith. We'll go out and get something to eat while your father fucks someone other than his wife."

"I told you once, don't talk like that in front of Keith."

"Fuck, fuck, fuck, bitch, cunt, whore. You asshole, you're a coward. You're worthless as a man. I hope your slut's husband rips your dick off and you die."

"Stop it," Tom yelled. It was the first time Keith had ever heard his father raise his voice to his mother. "If you cared about something other than making money, coming home, and changing into your pajamas, and then lying in bed every night and all weekend watching TV, this might not have happened."

"Oh, so it's my fault you fucked someone else."

"No, but it is your fault that you got so consumed by work and money that Keith hasn't had a mother to spend any time with him for five years, and I haven't had a wife I could talk to for ten years."

Kathy stopped and stared at Tom. Then she grabbed Keith by the wrist and dragged him toward the door.

"Think about it," Tom yelled as she walked toward the door. "When's the last time you went to any of his school events? When's the last time I talked to you? I answer your questions, but I don't tell you anything beyond what you need to know. Sexually, you died the moment I put the ring on your finger. So, yeah, it is your fault."

Keith remembered the door slamming shut. The latch never set in place, but the sonic concussion resounded through the neighborhood.

His mother walked to their oversized, custom-made Suburban.

He stopped halfway between the car and the house. The sun was setting. It was a west-facing house. The low-angle sunlight passed through the dust in the sky and threw a golden light on the façade. He wanted to go back into the house to make sure his father wasn't packing his clothes.

"Keith," his mother said, "come on. I want to hear about school."

He didn't know what to do.

"Come on, Keith."

He saw his father step into view in the living room window. Their eyes met, and then he waved.

Keith ran back into the house. "Dad, don't leave."

Tom held his son. "Keith, this is not your fault. I'm sorry you saw and heard all that. Your mother and I have clashed for years, but we tried to keep it away from you. Go with your mother for dinner. I won't be here tonight when you get back, but I'll pick you up after school tomorrow."

"No. Stay."

"It would be best if I didn't stay tonight."

"Keith," his mother spoke gently from the archway of the front door, "come on. I'm sure you're hungry."

"It's okay, Keith," his father added as he released the boy from his hug.

"Don't go, Dad."

"I'll see you tomorrow. We'll talk."

Keith heard Lupe crying in the kitchen. He ran to her. She turned away from him. He slowly turned and walked to his mother.

When Keith and Kathy returned from dinner, they found that Tom had taken most of his clothes out of the closet. His computers were gone, and so were a couple of photographs he'd had matted and framed.

Over the following few months, Keith saw Tom almost every day after school. He even spent nights at Tom's apartment. His dad was fun again. They played video games, went out to dinner, and went to several Triple-A Giants baseball games. They went to a family counselor a couple of times and talked about the divorce. Keith tried to understand all the things they talked about, but the only thing that made sense to him was when the three of them were there together. His mother had said she was sure there was someone better for each of them out there. The counselor said no, that the better way to say it was that there was someone easier to be with out there. That made sense to Keith.

Then Tom transferred to Seattle. Boeing bought the McDonnell Douglas Apache helicopter plant and offered Tom a director position. He left. Keith went there twice a year, spending a week each time. At first father and son talked and e-mailed every day, but their communication gradually diminished. Tom paid for Keith to go to Northeastern and get his degree. At that time, it had been four years since he'd seen his father.

His mother stopped working after a month and grew steadily reclusive at home. Tom said it was because she felt she was a failure, because the marriage didn't work out—and she couldn't accept failure. Money wasn't a problem. Both his parents had inherited substantial resources. Kathy did engage more with her son's schooling, though. Over time she started getting out, not on dates, but she did volunteer work with various organizations and joined a book club at the library.

Forward Operating Base Speicher

April 2003
Tikrit, Iraq

Between Hingham and Kuwait, Keith and most of the soldiers of the 1058th spent two cold months of training at Fort Drum in New York, while the unit's trucks transited the ocean in the hold of a cargo ship. Within sixty days' time, Keith experienced temperatures ranging from –30°F to 119°F.

He received e-mails from a couple of guard buddies who had traveled with the unit's trucks across the ocean. He was a little envious. Rather than the frigid conditions he was experiencing, they wrote of the comfortable accommodations and good food on the ship. Even better, one of them wrote, because it was a merchant ship chartered by the navy instead of a USS warship, the soldiers received an alcohol ration. They quickly consumed their allotment, and for the remainder of the voyage felt as though they had been unwillingly admitted to the navy's version of the Betty Ford Clinic. Otherwise, the passage from Charleston to Kuwait was easy.

The one thing Keith and everyone wanted when they got to dusty, hot, and humid Kuwait was beer. Their disappointment was palpable when they finally docked in Kuwait and were forced to face the fact that Kuwait is a Muslim country where alcohol is ostensibly forbidden.

Keith and all the 1058th soldiers were eager to get into the fight, but no one up the chain of command seemed to know what to do with the 1058th. For the first two months they were boots-on-the-ground in Kuwait, they did little more than run a few incidental trips, bringing supplies to the Iraq border. The rest of the time was spent in convoy training, weapons training, and resisting the stultifying boredom. Finally, after two months, somebody up the chain of command took ownership of the unit. It was absorbed into the 180th Transportation Battalion of the Fourth Infantry Division. At last, the 1058th received orders to cross the border into Iraq. Armed escort Humvees would meet them at the border and accompany them to their forward operating base. They were to make their way to FOB Speicher in Tikrit. The base was named for Commander Michael Scott Speicher, a navy F/A-18 pilot shot down over Iraq on the opening night of the Gulf War in January 1991.

Most days, the dust hung in the air like fog, but unlike fog it didn't burn off as the sun rose. It wasn't so bad that no one could function, but since the 1058th was a New England unit and the soldiers were used to the organically rich, moist soil that covered the earth—and knowing that sand lay only on the beaches—the ever-present sand and dust and wind of Kuwait made life miserable. It permeated everything. To many Americans in the Gulf, it felt as though the sand was wearing the enamel off their teeth.

The night before the unit was to head to Iraq, another sandstorm built up and rolled across Kuwait. The weather-guessers from all the services working out of the air base saw the satellite images of the dust rising over the horizon on their radar and computer monitors. Initial estimates put the height of the wall of dust at one thousand feet. Sand whipped around at seventy-five miles an hour on the desert floor. Two navy helicopters launched from a carrier and prowled over the top of the dust wall at twelve hundred feet. The aircraft paced back and forth above the storm for two hours. Satellites and photographers aboard the helicopters hovered above the storm and relayed imagery of the wall of dust back to the air base. It was a spectacular sight.

Whenever a dust storm was forecast, everyone on base worked to seal all cracks, intakes, and exhausts on vehicles of all types, including aircraft, and any air leaks in the tents. Keith and all the soldiers, including the officers, of the 1058th worked as hard to seal up their equipment, duffel bags, and personal gear. However, this time, Keith sealed his gear tighter than usual. The unit had been briefed that it might be weeks before they would be able to take a decent shower and find a washing machine. In anticipation of a showerless month, every soldier took an extra-long shower and washed every piece of clothing he or she had on the day before departing.

The storms were nothing for Keith. The dust storms of Arizona and the simooms of the Sahara and Arabian Peninsula were simply a fact of life.

Another National Guard soldier, this one from Guam, had transferred into the 1058th shortly before deployment. Previously deployed to Africa and stationed in Djibouti, he was part of the force-protection unit that traveled with the various civil affairs teams around the Horn of Africa. He said that in Sudan they called a sandstorm a *haboob*.

As the storm moved in, Keith watched the light change like he did when he was a boy and the summer monsoons of Arizona moved into the Valley of the Sun. It was like daylight during an eclipse; the brilliance, the luminance, and the very color of the light altered. It was not like the late afternoon light that shone from the sun low in the sky, creating the mysterious, magical light and long shadows of dusk approaching. The light of a sandstorm was odd. There was an eerie feel to it. The animals that usually scurried around the garbage pits on base disappeared as though night were approaching. The wind preceded the dust. It had an ancient smell to it, like a cover had been peeled off and layers of buried civilizations were stirred and moved about for the first time in eons.

Dust, obviously, accompanied the wind. The soldiers donned their goggles and scarves to cover every inch of skin. A few had made the mistake of trying to stand outside unprotected in the first sandstorm they encountered in Kuwait. They did not stay outdoors very long. One soldier tried to take a pee in the storm. His often-told account of the storm revolved around the fact that he said it felt like his dick was being sandblasted off, earning him the nickname Dumb Shit for the remainder of the deployment.

Before and during the storms, most of the soldiers of the 1058th were intrigued, indifferent, or slightly anxious. That night, Keith was simply glad that he was finally leaving Kuwait. He hoped that FOB Speicher would be less gritty, less boring, and less humid than Kuwait.

some equipment out of there when it was shut down. Went and saw the USS *Constitution* too. What else?"

"Got clam chowder."

"I'm from Oyster Bay, Alabama. I know all about bivalves."

"The town where I teach, Weymouth, spawned five Medal of Honor recipients," Keith said.

"Really?" Steele replied. "Now I can respect that." He pulled a notepad from his breast pocket and made a note.

"Here's what we're going to do. We're going to go for a thirty-minute run, and then I want to inspect every piece of gear you brought with you. I mean everything: your trucks, comms, weapons, body armor, underwear, tampons, condoms. Hell, I wanna see your toothbrush. Everything. I want to know what I've got to work with."

"Company, atten-hut! Be back here in ten minutes ready to run. Fall out."

Keith and all the 1058ᵗʰ soldiers settled into FOB Speicher. Like Kuwait, here the wind and dust blew in over the top of the twenty-foot-high, concertina-wire-topped dirt berm surrounding the base. The wind never stopped. It only changed from more intense to less intense, with unpredictable gusts. It was not a gentle, pleasant onshore breeze like Keith experienced on drill weekends in Hingham or during annual training on the Cape. The wind in Iraq was relentless. Its faint dust carried enough particulates and silica to irritate throats. To make things worse, dense smoky fires burned everywhere. Both Iraqis and US forces burned everything when done with it: paper, tires, ammunition, shipping pallets, DFAC leftovers, contaminated clothing, medical waste. Even the honey pots from the latrine were soaked with diesel fuel and set on fire. Iraqi garbage, too, burned throughout Tikrit. Iraq smelled like a burning dirty diaper. In fact, wherever the 1058ᵗʰ went, Keith thought Iraq smelled like shit.

For the first month, Keith's and everyone else's throat was sore. Their eyes burned, and they suffered a smoker's hack, regardless of smoking cigarettes or not. Sometimes at night, when the air was still, the guard towers disappeared into the pungent miasma.

FOB Speicher, in a previous iteration, had been a large training base for the Iraqi air force under Saddam. It was taken from the Iraqis in the first week of the war by the 1-10th Cavalry of the Fourth Infantry Division, and then it was handed over to the Fourth Aviation Brigade. It was a large forward operating base to defend and operate.

Speicher afforded ample room for the 1058th to stay together. They carved out a small corner of the compound where they set up their tents. Sleeping arrangements were set up by rank, not by gender. Only a few regular army noncommissioned officers complained about the lack of isolated billeting for the females. They insisted that the females needed to be protected. Keith thought the 1058th women rolled with the wartime circumstances as well as the men. Not once did he hear them complain about the lack of privacy, the filth, the vermin, or going for days without a shower. They shared whatever soap, shampoo, and tampons they had.

At first, once every couple of weeks, women showered by standing on a wooden shipping pallet in a muddy spot behind a tent with ten other women forming a protective screen around them. Every woman in the unit said that showering with two dozen 16-ounce plastic bottles of water was a luxury.

Every woman in the unit was also acutely aware of the possibility of assault and rape by the Iraqi forces. What they were not prepared for was the possibility of assault and rape committed by US servicemen. The rumors were rampant. The men of the 1058th heard the rumors, too, and developed a strong fraternal dedication to the women of the ten-five-eight. Out of all the hardships and inconveniences of Operation Iraqi Freedom the 1058th endured, peer rape was not one of them.

Keith knew a few of the regular army soldiers were pissed off because they had to work with a guard unit. Most of the regular army soldiers didn't give it any thought, but there were enough with the fucking guard attitude for it to be noticed. Without saying a word, the men and women of the 1058th knew the best way to beat that attitude where it could be beaten was to do the best job possible.

Convoy 1

April 2003
Iraq

At muster on his third morning at Speicher, Keith learned the 1058th was scheduled to go out on its first resupply run within a week. The mission: to deliver supplies to a marine company setting up a combat outpost west of Fallujah, offload, and return to Speicher by 0500, twenty minutes before dawn. The cargo was ammunition, small generators, fuel, and MREs. Stops at the isolated outposts for fuel were planned and timed. The longer the vehicles stopped, the greater the risk. Experienced active duty army soldiers would lead the convoy of fifteen army trucks and more than half a dozen Humvee gun trucks scattered throughout.

Five days later, exactly as briefed, the gates at FOB Speicher opened at 2130 and the 1058th departed on its first mission. Keith was in the driver's seat of his truck, and Private Harvey, another 1058th soldier, was riding shotgun. Keith's truck was about midpoint in the convoy, and he was nervous. In the compound there had been talk of ambushes at the fuel-bag farms. The resistance came from leftover Baathist soldiers, and according to the captain during the mission brief, a new trend was surfacing. Rogue groups of Shiite Muslims were reacting and seeking retribution for the years of repression they had suffered under Saddam. They hated the troops simply because they were American. Al-Qaeda was making a strong presence in Iraq too. Roadside bombs and homemade mines were a growing threat.

Moonless nights made the desert eerily dark. Keith and other members of the 1058th had trained with night vision goggles in

Kuwait. Now, driving in the dark Iraq desert, his night vision goggles were an invaluable tool. The night-optics equipment made the terrain surprisingly bright and revealed a remarkable amount of the detail, but the 1058th had been issued the monocular version, making depth perception difficult to gauge. More than once during training, the trucks of the 1058th had rear-ended each other.

In training, Keith had been told that his brain would adapt to the detailed but grainy green and tunneled view of his NVGs coming in through one eye and the full field of view and deep black of the desert night coming into the other eye. He thought his brain never quite adapted. Plus, the particularly ill-fitting set of NVGs he had been issued for the mission only fatigued his brain. Under the dash, a red filter had fallen off a light. The NVGs magnified the light so much that if he looked at the dashboard or anywhere other than through the windshield, he was temporarily blinded.

The Iraqi desert had more vegetation than he'd anticipated. The Sonoran Desert, where he grew up in Arizona, was the most verdant, lush desert in the world. He expected the Iraqi desert to be more like the Yuma Sand Dunes in California, but he was wrong. Centuries of irrigation and civilization had given Iraq desert vegetation. Palm and fig trees, and patches of crops and cypress trees, dotted the landscape. In spite of the NVGs and his sharp eyes, he jumped every time an underdeveloped palm tree suddenly appeared on the side of the road.

Keith was tense on the outbound trip to the marine encampment. His heart pounded; he could half sense and half hear it beating against his eardrums. Every few seconds he reached down and made sure his M16 rifle was in place. In Kuwait, he and the other drivers rehearsed the steps and competed to see who could unlatch his rifle and fire the first shot. He won, 2.7 seconds from unlatched to first round fired. Back on the Cape, he held the record for a year as the quickest draw and most accurate shot. He wished he could do just one more practice draw, just to make sure the gun wouldn't get hung up on anything. He felt that the countless times he'd practiced earlier in the day weren't quite enough.

The first fuel stop went smoothly. The second fuel stop was only thirty miles from the marines. The convoy commander wanted to fuel up, deliver the supplies, and get back to the first bag farm without stopping. During his premission meeting, the briefer from Intelligence had cautioned that if they were going to encounter enemy activity, it would be as the convoy neared Fallujah. No enemy activity was expected anywhere else on the route.

The activity at the destination was low-key too. The challenge was to find the marines. They were hidden in a location identified only by GPS coordinates. The convoy stopped, passwords were exchanged, and then came greetings followed by one hundred Marines materializing out of the dark. Within an hour the trucks were unloaded. The commanders exchanged unit coins, and handshakes and well-wishes passed quickly between the soldiers and the marines. The 1058th rolled out of the unnamed marine location and back into the menacing dark.

"This road is fucking terrible," said Keith. Throughout the entire trip, the undulations of the poorly engineered and poorly constructed road made the trucks weave out of line and sometimes careen toward the edge. "This is beyond annoyance. I'm getting more and more pissed off every time we slam into one of those fucking canyons."

"Yeah, I almost bit my tongue off on that last fucking crater we hit," said Private Harvey.

"Shit!" Keith yelled after slamming into a particularly fierce gorge. He fought to recover control of the truck before it hit the outer edge of the road and spun off into the harsh desert gravel.

Momentum forced the driver side's front wheel onto the gravel and triggered the mine.

The explosion tore the steering wheel from his hands before his brain processed the sound and he realized what happened. Keith lost control when the truck abruptly swerved. His helmet absorbed the impact when his head smashed into the metal surrounding the driver's compartment. He felt other pieces of shrapnel tear at his helmet, and the opposing forces of gravity, momentum, and weight hurl the truck completely off the road and, in rapid succession, beyond the shoulder, into the sand, and onto its side. During the roll, the truck had almost enough momentum to tip one hundred and eighty degrees, but its low center of gravity prevented it from completely flipping over. It settled on its side at about ninety degrees. Amid the tumult, Keith felt the chaos stop. Then the rasping sensation on his left arm took over his diminished awareness. From his contorted position, he rolled his head as far as he could and then continued to roll his eyes farther until he saw the mangled skin and blood on his left arm. A piece of metal had hacked through the skin and stuck into the muscle near his elbow. He could not see if his hand was still attached. The pain was so intense that it blocked the signal from his brain to try to wiggle his fingers. The pain worked in the other direction too. His left shoulder and the side of his neck felt on fire. In his flimsy consciousness, he guessed at what had happened: a bomb. His full awareness slipped for an indeterminate period, and then he saw Harvey trapped in his seat belt, hanging in the air.

He heard the other trucks decelerating, braking, and swerving.

Keith could see the muzzle flash of the .50-cal machine guns mounted on the Humvees through the shattered windshield of his truck. He didn't fully comprehend what had happened. He stared at the machine guns and knew he should be hearing the deep, loud bellow of each round being launched into the night. He heard nothing.

The concussion from the bomb made his body tremble. He felt nauseous and dizzy, even though he was motionless, held in place by his seat belt. He tried to break free, but it was impossible. After a mighty surge, trying to overcome the sturdy design and construction of the truck, he realized the futility of his situation and waited for help. Keith tried to yell for a medic, but the sound of his voice did not echo in his head. Moments later his brain registered faint audible activity and he sensed the muffled sounds of commotion. The delay was very confusing. He thought the activity he heard was close by. He heard other abrupt and indistinguishable sounds, but he couldn't tell if those noises were close by or far away.

He saw soldiers discharge fire extinguishers onto his truck. Some of the foam spread into the cab. He saw the medics arrive. Keith was feeling faint. The first medic he saw was Specialist Flora as he crawled in through the broken windshield glass. One of the younger guys, Flora lived in Quincy and was quiet.

"Okay, Sergeant Morris, I got you," Flora said. "Can you tell me where you're hurt?"

"He spends most of his time complaining about how much Iraq and the Iraqis suck."

"It does suck," Lopez said.

"True, but Stivdednek here thinks the problem is that they're Muslims and following a false prophet," replied Keith.

"Got that right," confirmed Stivdednek. "I'm willing to stand up for what I believe and to carry the message that believing in Jesus is the only way to know God."

The MP nodded. "I believe that too. I know Jesus Christ is my Savior too, but—" He paused. "I'd like to come back here after all this crap is done and work as a missionary. For now, I have to let my actions speak louder than my words, both as an American and a Christian."

"Good for you, but I ain't waiting. I'm on a mission now. As far as I'm concerned, the world would be better off with every sand nigger we send to meet Muhammad."

Stivdednek continued, "It's right in the Bible. 'They entered into a covenant to seek the Lord, the God of their fathers, with all their heart and soul; and everyone who would not seek the Lord, the God of Israel, was to be put to death, whether small or great, whether man or woman.' Second Chronicles."

"Whoa. You're taking selected verses and bending them for your own purpose," Sergeant Lopez replied. "With what you're saying, you're no better than the jihadi whack-jobs who think everyone who doesn't believe as they do should die. You're not thinking right."

"My thinking is absolutely correct. I know what the Bible says. I'm on a mission."

"You're right," Keith interrupted. "We're all on a mission now, and the mission is to do what the army wants us to do. Take your proselytizing crap and stuff it. You're not doing anything else tonight but driving your truck in a safe manner. You want to convert the world, fine. Do it in another place and at another time."

Stivdednek stared at Keith.

"Got it?"

Stivdednek continued staring at Keith and eventually replied, "Yes, Sergeant."

Keith turned his attention back to the other soldiers in the convoy. "How's everyone else doing?"

"Good." "Fine." "Gotta stretch." "Gotta take a leak," came the replies.

"I'm gonna step over there," said Corporal Diaz as she stepped back and walked between the trucks, away from the men, who were already unbuttoning and unzipping.

Keith moved to follow her.

"We're fine here. I don't need you standing next to me each time I have to pee," she said.

"You know the drill, everyone has to have a battle buddy close by, even to go to the bathroom. I always turn my back," he replied. "You don't have to complain each time."

"It's humiliating."

"You're vulnerable."

"Guys are vulnerable too."

"You're more vulnerable. If you had to move in a hurry, you might trip. I'm not going to have this conversation with you again. That's the way it is. Believe me," he added, "it's not the high point of my day either."

Keith looked at Lopez.

"These Iraqis can hide in the desert really well," said Sergeant Lopez. "We scanned this area with our thermal camera when we stopped, but still, if they're hidden behind one of those little mounds, sometimes we can't see them and they sneak in." He shrugged his shoulders.

Corporal Diaz glared at him and said, "I know."

She turned and walked to the other side of the trucks, where she started unbuttoning. Keith followed her, stood several feet away, and stared at a distant light on the horizon.

The soldiers gathered near the trucks. A couple smoked. A couple stretched. All of them walked around, shaking off the road fatigue.

"What else can you tell us about the PWs we're picking up?" Doyle, another 1058th soldier, asked.

"Not much. I've got GPS coordinates where we'll meet some guys. We'll exchange passwords and that whole drill. Then he'll disappear, and a couple of minutes later a few more guys, a couple dozen shackled Iraqis, and whatever else they've caught will walk out of the desert. We'll put them in the truck, they'll radio someone and tell them the exchange is done, and they'll disappear."

"Are these guys other MPs?"

"No. They're Special Forces. They're grabbing as many fighters as they can coming over the Syrian border."

"What are the PWs like?"

"Most are young guys. Stupid. Full of themselves. Don't know shit. But in almost every group we've picked up, there's one or two who seem smart and, I don't know, up to something."

"How come you need us?"

"We usually do this ourselves, but two of our trucks got blown up last week in Baghdad and you guys were assigned to us."

The MPs went back and relieved the gunners. Ten minutes later the convoy was moving again. At daybreak they stopped at a bag farm, found a piece of desert near a guard tower, set up a sentry cycle, and pulled out a foam ground cloth. With weapons close by, they fell asleep in the shade under the trucks.

"Watch out," Diaz yelled.

Even though the trucks were heavy reinforced steel, Keith felt the bump.

"Tell me it wasn't a kid," he mumbled.

"I think you nailed a couple of goats," Diaz said, looking back in the side-view mirror. "What do we do?"

"We gotta stop. Crap. I didn't see the herd. Where were they?"

"I don't know. I just them saw them out of the corner of my eye for a second."

"I bet they threw the goats under the truck to get us to stop," said Keith.

"Why would they do that?"

"Money."

Keith reached for the radio and spoke to Lopez in the lead Humvee. "Pull over as soon as you can."

"Copy," came the reply.

The convoy continued past the settlement and stopped.

"I'm going to talk with Lopez for a moment. Keep an eye out," Keith said as he released his machine gun from its rack and left the truck.

"What's up?" Lopez asked.

"We ran over a couple of goats back there. We're going back. If we can figure out who the leader is there, we'll give him some cash and get out of there," said Keith.

"Happens a lot," said Lopez. "How do you want to handle it?"

Keith pointed to a tree near the road. "See that tree? We'll pull up about a hundred feet from that palm there on the very right-hand edge of the road. It's close to the village. We reassess there," he said.

"Looks pretty straightforward," replied Lopez. "What do you want to do from there?"

"I don't want to go in with everyone and everything. I'll walk in with one Humvee next to me."

"You sure? Why don't you get inside with us?" Lopez said. "We can approach them, talk with *el jefe*, give them some money, and get out of there."

"Yeah, I like that idea a whole lot better," Keith replied. "But I think if they see us walk up, we may get a better reception."

"Okay, but if it looks like any shit is going to happen, jump in here."

"Bet your ass I'll be in there in less than a half a second."

"Let's brief everyone."

Keith directed Doyle to keep his eyes downrange into the desert. "Anything moves, call it out. Diaz, Stivdednek, stay with the vehicles. Keep your weapons ready. The other Humvee will stay with the convoy. Keep the engines running. Anything happens, head west and we'll rally four miles out. Got it?"

"Ready?" Keith asked Lopez.

Lopez nodded.

Keith turned toward the town and began to walk. The rear door to the Humvee was open.

The Iraqis swarmed around the dead goats, their arms waving

and their fingers pointing toward the American trucks. The setting sun threw an orange light at the Iraqis. The dust formed its own odd diffuse layer that reached from ground level to about twenty-five feet in the air. Although the air was still, it seemed to Keith as though everything was slightly out of focus. He could see one of the men already skinning one of the goats. *Roadkill stew, yum,* he thought. It was a small village, no more than two dozen huts. No one could sneak up on them, but someone could leap out of a hut. As he walked closer, the din increased. Most of the men wore long white robes. The boys were young enough to still wear shorts and T-shirts. Extreme Islam had reached into this village too. The women were shrouded. They retreated to the huts as he approached.

"Looks like the boss is expecting us," said Lopez.

One man stood with his arms crossed in the middle of the road. He didn't move. The others swarmed and gathered around him, like bees near a hive. A few moved in front of him. He waved one arm in a gesture like he was shooing a fly, and they moved out of his way. He was armed, but the old carbine was slung across his back. He wore a full beard and was taller than everyone else.

"Looks like that guy with the sword in *Raiders of the Lost Ark,*" said Lopez. "Got your whip?"

The soldiers stopped a few yards in front of the crowd. Keith drew a breath, slung his weapon, and walked toward the boss. He didn't bow his head.

Another man held the mangled goat's body. He dropped it on the ground at Keith's feet.

"We apologize for what happened to the goat. I can give you fifty dollars for it." He reached into a pocket, pulled out five ten-dollar bills, and extended his arm to the leader.

The man shook his head. "Four goat dead," he said.

Keith barely understood what the speaker said in his heavily accented and broken English. "Let me see the dead goats," Keith replied. He pointed to his eyes and then gestured to the dead goat.

"Four goat dead," came the response.

"Two," Keith said. He held up two fingers and then reached into his pocket and pulled out five more bills.

The chieftain shoved the body of the dead goat toward Keith. "Four."

Keith looked toward Lopez.

"If we give in, then every vehicle that goes through here is going to pay the toll, and it'll only get more expensive when every village figures out it can get us to kill their goats. We pay for it, and they still get to eat it."

"Yeah. Give him the hundred bucks. We'll throw a box of MREs at him and get out of here."

A box of MREs dropped out of the door of the Humvee. Keith extended his hand with the money.

"Four dead goat," the man replied. He spoke in his language to the crowd. The gibberish grew louder, and the line of male residents began to shift into a circle around the vehicle and soldiers. The female voices grew louder and shriller.

"We need to get out of here."

"Yeah."

Keith took the money and tucked it under the plastic straps securing the box of MREs.

"Four dead goat," the leader said again, louder.

The crowd picked up on it and began to clamor.

"Four dead goat, four dead goat, four dead goat ..."

The circle closed in around the soldiers.

As Keith moved toward the Humvee door, a burst of rounds from a machine gun pierced the cacophony. He dove in and slammed the door behind him. Lopez hesitated. The crowd was scattering, but there was no clear exit for him. The gunner on the roof spun around looking for the source of the shots.

"Everyone okay?" Keith yelled.

"Who was shooting?" yelled Lopez.

"I don't know. It sounded like an M16," said the gunner.

"Guns, do you see anything?" asked Lopez.

"I think it came from one of our trucks."

A path had opened through the stampeding Iraqis. Lopez spun the Humvee around and headed back to the trucks.

"Anyone hurt here?" Keith yelled at the soldiers when they rolled up to the convoy.

She looked at Sergeant Morris and ever so slightly nodded her head. She stopped resisting. She was breathing hard, glaring at Stivdednek.

"He's going to get us killed, Sergeant," she said.

"You're a woman," Stivdednek said. "You don't even belong here."

An enormous silence descended. The engines of the vehicles droned on. That statement was dumbfounding.

"What?" Lopez asked, incredulous.

"Where do you get all those fucked-up ideas in your head?" Doyle yelled. The machine gunner tipped his helmet back and let go of the handles on the .50-cal. He pulled out a cigarette, lit it, and quietly watched the drama.

"It's all in the Bible," Stivdednek responded. "Women should be at home, making clothing, preparing for visitors, taking care of children. War is no place for women. Home is the place for women."

"You are twisting so many Bible verses. What you're doing is blasphemous," said Lopez.

"No. My preacher makes it perfectly clear, and he told me to expect trouble from those who have modernized the Word of God, when, in fact, the Word of God is perfect. It was perfect. It is perfect."

"Enough. You're riding with me," Keith ordered. "Diaz, take his spot. Doyle, you're driving."

The convoy resumed.

Keith was furious. The Iraqis in the village were agitated, but they had posed no threat. Who could blame them? They lived under a regime that either ignored them or sought to kill them. Whether the goats were thrown under the truck or ran out into the road didn't matter, and the three hundred dollars he had thrown on the ground when the crowd started scattering wouldn't make a difference to the unit or the war effort.

But Stivdednek had made everything worse.

"What's the real reason you fired your weapon?"

"It looked like you were in danger."

"Bullshit. I think you want to get in a fight and kill as many Iraqis as you can."

"We're here to fight a war."

"The war we're fighting is questionable, but since we're here we can make a difference, and I think we can do some good. But stupid shit like what you just did only makes things worse."

Keith caught himself yelling as he spoke. He forced himself to calm down. It was like when his students were particularly rambunctious. He would grow irritated at the children and start yelling, and then force himself to speak stronger but softer. He had trouble respecting leaders who yelled in response to every annoying situation, in both the civilian and military worlds. It was as though they viewed every problem as a nail; thus, their only solution was a hammer. The leaders he respected spoke with authority and expectation. The leaders who only yelled were petty blowhards. It had taken time, but for the most part he had developed the discipline to keep his anger in check.

He thought about his own limited religious upbringing. Before his parents divorced, they went to a community church. It was boring, quiet, not very convincing, ineffective, and uninteresting. His Baptist friends seemed more enthused and obnoxious. But, he wondered occasionally, weren't Baptists, Catholics, Episcopalians, and whatever else all supposed to be practicing the same values?

"I'm not a religious guy, so it's not my place to be preaching, but aren't Christians supposed to be patient and kind?" Keith asked.

"There's a time and place for that, and this is not that time or place," Stivdednek replied. "Besides, I don't just talk about it. I live what I believe."

"You cannot put us or this mission in jeopardy."

"And you cannot interfere with me practicing my religion."

The display on Keith's GPS unit abruptly lit up. In a different situation the light might attract unwanted attention. A moment later Lopez was on the radio, saying, "Watch for a turn."

"Yeah, I got the indication too."

The trucks slowed.

"I see the turn. There's no traffic at the moment. Kill the lights.

Get your NVG on. Everyone except Morris, stay put," Sergeant Lopez said over the radio. "Morris, meet me up here."

Keith was glad for the chance to stretch his legs. They had gone a hundred miles without seeing a village, a gas station, or a turnoff. Traffic on the road had been steady, but after midnight it diminished. There were long gaps of tedious, tense isolation on the road. The new moon was but a sliver, and no lights shone on the horizon or punctuated the taunting dark desert.

He put on his night vision goggles and stepped down from his truck. His eyes were adjusting to the dark and peculiar green light of the goggles. He walked up to the front of the convoy. It was creepy. There was movement in the desert, but it was too far away for him to discern what it was. Perhaps it was an animal, he hoped.

"What's up?" he asked when he found Lopez.

"We're looking for a small cairn. If we find it, we're clear to go in. If we don't find it, the SF guys have not made it here." He paused. "Or it's unsafe. Then we turn around and get out of here."

"A cairn? There's all kinds of rocks piled up around here. How do we know which one is ours?"

"Because it'll be stacked in an unnatural way and there will be something under the stones. A penny or a piece of gum or something so totally out of place you'll know."

Five minutes later Lopez said he found it. Keith walked to him.

"What kind of treasure did they leave?"

"You know those machines, the ones you put a penny in it and then for fifty cents more you can press a shape into it?"

"Yeah?"

"It's a naked chick, and it says, 'Feathers and Boas Show Club, Rapid City, South Dakota,'" Lopez said. "I would say this coin is out of place."

"Yeah. Me too. Let me see the coin," Keith said. He flipped his night vision gear aside and turned on a small red-light flashlight. He studied the coin, turning it over slowly between his fingers. "It's been a while since I've seen anything female and naked that's worth looking at, and I'm getting tired of the sausage festival in the men's showers."

He studied the coin more. "Getting a boner."

"That's pathetic," said Lopez.

"I know."

"Road trip to Rapid City when we get back?" Keith said, passing the token back to Lopez.

"Sure."

"You're a Christian. Isn't that against the rules?" Keith asked.

"I'm not like your boy back there. God knows, I like the female form. I believe in God's grace. He believes in God's retribution," replied Lopez. "What about you? What do you believe?"

"I don't know what I believe. Growing up, I went to church, but it was something I never felt strongly about. I know, like politicians, the loud and intolerant voices are the only ones being heard now. I know there's a lot of decent, compassionate people who belong to a church. But it's not for me, at least at this time in my life.

"All I know for sure," Keith continued, "is that those people with a Christian fish symbol on their cars are the most aggressive drivers on the road."

"Yeah." Lopez laughed. "I've noticed that too. The parking lot at church is more dangerous than being here in Iraq."

Lopez then asked, "What are you going to do about your boy?"

"We need him so we can finish this job. When we get back, I'm going to take it up with the first sergeant and the chaplain."

"I can arrest him. That'll get his attention."

"I'd rather not. Maybe Chaplain Rick can talk some sense into him. But if he does another reckless thing like he did back there, then, yeah, arrest him," said Keith.

"Deal."

"So now what?"

"We roll to another set of GPS coordinates I have, and they'll come to us."

The tires rolled easily across the first part of the road. The sand was packed hard. There were no ruts, and easy curves. Along the way there were a few wrecked and stripped vehicle hulks. When the road curved around the base of the Sinjar Mountains, their vehicles' progress slowed significantly. Jagged, pointy rocks threatened to pierce the tires. Large deep ruts forced the trucks into a line of travel.

Off the road was not much of an option. Larger rocks would have slowed their speed to a point of considerable vulnerability.

Stivdednek was driving and skillfully maneuvered the truck. Keith studied the road ahead. He thought he saw human movement behind a couple of rocks. He tightened the grip on his weapon and flipped the safety off and on, off and on, off and on.

They stopped at a wide point in the road. Shades of black revealed that, to the north, the desert opened to its great expanse. To the south, the mountain formed a darker sheer wall.

"Morris, over," the radio crackled.

"Morris, copy," he replied.

"Turn your vehicles around. Then meet me at the rear. Over."

"Roger."

"Okay," Keith said to his squad. "You heard him, one at a time. Diaz, you first."

With that, the engine growled and the truck moved. In an easy three-point turn, she was done: up against a cliff at the base of the mountain with just enough room for one person to pass between the truck and the cliff at the mountain base. The Humvee turned with her and the truck, the gunner slowly spinning his turret and studying the desert for the slightest movement. Stivdednek followed and slid in easily behind her.

Keith stepped out of the truck and met Lopez in the dark, ten feet behind the rear Humvee.

"Well?" he asked.

"We wait," Lopez replied. "I hate this part."

"How long do we have to wait?"

A voice from the dark answered, "Not long."

Keith and Lopez raised their weapons.

"Don't," the voice replied. "You don't stand a chance."

They didn't lower their weapons.

"Bruins," Sergeant Lopez said.

"1970 Stanley Cup," came the response.

"Bobby Orr, overtime goal," Lopez replied.

"Swept the Blues."

"Okay." He lowered his weapon. "The response is correct. Keith, we're good. You can lower your weapon."

Perfectly concealed until he moved, the body belonging to the voice emerged from the darkness. He was of average height, build, and manner. His weapon was slung across his chest. After lowering the black *shemagh* that covered his face, he walked up to Lopez and Keith and held his hand out. "Mark Gillespie. Pleased to meet you."

He turned to Keith and shook his hand too. "I know you guys are out of Hingham."

"Yeah. How'd you know that?"

"I like to know who I'm dealing with at all times."

"I hear a Boston accent. Where you from?"

"If I told you that, I'd have to kill you."

Keith hesitated. "Really?"

"No. I say that 'cause I can." He smiled. "Startles some people. I was born at Boston City Hospital. Grew up in Hyde Park. Moved to Quincy after I graduated BC."

"That explains the Bruins passwords," Lopez added.

"No shit, Sherlock," a voice from the dark added.

"Yup. I even gave more than a passing thought to joining the guard, back when there were units in Quincy, Braintree, Weymouth, and Hingham, but regular army was the better choice for me."

"So you ended up in Special Forces."

"Maybe I am and maybe I'm not," he said, smiling. "Did I scare you? Yeah. Been in for more than twenty years now."

He held his hand up in a stop gesture and spoke. "We're good. Bring 'em forward."

It was then that Keith noticed the clear plastic microphone tube positioned at the corner of Gillespie's mouth. He also saw the coil going to the receiver in his ear.

Keith suddenly became aware of three more people who had emerged from the dark and were standing directly behind him and Lopez.

One of them spoke up. "Has he been talking about Boston again?"

"Yeah. I'm used to it," said Keith. "I grew up in Arizona, but I teach in the Boston area. They all like talking about how special Boston is—all of New England for that matter."

The sound of shuffling feet and clothing grew louder as a dozen men and four women hobbled out of the dark. They were shackled together with zip ties looped together in a tight figure eight around their ankles, and with more zip ties binding their arms behind their backs and to each other. If one stumbled or stepped out of rhythm with the rest, the whole group teetered and lurched.

The stench of body odor that permeated all gatherings of Iraqis quickly attacked Keith's nose. This was a particularly powerful saturation of filth and stink.

"How long you guys been dragging them around?"

"We picked up the first ones about a week ago and the others a couple of days later."

He turned to the other operators. "Let them rest. Get them some water. Cut the zips off their arms." He turned to Keith and Lopez. "They won't go anywhere."

Most of the men were silent, their eyes looking down or to the side, followed by a quick glance at the soldiers and then another glance at their surroundings. There was no anger or desperation, just sullen resignation. Two of the men muttered in a language that did not sound like the language Keith had grown accustomed to hearing Iraqis speak. By the way their volume rose and fell as they spoke, Keith guessed they were cursing the soldiers. He didn't need a translator to interpret the tone of contempt in their voices.

One of the Special Forces soldiers spoke, and the group sat down near the rear of the trucks. As soon as they sat down, the Iraqi females started talking. The men started talking back at them. They seemed to be saying, "Be quiet," but the women spoke louder and more aggressively in response to the men.

"You got a female with you, yes?"

"Yup."

"Bring her forward. Let the other females see her."

"Diaz, front and center."

She appeared from the dark and walked up to Morris.

"Yes, Sergeant?"

"Walk over to the females there. Let them see you," Gillespie said.

She looked at Keith for confirmation.

"Yeah, you and Stivdednek stand guard nearby. You, near the females."

"They won't be nice to you," one of the Special Forces men yelled. "Don't get too close."

"If they gotta go to the bathroom, escort them away from the men," said Gillespie.

Diaz left, called out to Stivdednek, and walked toward the prisoners. The group fell quiet. The women murmured, looking and pointing at Diaz.

Stivdednek joined her.

"May the Lord have mercy on your souls," he said to the bedraggled group of prisoners.

"Knock it off," Keith yelled. "You're on guard duty, not at a revival." He said to Diaz, "We'll keep an eye on you. Anything comes up, just give me a signal."

Diaz stopped about ten feet away from the women. She kept her weapon shouldered and treaded softly toward them, unsnapping her neck gaiter, tipping her helmet back, and looking at each one of the female prisoners. Three of the Iraqi women studied her as though they were trying to understand why she was there and what she was going to do. The fourth female flashed the briefest, smallest smile at Diaz, who did not return the smile. She reached into her pocket and passed the woman a tube of lip balm. The Iraqi woman did not reach for it. She stared at it as though it was an unknown meat she had to render for the cooking pot. Diaz touched her lips with the capped stick of balm and then circled her lips with the tube. She pulled the cap off the tube and handed the tube back to the female. The dirty, tired, sore woman took the stick and applied the balm to her lips. She smiled and nodded her head at Corporal Diaz.

Stivdednek stood, immobile, slowly panning his head right to left as he studied the group, his weapon waist level, his hand inside the trigger guard, the stock tilted upward and the muzzle pointed down. He stepped close to the circle of male prisoners, kicking their feet and legs if their limbs lay in his path.

One of the SF soldiers stepped out of the dark. "You guys want a beer?" he asked. He had a beer in each hand and gestured it toward Lopez and Keith.

"Yeah," Lopez answered. "That's the reason I like these missions."

He reached out and took one. The motion caused his weapon to slide down his shoulder a little. He shrugged it back into place. With his other hand he held the beer. Cupping the bottle top between his thumb and index finger, he slowly twisted the cap.

"Ah, the sweetest sound," he said as the cap released and a tiny burst of pressure released into the cool desert night.

"We're in the middle of Iraq and you've got cold Sam Adams beer. How the hell did you do that?" Keith asked.

"Magic," Mark replied, smirking.

"That's not all we brought with us," one of the other soldiers said.

"What else?" Keith asked.

"Adult entertainment," Mark said.

"Porn," said the other soldier, dropping a twelve-inch-high bundle of magazines onto the desert floor.

The cover was missing on the magazine on the top. In the dim red light of the headlamp attached to his helmet, Keith saw the first naked woman he'd seen in months. There was movement below his waist, behind the genital-protecting piece of his body armor.

"You're kidding."

"Nope. It's pretty tame stuff. *Playboy*, *Penthouse*, a couple of issues of *Hustler*, and a couple of European ones."

"There's one in there, though, *210 Photos: Nothing but Pink*," said another voice from the dark.

"That is the perfect porn title," added another voice.

"The beer's good, but I'm not sure what you want me to do with the magazines," said Keith.

"You got a company full of males, yes?"

"Yeah, mostly."

"Give them these. They'll figure what to do with 'em."

"Great. There'll be little swamps of cum all over the base."

"Yup. But the guys'll all be in better moods."

"Okay," interrupted Sergeant Gillespie. "We can't hang out here forever. Get the rest of your guys up here, give them a beer, and then get ready to get out of here."

"Doyle, relieve Stivdednek," Keith ordered.

"Okay," he replied. Doyle stood up and walked toward Stivdednek. He quickly closed the distance between himself and the detainees.

"Wow, he's tall. Moves like Larry Bird," he commented. "Looks like him too. Is he good at basketball?"

"No, he sucks. He's gangly. Even when we're doing PT, he invariably stumbles over something. I swear, sometimes he seems to stumble when he's standing still."

They talked for a moment. Stivdednek moved his hand in a dismissing gesture. A moment later, Doyle was talking to Diaz. She started moving toward Gillespie, Morris, and Lopez.

"Yes, Sergeant?" she asked Keith when she got to the group.

"Want a beer?"

"Really?"

"Yeah, here you go."

"Thanks."

She turned to go back to guard duty.

"Stop. Relax. You can chill for a few minutes before we have to get going. Enjoy the beer."

She slung her gun and stepped back to the group. She opened the beer and took a big swig.

"That's good," she said. She took another swig. "That's really good."

She visibly relaxed; her shoulders dropped. She lessened the firmness of her stance so much that in spite of all the body armor, her pelvis settled into a different position, her feet shifted, and her head tilted ever so slightly. The muscles in her face released, and she smiled. She took another drink and looked around. She saw the pile of magazines. She looked at the top of the pile and then looked at the males. Picking up the pile, she flipped the top few magazines back and looked at the men again.

"Really?" she said to the men. It was more of a statement than a question. She kept flipping through the pile. "And nothing for the ladies?"

"Yeah," drawled Gillespie, as much as one can drawl a Boston accent. "I've been married a long time, and I know for females it's all about the mood in that moment. Pictures of naked men do not have the same predictable, guaranteed effect on females like pictures of naked women have on men."

Lopez and a voice from the perimeter agreed.

"That's gross," Diaz said when she saw the *210 Photos* title. She opened the magazine and glanced at one of the pictures. "I've never understood what the fascination of just looking at it is for men."

"That's 'cause you have one," the same concealed voice said.

"Respect," Sergeant First Class Gillespie barked.

"Oh, please, that's nothing compared to some of the crap I hear around base," Diaz said.

"So what do you mean? It's no big deal?" Keith asked.

"Strip clubs and dirty movies and such have such a strong effect on guys. I mean, all girls like to be thought of as attractive and sexy, and I think we all want to show it off to varying degrees, but you guys can be totally controlled by it."

"I think it's because we have a steady drumbeat of testosterone and so we're always looking for a way to relieve that pressure. With you females, I think it comes in inconsistent waves," Keith offered.

"That makes sense. I listen to the other females back at Speicher. There are a lot of good-looking young men around, but they're so stupid," she said. "Don't get me wrong, they're great soldiers and knowledgeable. I trust them to do their jobs, and the eye candy is good, but so many of the things they say and do around females are just dumb."

"The girls respond to their stupidity," Lopez said.

"Yeah, we do, and when I figure out why, I'll let you know. Young females aren't much better."

"Here's a tip for you," Gillespie said. "I've been in charge of lots of young males and a few young females for years, and I can tell you this: young males are stupid and young females are crazy. But I can see stupid coming. I can manage stupid; I can tell stupid what to do. The only thing I have to worry about with stupid young males is a rash and often violent act. But with females, crazy just happens. I can't see it coming. It just happens, and I can't do anything about it."

"Diaz, by the way you talk, you must be older than you look," Lopez said.

"How old do you think I am?"

"Midtwenties."

"I'm thirty-two."

"Really? You don't look it."

"Thank you."

"You're an E4. Did you have a break in service?" asked Keith.

"Yes. I was in for a couple of years, several years ago. Then my country was attacked and I joined the guard."

"Why did you sign up as a mechanic?"

"It's what I did in the civilian world. My father owned a garage outside Blythe. It's what I know."

"So you were the bookkeeper?"

"Yes, I ran the office, but I worked on the cars and trucks that came into the shop too."

"No shit. I don't see many females doing dirty work or heavy lifting, and working in a garage involves both."

"Running a garage on the outskirts of Blythe wasn't easy. My father needed all the help he could get. After my mother died, it was just the two of us. After school, I'd go and help him. I'd work the register, get parts he needed, and if he needed me to finish a job for a customer, he'd tell me what to do and I'd do it." She looked at Gillespie and said, "I lifted everything. I had to and got lots of grease under my fingernails."

Sounds of a skirmish broke the conversation.

"Need some help here," Doyle yelled.

Gillespie, Morris, Diaz, and Lopez dropped their beers, grabbed their weapons, and ran to the group of prisoners, while the beer gurgled out of the bottles and was absorbed into the arid desert in an instant.

The gunner in the turret of the Humvee spun around, and cocked and aimed the machine gun toward the cluster of soldiers and Iraqis. He kept the barrel pointed over their heads while he scanned the dark for any unusual activity.

Stivdednek was on his back, slashing his knife wildly in whatever direction he saw movement. One prisoner was on the ground next to Stivdednek, not moving. The other circled prisoners were trying to kick him, but, still bound by the zip ties, the circle only warped as they thrust their legs.

As the soldiers reached the group of prisoners, they tried to get them to stand, but the entire group fell to the ground. Stivdednek slashed two more when they fell on top of him. The mass of bodies squirmed like bugs when a rock is first turned over.

Diaz ran to the females and herded them away, but their crying, chattering, and wailing pierced the night. She tried to calm them down. As soon as they were unable to see the commotion, their crying reduced to a whimper.

The soldiers formed a circle around the prisoners, leveling their weapons at the group; all movement stopped.

"Stivdednek?" Keith asked. "You okay?"

"Yeah, thank God."

"Can you get yourself out of there?"

"Yes."

"All right. Come on out."

Stivdednek stood slowly. He looked around, and then moved toward the soldiers, kicking a downed prisoner as he walked.

"Doc," Gillespie spoke into the clear plastic tubing microphone near his lips. "Come on out here. We got at least three wounded PWs."

"What happened?" Keith asked.

"Bastards jumped me," Stivdednek replied.

"Bullshit!" Doyle shouted. "You were saying your religious crap to them. Then you slung your weapon and threw water on them, saying that you were baptizing them. You got too close and one of them tackled you. You stabbed that one."

The medic arrived. The soldiers directed the prisoners away. Doc knelt down next to the wounded men.

"What do you think?"

"Two of them are okay. They'll need stitches. I can bandage them and they'll be okay until we get some help, but the other one looks bad. He's bled out a lot. I got it under control, but he'll need to be medevaced right away."

"How long for a chopper to get here?"

"Hard to say."

"How long will it take to drive back to your FOB?" Gillespie asked.

"If we push it, five hours straight through."

"Doc, will they make it?"

"Yeah."

"Good. Here's the plan. We call in a helicopter to get the bad one out of here. Can he travel at all?"

"Yeah."

"Okay," acknowledged Gillespie. "Dead or wounded, we're still going to have to report it.

"We're going to get out of here and rally with the helicopter on the road," said Gillespie. "Doc, you, Dalley, and Belkamp will go out on the helicopter when we meet it."

"Morris," Gillespie said as he turned toward Keith, "your boy is too unstable. Put him in one of the Hummers with the MPs. You'll need another body, so I'll ride with you back to Speicher. You can pick up another driver once we're there and finish the delivery to Baghdad. Anyone want to add anything?"

"Works for me," Keith replied.

"Me too," Lopez added.

"Good. We gotta get out of here. Call for the chopper and get the Hajjis into the trucks. I want to be out of here in five minutes. One last thing: your boy is going to be charged with a few UCMJ articles when we get back to your FOB."

"Yes, he will."

In the distance, call signs and coordinates were sent on a secure channel.

Keith directed the prisoners to the trucks. The Special Forces soldiers loaded the wounded onto the truck. The site was swept clean. Stivdednek sat behind Sergeant Lopez in the lead Humvee with his head tipped onto his folded hands, saying a prayer.

Within five minutes, the convoy rolled out.

Soccer Balls

Fall 2003
FOB Speicher

Dear Kids,

Thanks for all the get-well notes and drawings and candy you sent me. I shared the candy with everyone in the unit. Actually, I didn't share all of it. As you know, I really like fireballs. I kept those for myself. Anyway, all the soldiers here loved it. Every single one of them wanted me to make sure I thanked you for them. Our commanding officer (he's like the principal) wrote you a note too. We saved some of the candy and gave it to the kids who live close to the base. They loved it! I don't think they get candy very often.

The kids here make me think of all of you.

Oh, by the way, don't send chocolate or anything that can melt. It's hot here, and all the chocolate dissolved into a puddle in the bottom of the box. And, wouldn't you know, someone scraped out all the chocolate goo and ate it.

I'm not sure how you found out I had been hurt, but I want you to know—*I'm okay.* I was hurt a little, not a lot.

Do you remember when that car flipped over in front of the school last year? It looked really bad, but the driver and passenger were able to get out of the car with only a few cuts. It was like that. My truck tipped over and I got a few cuts.

Things are okay here. There are other places in Iraq where things are really bad. Saddam is a bad person and has hurt a lot of people. Although Saddam didn't attack us on September 11, it's a good thing we are here. We can help and do some good for the kids and grown-ups. Many of the people in Iraq are poor. They don't have nice houses like most everyone in Weymouth, but they seem happy with what they have. I don't know what Iraqis eat, and I'm not sure I want to know. When they're cooking their meals, there are lots of odors. Some are really tantalizing (you'll have to go to the dictionary and look up the definition), but some of the other smells are *gross!*

The kids here are great. I have an idea and I hope you all want to help. Mrs. Wells asked me if I needed anything. I don't, except more fireballs, but the kids here can use some things like old or new sneakers, colored pencils and paper, toothpaste and toothbrushes, and balls, any kind: baseballs, basketballs, superballs, but most of all, soccer balls. They love playing soccer. So if you want to, and your parents let you, look around your house and see if you have anything you can send to the kids here. Bring it to school, and Mrs. Wells will take care of mailing it to me. There's a photographer here, and I'll ask her to take some pictures when we give what you send to the kids. I'll make sure you get a copy.

That's it for now. Take care and study hard. When I get back, Mrs. Wells said the whole school will have a big cookout.

I can't wait to see all of you.

Fondly,

Mr. Morris

To Keith, at first, the gulf of suspicion, wariness, and mistrust between the soldiers at FOB Speicher and the Iraqi locals seemed insurmountable. The Iraqis steered clear of the base. Men slowly walked past at a distance they thought was safe from the .50-cal. machine guns in the towers at each corner of the base. Their vibe flung contempt-accented gestures with every stride they took toward the soldiers and the base. Women scurried past as quickly as they could, fearing to look at the base as if a glance would draw the ire and bullets of the soldiers. It was, however, the children who crept steadily closer to the fortified base, controlled access gate, and heavily armed soldiers.

It was one of the armed sentries who first gave a group of children a half dozen leftover sugar cookies he had received in a package from his girlfriend. He handed the small paper bag containing the cookies to the closest boy. Slowly, like a badly beaten dog, the boy reached for the bag. The murmuring of the other children ended when he held the bag. He carefully peered into the bag and then pulled out a cookie. He put it to his lips and smiled when the first crystal of sugar dissolved on his tongue. He knew he would be swarmed by the other children, so he quickly consumed the rest of the cookie as the pack descended on him.

When the soldier was on duty again, there were more kids. They crept closer and stayed longer. Another soldier reached into his cargo pockets and tossed a handful of SweeTarts wrapped candy packages at the kids. The kids ran after the candy, tumbling into a heap of feet and hands. The heads of the various children alternately percolated up out of the pile. As each child emerged with candy, they smiled as they tore the package open and ate. The soldier threw enough so each kid could have more than one package. Mothers screamed, yelled, and gestured at the children to get away from the soldiers. The children slowly returned to the Iraqi side of the road. Three of the children smiled and waved at the soldiers.

Each day the children hovered around the barricaded entrance. Some of the soldiers remained stoic, unflinching, and disengaged from the children. However, most looked forward to the daily gaggle of children. More and more candy emerged from the base.

Leftover food from the DFAC found its way to the children, as did Band-Aids, coins, and bracelets made from 550 parachute cord and paper clips.

As the interaction of soldiers and Iraqi locals thawed, the commanding officer of the base recognized the opportunity he had to create goodwill with the community. He ordered the formation of a civil action team. The civil action team leader, Captain Delsignore, proposed three community involvement projects. Number one, the base would operate a community health clinic. Second, they would create a classroom for community education. And third, in an undeveloped field within the walls of the base, they would create an athletic field to play soccer and also teach the kids how to play baseball. All of this would take place behind the sandbags and concertina wire, to control access.

Somehow the CO had learned there was a teacher in the guard unit under his command. By way of First Sergeant Steele, Keith was volun-told he was part of the civil action team. He was to teach the Iraqi children, with the help of a translator, about basic math, health, nutrition, and other things American without being overtly propagandizing.

"Any questions?" Steele asked.

"Yeah, a few. First, do I get to meet the translator, and do I get the same translator each time? That would be best. Second, do I still get to do my job with the ten-five-eight, or is this what I do for the rest of my deployment? Lastly, what kind of stuff do I have to work with? A chalkboard? Books? Pencils and paper? A map?"

"Good questions. I'll find out about the translator. Yes, you will still report to and drive for your unit. As far as supplies go, let me know what you want and how much you want. You'll get what you need," Steele replied.

"Thanks," Keith said. "I'll need someone to help."

"Doing what?"

"Just help. Keep an eye on the kids, work one-on-one, pick up supplies. Whatever. I'm sure there's someone around here who'll help."

"I'll do it."

"Really? I wasn't expecting you to volunteer."

"I've been thinking about the Troops to Teachers program for a long time. This might be a good way for me to get a better idea if that's what I want to do when I'm done with the army."

"Getting short?"

"Yeah. This is my last deployment."

"How long you been in?"

"Twenty-eight years. It'll be thirty by the time I'm done."

"What makes you think you want to teach?"

"I like training soldiers. I like helping them get their shit together, and I really like turning some punk kid around."

"That's great, First Sergeant. I can use the help. You got kids of your own?"

"No. Been married a half dozen times, but no kids."

"That's probably best," he added after a long pause. "Every base I've been to has a program to help pain-in-the-ass teenagers, and I always volunteer to work with them. I've seen some of them turn around. I like that."

"When do we start?" Keith asked.

"I'd guess within a month or so. I'll let you know."

Keith heard First Sergeant Steele before he saw him.

"Morris," Steele yelled as he walked into the tent that the ten-five-eight was using as an office. "This place is a fucking dump. Every time I'm in here, it makes me feel like I'm going to puke. Make sure it's clean the next time I come here."

"Yes, First Sergeant."

"Let's go."

"Can't. I'm scheduled to drive in an hour."

"What do you think I am, stupid?" Steele yelled even louder. "I set the schedule for you and I schedule the time you take a shit, so if I come in here and say you're coming with me, you should be smart enough to figure it out that you're not on a mission."

"My bad," Keith mumbled, feeling somewhat diminutive in front of the six-foot-six-inch, two-hundred-and-thirty-pound, eardrum-busting first sergeant.

"We're going to take a ride with Captain Delsignore and meet with the caliph, grand sultan, almighty poohbah, or whatever the fuck they call the neighborhood boss here, about getting the kids in town to the clinic and school. Be ready in fifteen minutes, full armor. We got four gun trucks and sixteen soldiers going outside the wire with us.

"Also, bring Diaz. Those walking body bags will respond better if there's another female around."

Fifteen minutes later they met at one of seven staging areas for patrols and convoys going outside the wire. The soldiers from the Fourth Infantry Division were already there.

"First Sergeant?" called out one of the Fourth Infantry Division soldiers.

"Yeah."

The soldier walked to him and held out his hand.

"Master Sergeant Evans," he said. "Pleased to meet you."

"Likewise. This is Sergeant Morris and Corporal Diaz."

They all exchanged handshakes. Evans introduced the other soldiers.

"I know where we're going. My question is, why?"

"We're setting up to do some civil affairs work with the locals, and the guy we're meeting is the village leader. It's a done deal, but we'll sit and chat, take a few hits off the hookah, and pretend to listen to him talk about something meaningful, and then we're out of there. We're bringing some tchotchkes with us."

"Okay. Sounds good. I know the alley and the guy in charge. I don't expect any problems. Watch out for wild dogs; they're everywhere, and they love those alleys. Lots of garbage to eat. If one gets close, first try to kick it. If it doesn't leave, shoot it with your sidearm. Don't unleash the M4 in the alley. Lots of people around. Things don't go well with a lot of 556 bouncing around."

They all nodded. Next came the mission brief, then a weapons check, and finally rally point info.

"Okay, load up," said Evans. "First Sergeant, can I see you for a moment? Morris too."

soldiers, from the Fourth Infantry Division, were thoroughly trained and experienced with foot patrol in the streets of Iraq.

Keith was trying to remember all the subtleties and procedures he had learned for dismounted patrol years ago at basic training and the refresher training the 1058th had completed prior to deployment. He glanced across the alley at Diaz and saw her concentrating deeply on the nearby buildings. The soldier behind her raised his rifle and pointed it at the base of her skull. He looked at a soldier on Keith's side of the alley and mouthed some word. He jerked back a little as though the recoil punched into his shoulder.

"Hey. Knock it off, Nguyen," Keith yelled.

He smiled a sadistic grin and lowered his weapon. "Don't shit your pants," Sergeant Nguyen yelled back. "Your bitch is okay."

Diaz turned and stared at Nguyen. Keith could see she was about to speak, when she stopped, turned back, and redirected her attention to the patrol and alley. She glanced over at Keith. She did not have a scared or angry look. It was more like a look of resignation.

Keith hadn't said anything to Diaz simply because he couldn't believe what Evans had said was real. He worked with women, and even reported to a female in both his civilian and military jobs. The women in the 1058th were as unremarkable as the men. Some were pains in the ass, some were inspiring, but most were ordinary and forgettable. He couldn't process the idea that someone would hate a woman simply because she was female.

Ten feet in front of the point man on the patrol, a cacophony of dog barks, cries, and whimpers erupted. Keith could see a pack of at least ten scrawny dogs leaping and darting at a bigger but no less scrawny dog.

"Ten bucks says the big dog gets away," yelled the point man.

"You're on," came the reply from someone behind Keith.

The yipping and barking increased as the smaller dogs snipped at the big dog's heels. The big dog, a sandy-colored, spotted mongrel, tore open the neck of a dog that got too close. It mangled the haunches of another.

The squad moved closer. Iraqi men standing nearby watched the fight. Money moved between the spectators.

"How's he doing?"

"He's taken two of them down, and the other ones can't get close enough to get at his neck."

Keith was appalled at the brutality. His dog, Caisson, was a big, happy, slobbering dog whose sole purpose in life, it seemed to Keith, was to eat, nap, and find someone to scratch behind his ears and at the base of his tail. Caisson wouldn't stand a chance. Just then another small disemboweled dog flew through the air and crashed into the side of a building. It lay there panting, struggling to get to its feet until it bled out and couldn't move. The rest of the dogs ran away. The big dog tore into the dog whose neck it had exposed and gnashed his mouth in the hole. Then it ran off with the small dog in its mouth.

As Keith neared the other eviscerated dog, it died. There was no whimper and no tap of its tail; it simply expired.

"Shit."

"You owe me ten bucks."

"I know. Crap. When we're done here, I'll get it to you."

The soldiers stepped over the dead dog. One of them kicked it out of his way.

"We're here," said Evans. "First Sergeant, Morris, Diaz, come on up here. The rest of you, you know what to do."

A trimmer, better-groomed man standing next to the fat one stepped forward from the crowd of Iraqi men.

"Welcome. I am Abu al Khayr. I'm your translator."

Keith guessed that he and Abu were about the same age. Abu was wearing a thawb and a keffiyeh. His beard was neatly trimmed, and the little hair that was visible looked gelled. He looked like he worked out. *Could be a grad student at any college in Boston,* Keith thought.

The one in charge spoke. Abu turned, listened, and nodded.

"Jumah welcomes you to his home and wishes you to come inside. He assures you that you are safe," said Abu. He gestured to the man beside him.

"Tell him we appreciate the opportunity to talk with him," said Captain Delsignore. "You speak English well. Did you study or live in America?"

"Yes. Many of my father's family left when Saddam came to power. I joined them in Michigan and lived there for fifteen years. I came back to help my father when the Americans came to rid us of Saddam."

"Your father is a good man."

"Yes." Abu smiled. "He's waiting for you to enter his home."

The soldiers looked at Jumah. He turned and stepped through the door. They stepped forward to the brick structure. The other Iraqis stepped aside and let the Americans pass. Once inside, Jumah turned. He shook the hand and kissed the cheek of each one of the four soldiers entering his home, except Diaz. As she entered, an older woman appeared from one of the rooms and presented a piece of colorful fabric to her.

"That is my mother, Lufti," said Abu. "She wishes for you to wear a hijab in the house of Jumah."

Diaz did not take the scarf. Instead, she looked at Keith.

Abu spoke again. "It is not a symbol of repression in this house. Accepting it is respect for Lufti and her Islam. You may keep it when you leave. It is a gift as well as a symbol of respect. It is no different than bowing your head when someone says grace, whether you believe or not."

Keith nodded.

All eyes were on Diaz. She reached for the hijab. "It is gorgeous," she said. She lifted her helmet, set the scarf on her head, and looked back at Keith.

"I think we all can remove our helmets here," Steele said.

Jumah gestured for everyone to sit down. Lufti disappeared down a dark, short, arch-shaped hallway and turned into a bright living room. There were several stuffed chairs, a large sofa, and an elegant dark-colored wooden table. Keith noticed there were no photographs in the room. It seemed uncluttered compared to American living rooms. There were several hallways stemming off the living room, but they were covered with beads and drapes.

Captain Delsignore spoke. "Thank you for inviting us into your home. As a symbol of our appreciation, we offer a box of America's finest chocolate for you, and a box of fine cigars. For your wife, we wish you to give her this scented soap and perfume."

Jumah nodded as Delsignore spoke. As Abu spoke, Jumah beamed and stood tall when he accepted the gifts. He yelled something and his wife appeared in the hallway. He spoke again, and Abu gave her the basket of scented products. She beamed, giving the basket to a small woman standing in the shadows behind her. She spoke again. A moment later, three young girls entered the living room and presented a tray of foods and drinks to the guests.

Acknowledgments of hospitality and appreciation passed back and forth through Abu. Jumah gestured for everyone to sit.

The conversation began about sports, the school, and the clinic. Captain Delsignore explained the goal and how important it was for Jumah to allow the community to participate.

"We can clearly see why your reputation as a strong man precedes you. It is easy to see that you are a kind and intelligent man too. Because the strength of your word is important, not only to us but also to your community, we ask that you allow the boys and girls to come to school and the clinic."

Jumah leaned back and struck a pondering pose. He spoke to Abu and shook his head as if he were saying no.

Abu nodded, turned to Delsignore, and said, "Boys may attend, but no girls."

Lufti turned around and yelled at Jumah. She stopped talking, glared at him, turned abruptly, and walked away.

Jumah scowled at Lufti's back until she turned a corner. Slowly turning his attention back to Captain Delsignore and Abu, he spoke to the latter.

"Jumah says both the boys and the girls will go to your classroom and clinic," said Abu.

"That is excellent," Delsignore said as he stood to shake Jumah's hand. Once Jumah stood, handshakes went around the room. Delsignore reached into his pack and pulled out a box. "I heard you are a man who appreciates good scotch. Here you go, my friend."

Jumah reached for the box, opened it, looked inside, and smiled.

Steele leaned over to Keith and whispered, "I don't understand Iraqi, but I've been on the receiving end of that look a thousand times. She was pissed."

"Yeah, I know," Keith whispered back. "I've been on the receiving end of the stink eye a few times myself."

"Yeah, the hairy eyeball."

"A buddy of mine back home was dating an Italian girl. He called it the *malocchio*."

"So it's in their chromosomes; women around the world can deliver it with no training."

"Great," Keith whispered, sighing.

"Let's wrap it up and get out of here," said Steele.

Amid the chatter, the crowd shifted, shuffled, and moved slowly toward the door.

Keith sensed some motion and saw Lufti. She stood in the arch leading to other parts of the house. Keith watched her. She smiled at the guests in her house as her eyes swept the room, making eye contact with everyone. When Jumah's and her eyes met, there was a stare-down. It wasn't a challenge, nor was it malicious or even annoyed. An unspoken message passed between them.

"What do you think they just said?" asked Diaz.

"I don't know. They're married. They probably have all kinds of codes and things they understand about each other."

"I think he said something like, 'I did what you wanted, Wife,' and she said, 'You're a good man,'" said Diaz.

"Really? What makes you think that?"

"My father told me sometimes he would do things he really didn't want to do so he could hear my mother say, 'You're a good man.'"

"Yeah, whatever," Keith replied as he looked askance at Corporal Diaz. "I think we're done here."

The first sergeant looked at Keith and motioned his head toward the door.

As the civil action team stepped out through the door and onto the stoop, the soldiers guarding the meeting broke up their circle and moved toward positions to escort the team out of the alley. As Diaz stepped out of the door and before her foot landed on the stoop, Nguyen stood and swung around, perfectly timing his act to knock her off balance and land her in some of the alleyway garbage.

As Keith stepped over to give her a hand up, he saw Nguyen smirk as he mumbled, "Oops."

Corporal Diaz didn't look at him. She returned to her position in the squad and focused on a point in the distance, beyond the alley.

"Fuck you," said Keith, staring at Nguyen.

"Fuck off, douche bag," replied Nguyen. He returned to his position in the squad behind Diaz.

The team emerged from the alley, climbed back into the Humvees, and returned to FOB Speicher without incident.

After the soldiers of the Fourth Infantry Division departed, Keith approached Diaz. "Why'd you take that from him? You don't take shit from anybody. Hell, I saw you tackle Stivdednek."

"Stivdednek was an idiot. That guy was scary. What was I going to do, tackle him? He would have killed me," she replied.

"I don't get it."

"I don't expect you to," said Diaz. "There's more than one guy in the world like that. I'm going to take a shower and call it a day," Diaz stated.

"Okay. See you tomorrow. You okay?"

Walking away, she did not look back. She simply waved at Keith with the back of her hand.

Keith watched her walk away. He turned and walked to the Fourth Infantry Division's section of the FOB. He asked various soldiers he saw on the way where he could find Nguyen. Eventually, someone told Keith that Nguyen was at the fight pit. As Keith walked close, he could see five soldiers cheering on a wrestling match in the sand-filled pit.

Nguyen saw him coming. Sweaty, with a veneer of sand, he stepped out of the pit. He strode aggressively toward Keith. "What do you want? Your bitch come crying to you and you're here to make things all better?"

Without a word or a foreshadowing stance, Keith used his limited martial arts training to hit Nguyen and drop him to the ground. Two seconds later Nguyen spun his legs at Keith and swept his legs out from under him. Keith fell. He scrambled to get up, but two of the spectators had his arms pinned behind his back and were pushing his hands up between his shoulder blades.

Nguyen stood and waved the knife he had pulled from his boot in front of Keith's face. He stopped with the point a millimeter away from the corner of Keith's left eye.

"Your spic bitch doesn't mean anything to me, but I'll fucking kill you if you ever come near me again," said Nguyen.

Keith didn't say a word. He stared at Nguyen.

Nguyen nodded and the soldiers released Keith's arms. The rush of blood back into his arms and the sudden absence of excruciating pain almost made him collapse. He stumbled and then stood, turned, and walked away.

"Hey, Morris."

He kept walking.

"Your bitch, she's nothing more than life support for pussy," said Nguyen.

The soldiers around him started laughing and giving Nguyen high fives.

Childproof

Winter 2003-4

Keith always knew when First Sergeant Steele was calling on the phone. He could hear Steele yelling the moment he had a connection. Before Keith had a chance to break in and say good morning, identify himself and the work center, and state it was a nonsecure line, Steele had already communicated at least a paragraph.

"Morris! You got half a dozen boxes at the post office," Steele yelled into the phone.

"That's great news, First Sergeant. I'll head on over and get them," Keith replied as he distanced the handset from his ear, wondering if Steele ever spoke softly.

"Did you not fucking hear me?" Steele bellowed. "I said you got six boxes there. Do you think I'd call you if you could walk over and grab them? Shit, with you as a teacher, no wonder the country is going to ruin."

"You'll need a truck to bring them back to your school room," Steele added.

Keith wondered what it was like in the house where Steele had been raised. Did the one who yelled the longest and loudest win?

"Oh. They're that big?"

"Yeah, that's why the LT running the show there called me. Your boxes are filling up his storage room. Grab the Gator and pick me up."

"Be right there."

Keith had received a couple of e-mails from Sharon back at the school in Weymouth, so he knew the kids were sending some sneakers, soccer balls, and other incidental stuff. But how much did

launched missile could be lethal. When the 1058th first arrived at Speicher, the RPGs were more frequent, but as time passed, routines developed, and familiarity with the community grew, the missiles became less frequent.

Keith pulled out his knife and cut through the packing tape. The kids and parents had come through, indeed. There was a large envelope with Keith's name on the top of a pile of sneakers inside the fourth box. Inside were four other letter-size envelopes. In one envelope, Keith found a copy of the *Weymouth News* and a letter signed by dozens and dozens of people. He studied the penmanship, from first grade scrawls to swirly, festive, sixth-grade-girl cursive, and concluded that every kid at Academy Avenue Elementary School had signed the letter. There was a group photograph with every kid attending the school standing in front of the school and waving; a photo of the kids in his class saluting; a picture of Caisson; and a handmade coupon for ten thousand fireballs.

In the second envelope were two pieces of paper. One was a handwritten note to Keith. The second sheet was typed.

Dear Keith,

The kids in all of the six grades here wrote these letters. One is to you, another is to all of the soldiers who serve with you there, and the last letter is to the kids in the community around your base. Each class drafted their thoughts, and then one student from each class wrote a letter. I combined their letters into one and made some corrections to the grammar and structure. (Hey, I was a teacher before I was the principal!) I think they wrote an amazing letter to the Iraqi children. The children of the world should be our diplomats.

Stay safe. I pray for you and all of our service members every day. Come back soon.

FYI, all of your students advanced to fifth grade.

Sharon

He sat down and opened another envelope. The letter he found read as follows:

Dear Mr. Morris,

We think of you every day. We hope you are safe and will come back soon. We were very worried when we heard you were hurt, but after Mrs. Wells read your letter to us at assembly, we all felt better.

The whole school decided to help the children in Iraq near your base. We asked our parents and had a car wash and a bake sale and raised over $1,000! The *Weymouth News* sent a reporter and a photographer. We were on the front page! There's a copy of the paper in the box in an envelope for you.

We loved the letters from all the soldiers you work with. One of the boxes has lots more candy and letters to your soldier friends. There are fireballs for you too. They are in the box with the word *candy* written on it.

Keith paused, looked at the boxes, and found a very decorative and colorful word *candy* drawn on the outside of one of the boxes. He noticed that all the boxes had been creatively labeled and the contents identified with various symbols and drawings. He continued reading the letter.

We wrote a letter to the kids you teach over there. Mrs. Wells said they might not be able to read English but that you have a translator. If they want to write back to us, that would be *way cool*. We didn't know if they had paper and pencils, so we put tons of paper and pencils in one of the boxes. Can you take a picture of the Iraqi children and send it to us?

There's a picture of us in front of the school in the *Weymouth News*.

Please come back soon. Mrs. Wells promised we would have a big party and cookout when you come back.

Love,

The Academy Avenue Elementary School students

Keith felt a lump in his throat. He passed the letter to Steele and opened the third envelope.

Dear Iraqi Children,

Hello from America. We're sorry to hear you have such a bad person for a president. We hope our army soldiers can help you get a nicer president. We get to change presidents every four years. It's confusing and people argue.

What is your country like? Is it hot there? Our teacher, Mr. Morris, is there in the army and says it is hot and dusty. Can you write to us and tell us what you do when you are not in school? What kind of candy do you have in Iraq? What are your favorite TV shows? Do you play video games? Does it rain? Mr. Morris told us you get dust storms. Do you not have to go to school on dust days? Do you get snow? We don't have to go to school on snow days.

We sent some pictures of what our country looks like. Can you send us some pictures of your country?

We see the news on TV, and it looks scary. We hope you are safe. Maybe someday you can come to America and we can go to Iraq.

Friendly,

Your Pen Pals at Academy Avenue Elementary School in Weymouth, Massachusetts, in the United States in the Northern Hemisphere, west from your country across the Atlantic Ocean

Keith stopped again and dug deeper inside the envelope. He pulled out drawings and a few photographs. The pictures were taken around Weymouth: Wessagusset Beach, the view to Boston from Great Hill, someone running a snowblower clearing a driveway, trees, flowers, parks, and backyards. The drawings showed the Statue of Liberty and the Liberty Bell. Someone tried to draw the *Mayflower*, and pilgrims and Indians having a meal.

"You're going to love this letter," Keith said as he passed the note to Steele. The fourth envelope was thick. He opened it and pulled out a piece of construction paper folded small enough to fit in an oversized envelope. He unfolded it. In very large colorful print, it read as follows:

Dear Soldiers, Sailors, Marines, and Airmen,

Thank you.

Sincerely,

Your Friends at Academy Avenue Elementary School in Weymouth, Massachusetts

Every inch of both sides of the paper was covered with drawings and short notes. The drawings included colorful hearts, orange skulls and crossbones, green and yellow four-leaf clovers, stars, airplanes, jets, tanks, ships, rainbows, and trees—everything a child would ever want to draw.

The notes expressed sentiments like "Be safe"; "Come home soon"; "If you see my dad, tell him I said, 'I love you'"; and other random thoughts.

"This is impressive, Morris," said Steele. "We'll hang this poster in the DFAC for everyone to see."

"Yeah. I wasn't expecting this much."

"You got a lot of people interested, both back home and here, in helping with your school."

"Yeah. About twenty-five people showed up at the meeting this morning."

"Good mix?"

"Yeah. Most of them already volunteer where their kids go to school back home. Some are interested in the Troops to Teachers program. About half of them are females. Even that hard-ass air force major running their admin shop volunteered."

"Hicks? Really? She's pissed off everyone here, walking around like her shit doesn't stink, snapping her fingers, and jabbing and pointing her finger at everyone she talks to."

"Yeah, I know. She's a real boner-killer," said Keith. "But she was different when we were setting up the classroom. She was, like, human. Very curious about what she is supposed to do around the kids. I told her to be herself."

"We don't want that. She'll scare them."

"Yeah, that's for sure. However, she didn't say much. Said she used to be around kids a lot. She thought about being a teacher at one time, but she hasn't been around kids much for years."

"Whatever. She probably scares them," said Steele. "What do you want to do now?"

"Unload these boxes."

Steele and Morris stopped outside the classroom. There were at least a dozen soldiers inside painting, adding color to the room.

"Nice," said Steele as he stepped inside. "Where'd you get colored paints?"

"The Seabees," replied a very, very large soldier. "The Combat Camera guys dropped off some prints to hang on the wall. Seems like everyone wants to help in some way. The S4 guys scored a shitload of paper and pencils. Hell, they even scored some hats and T-shirts. Supply is outfitting the kids better than they're outfitting us. The spooks in S2 dropped off a ton of jelly beans."

"I'm not surprised," said Steele. "Everywhere I've been, any time we reach out to the kids, so many people, even some of the meanest sons of bitches, step forward in some way."

Half the soldiers in the room set down their paintbrushes and moved the boxes. The atmosphere became almost festive as they unloaded the boxes. An impromptu kickball game started when one the boxes tipped over and one of the balls rolled away. Unpacking the box of stuffed animals brought forth words like *cute* and *adorable*, and comments like, "My daughter had this one when she was a little girl" and "My son still sleeps with one like this."

One of the volunteers tilted his head upward and looked at the sky. "Medevac," he said. "Coming fast." He set his hammer down and moved toward the door.

"Need me to go with you, Doc?" one of the other volunteers asked.

"No. I'm not on call today, but when I hear one coming like this one, I want to be there, just in case."

"I'll walk with you."

"Okay."

"How do you know that helicopter is a medevac? How can you tell it's coming in fast?" asked another one of the volunteers.

"It's hard to describe," Doc answered. "They're not always bringing in wounded, but sometimes, I don't know. Maybe the pilot is pushing the chopper harder than usual, or maybe it's the direct approach to the LZ as opposed to the normal approach, which comes around the end of the runway. I bet you this one comes directly over the runway, fast. It's like the pilot skids the helicopter to a stop right next to the door. When that happens, they're bringing us someone who's badly wounded."

"Like you, Morris," Doc added.

He looked up. The helicopter was going fast and was barely over the rooftops. Then it dropped from sight and the sound of the rotors changed as the pilot adjusted the pitch. Two other medevac helicopters approached around the end of the runway.

"Gotta go."

The classroom working party had fashioned some benches and desks out of wood taken from the KBR compound. When the painting was done, they moved the desks inside.

When the unpacking and arranging was done, all the servicemen and servicewomen stepped back and assessed their work.

Keith was the first one to speak. "This is great. It's bright and colorful, and everything is made kid-size. I think we'll make a difference. Everyone, thanks for your help."

"When are the kids going to start coming here?" asked one of the soldiers.

"We're still working out the security details," answered Steele. "We can't just send a bus out to pick them up. Some of the parents want to come along, and many of them are mistrustful. And we can't just let anyone walk through the gate without screening them. We don't have enough females around here to screen all the women and girls. We got details to sort out."

The area around Speicher was mostly calm. Most of the problems in the area were among the Iraqis themselves. Intelligence reports noted a growing rift between the Sunni and Shiite Muslims throughout Iraq. Also, local and foreign al-Qaeda fighters were murdering Iraqis whom they felt were friendly or not hostile enough to the Americans and coalition partners. There had been an attack on a mosque in the village, and a dozen young men who fueled American vehicles or worked on the base had been murdered over the course of the last three months.

Two weeks later, thirty-two children ranging from six to twelve years old passed through the gate. Jumah and Lufti led the parade. The base access point retained all the weaponry and barriers, but a special entry point was created for the children. The line to pass through the metal detector was short. The soldiers bore no visible weapons. Once through the gate, the children were issued a very colorful ID badge that looked nothing like the standard DoD ID card.

Jumah had been on base once before. Colonel McNab, FOB Speicher's commanding officer, invited him to tour the facilities. McNab had also hosted a luncheon in Jumah's honor to acknowledge his leadership in creating a bond between Iraqis and Americans. The CO was there to greet Jumah and Lufti and as many of the children as he could.

The parents stayed by their children. It was the children who drifted away from the pack, noticing the insignificant but colorful things, like the barber's pole.

The base barbershop was staffed by five barbers, contracted by KBR. They were perfectly groomed men from India. They all had precisely gelled hair, manicured fingernails, high-pitched voices, and effeminate gestures, and they always wore cologne. Most of the soldiers did not even bring cologne with them. They were stationed in a war zone. However, somehow the barbers had come into possession of a small barbershop pole and mounted it on the outside wall near the otherwise nondescript door. Hardly anyone noticed it after their first day on base or after the first time they went looking for a haircut.

The children's first stop was at the medical clinic. The second stop was with the base PA shop photographer. She lined up all the kids, parents, and soldiers, nearly one hundred all told, on a set of bleachers. She made prints for everyone and a couple of extras for Keith. As requested, he sent a copy of the photo to his students. The next stop was the DFAC for a snack. There was another stop at the classroom, and the last stop was a game of kickball on the recently graded and leveled field, refereed by Steele. Dozens of the soldiers not on duty participated. For many it was a chance to elude the boredom of life on the FOB.

In the classroom, Major Hicks sat between a brother and sister, two of Jumah's large pool of grandchildren, and tried to guide them through the map lesson Keith was presenting. Keith noticed that she smiled at the children often, stroked the girl's hair, and listened attentively as the boy talked about something in his language. Hicks did not know what he was saying, but she understood it was important to him. As soon as the boy was done, he plopped back into her lap. The two children settled comfortably in her lap as she pointed out the various places on a map. She had an Iraq–English dictionary she referred to, but soon she gave up and pointed to places and said the names and colors in English. The children were fascinated if not comprehending. Keith knew from personal experience that children are very forgiving of mistakes. At the end of the class, Major Hicks very tentatively hugged them, patting them on the back as they left.

"Those kids seemed to click with you, Major," Keith said after the class ended.

Hicks snapped her head in Keith's direction. She almost scowled at him. She had a noticeable jerk to her body as she stood and turned to Keith. She lowered her eyes and looked at him as if she were expecting a fight.

"What did you say, Sergeant?" she asked.

"I said that those kids really clicked with you, ma'am."

She stood still for a long, tense moment.

"You think so?" she asked. Her question had an ever so slight vulnerable quality to it.

"Yes, I do," Keith assured her. "I've been a teacher for a few years. If kids aren't getting the right vibe, they quickly migrate away. Those kids worked their way into your lap and stayed there."

"Thank you, Sergeant. That's nice of you to say." She turned away and walked toward the door.

"You got kids, ma'am?"

She kept walking.

School was in session two days a week, on Mondays and Thursdays. Keith was not required to work with the 1058th on school days. Having the children on base abated the thoughts of war for a while. The dental department cleaned every child's teeth and passed out toothbrushes, toothpaste, and floss. The Seabees and soldiers squared off in a game of kickball with the Iraqi children, evenly divided between the army and air force teams. Keith tried again to teach a lesson on geography to show where Iraq and the United States lay on a map. It was very slow going because the children were at different levels of knowledge, education, literacy, and maturity.

Working through a translator was frustrating too. It became increasingly difficult to lead a class. The language barrier made it difficult to reach the children. Keith's lesson plans steadily devolved from attempting to teach math concepts to allowing the various translators to try to introduce the children to the most fundamental concepts of arithmetic. The younger kids loved the class with the reading and artwork as they explored coloring books. The older boys tended to stay outside and get a pickup baseball, basketball, or football (soccer) game going with the soldiers. The older girls tended to stay in class.

During the authorization process to build the school, Keith had been surprised to learn that prior to Saddam, Iraq had one of the most literate, nearly gender neutral, and effective education systems in the Middle East.

Once the children came to class, it was obvious that education mattered. It was often the grandparents leading the children to school and then sitting in class themselves, seemingly pleased to be in a classroom.

Often while the children were in class, the parents went to the health clinic. The dentist was the busiest place on base. There was one female and one male dentist, both reservists, running the show with about ten support staff. The normal pace with the soldiers was steady but by no means overwhelming. On the community health days, they were swamped: pulling teeth, applying fillings, treating various mouth diseases, and teaching the basics of brushing and flossing. It seemed to Keith that North America and some European countries were the only places where people cared about their teeth. The British were nearly as bad as the Iraqis.

After a few weeks, the stream of children attending class stabilized and became a predictable number. The parents, too, were not coming as often, nor were they accompanying the children as frequently. Speicher's commanding officer was pleased with the program and sought the funds to repair and upgrade one of the primary education schools on the edge of Tikrit closest to the FOB. A different Seabee battalion was deploying to Speicher, replacing the outgoing Bees, and their first task was to rebuild the school. Within two months, they had it functional with electricity, running water, and a roof.

The number of volunteers dwindled. Steele couldn't be there all day, every day, but he would show up and participate as much as he could. Major Hicks was always there, quiet and seemingly happy to be around the children, and yet, Keith thought, she exuded a sadness. The same two children found their way into her lap every session. Often, other children gathered around her too.

A half dozen other volunteers consistently helped.

"Sergeant," Hicks said one day after the children left. "Do you have children of your own?"

Keith was always surprised when Major Hicks asked a question. It was rare that she engaged anyone in conversation, particularly an enlisted member. According to the airmen in her shop, even when a new airman was reporting, she never inquired about the new report's background or interests. She told the new member what was expected, who the senior enlisted member for the air force was, and where to find that person on the FOB. Then she closed the door to her office.

"Uh, no, ma'am," Keith responded.

"Married?"

"Nope. Came close once."

"Do you want kids?"

"I haven't given it much thought either way," he replied. "I guess some day it'll probably happen. What about you, ma'am?"

She turned and stared at Keith, and then looked away.

Keith thought she was going to walk away again like she did the last time they spoke. But she didn't.

"I want children very much."

She stared at Keith until it became uncomfortable for him. He turned away and moved to grab the broom near the door, when she let loose another statement.

"My husband doesn't."

"I'm sorry to hear that, ma'am," said Keith. "Kids are great, but I see parents every day who shouldn't be parents."

"He said he wanted children before we were married. He won't tell me why he changed his mind."

She stared at Keith again. Maybe she wanted him to respond, but he thought it would be too easy to say the wrong thing.

"I'm sorry to hear that," he said again.

She turned and left. She never looked back and never broke her stride.

Keith let out a deep breath. *She's so intense,* he thought.

Keith noticed his students were often tense when they arrived. Each day at the morning brief, he heard how tension in the community had increased. Briefers stated that Iraq was in turmoil in ways the Americans had not considered. Sunni and Shiite neighbors wanted to kill each other for not adhering to the same sect of Islam. Everyone wanted to kill the Baathist, and Muslim extremists wanted to kill only for the sake of killing.

Murders and explosions rocked Tikrit frequently. Keith and the students had to evacuate to a nearby bomb shelter a couple of times when RPGs came too close. His heart pounded as he led the children to the shelter. The children, he noticed, did not seem to get as anxious as he did.

After a month, classes were canceled. The S2 had human intelligence that al-Qaeda in Iraq was in Tikrit and terrorizing the local Iraqis for accepting favors from the Americans. Al-Qaeda was looking for a target, and anyone or anything was fair game. The base increased its defensive posture and forbade anyone to be on base who didn't have a clear and preapproved reason.

Jumah was considered a friend of the CO and had expedited access to the base. On January 14, 2004, he arrived at the gate seeking an appointment with the commander to discuss the violence in Tikrit and in his neighborhood in particular. There had been ten murders in four days. Women and children had been hurt. The guards recognized him and allowed him access, but only him. Some of his entourage waited outside the checkpoint, while others wandered away.

The commander cleared his existing appointments and genuinely welcomed Jumah. The two were the same age, were of similar build, and exuded the same confident aura. The meeting lasted two hours while Jumah expressed his concerns for the safety of his community. The commander promised to redirect as much of his resources as he could and step up patrols the next day in Tikrit, particularly in Jumah's community.

The commander escorted Jumah back to the gate and offered him an armed escort back to his home. Jumah refused, saying he was safe, but his concerns were with the others who were not as strong as he. What would they think if he arrived with US Army soldiers as his bodyguards? They would think he was afraid, and then fear would grow.

The commander nodded, and waited until his friend disappeared from sight.

Cultural Numbness

Spring 2004

The school reopened. Keith was getting the classroom ready for the kids' return. The previous day, he had received a box of donated musical instruments. He knew there was sure to be a cacophony in class that day with the children experimenting with the kazoos, harmonicas, three flutes, tambourines, bongo drums, triangles, maracas, jaw harps, kazoos, and other assorted noisemakers.

Steele quietly came into the classroom. "Morris," he said. "We're suspending the classes and stopping the children from coming on base." Steele spoke softly.

"Why?"

"Jumah was killed last night. The Iraqi equivalent of a drive-by while he was having tea at some hookah joint. Five others were killed too, and several more were wounded."

"You're shitting me? Jumah was a stand-up guy."

"Yeah, I know. What's worse ..."

"Worse?"

"Yeah, his wife and grandchildren were murdered at their home."

"You're kidding me." Keith felt nauseous and his eyes stung. He started to rapidly blink his eyes.

Steele gave Keith the courtesy of looking away and walking over to a piece of paper that had fallen on the floor. Keeping his back to Keith, he bent over to retrieve it, slowly searched the wall in front of him for a thumbtack, rehung the fallen paper, and straightened up the rest of the items on the bulletin board.

Keith let out a heavy breath. "This place is fucked up. Bad."

"Yeah," said Steele. He paused. "The community is scared shitless, and they're blaming us, our presence, as causing the killings. We have put a hold on the program until we figure if what we're trying to do with our civil action programs is helping or only making things worse. In this case, even with the best of intentions, things got worse."

"I still can't believe what you're telling me."

"Believe it. I was in Bosnia a decade ago. Same kind of things happened there. So many people killed in the name of God."

Not God, Keith thought. *In the name of power and hatred.*

Major Hicks walked into the classroom. "Good morning, First Sergeant, Sergeant," she said.

"Morning, ma'am," they responded.

"I must be getting used to seeing the children. When they weren't here last week, I found myself thinking of them. It'll be nice to see them today." She paused before adding, "I think we make a difference."

Keith and Steele did not respond. Keith knew she was very attached to the children. He noticed that only when she was around the children could she set aside her sternness. His gut told him she was going to take the news of the murders very hard.

"Ma'am," Steele said. "This classroom and this whole COMREL effort is ending."

The hint of softness, present on her face when she said she was looking forward to seeing the children, vanished.

Steele continued, "Jumah and his whole family were murdered last night by some al-Qaeda fighters because he was working with us and encouraging his community to work with us too."

"Ma'am," Keith said, "I'm very sad and sorry. I know a couple of Jumah's grandchildren had taken to you."

She seemed to shudder. Then she forced her head up and made her body rigid as though she were at attention.

"I'm sorry to hear it too." She nodded her head for a moment. "I have work I can tend to now. Have a good day, gentlemen. Please let me know if there will be a memorial service."

Word of the murders spread fast. Many of the soldiers who helped create the classroom and ball field went to the classroom. Little was said. Steele went to the gym and worked out all day.

Keith tried to read, to work out, to nap, and to eat, but nothing diluted the awful feelings churning inside. He felt as if he would fall over at any moment. If he were lying down, he felt he might not have the muscle and bone necessary to rise again. He pictured the children's faces all day—the parents' too. Eventually he fell asleep in his rack.

The following day, Keith went to the DFAC. He was sitting alone. In front of him was a paper plate with two pieces of cold toast on it. Steele walked over to him.

"How you doing?" Steele asked.

Keith shrugged.

"Been looking for you."

"Been in my rack."

"Morris, I know that what happened sucks, but you're on a run today. You have to be 100 percent. Here's your assignment."

Keith didn't take the paper when Steele held it out.

"You have to punch through this now, Sergeant. If you don't, it will take much longer to get distance from it." He pushed the paper closer to Keith.

Keith shook his head and looked away.

"I'm not telling you to forget it. You will never forget. I'm not telling you to not feel sad. You will for a very long time. But this day is the day that you will either get something of a grip on it or you will be on the medevac flight with Hicks."

Keith looked at Steele.

"Hicks took it really hard. She tried to kill herself last night," Steele explained. "She got some sedatives from Medical and took all of them. One of her staff went to check on her and found her in a heap on the floor, barely breathing. They got her stable, but she's out of it.

"So you can either get some leverage against this shit and force some kind of a reconciliation into your head now, or you can't. And if you don't push through it now, you're going to have an even harder time readjusting when you get back to your normal life. I know. I've lived through this kinda thing once before."

Keith sat there.

Steele placed the paper on the table and left the building.

Five minutes later Keith picked up the piece of paper and walked out the DFAC door. Steele was standing there.

"Good. This is the first and most important step you're going to take. Drive carefully."

Home

April 2004
Weymouth and Hingham

When the order to redeploy came at the end March, Keith made an entry in his journal, "Going home." On his last day with his students in Weymouth, the school nurse, Natalia, gave him a journal. He tried writing in it while at Speicher, but he grew frustrated with himself because he thought his entries were inconsistent. Worse, he felt like he was making entries in a log more than capturing his feelings and observations.

He lay in his rack and considered returning home and resuming his life. Fourteen months had passed since the 1058th had left Hingham. Deployment was a significant life event, but his mental efforts to wrap it all in a neat bundle were futile. He wondered if his haphazard thoughts were an effect of the concussion he experienced. Sometimes light, noise, and smells affected him in ways he knew that, prior to the bomb, did not bother him. In fact, members of the unit regularly asked how he was doing, and some commented on what seemed to be an increased irritability level he had. He shrugged it off and responded by saying that everyone was irritable and cranky in a war zone or that everything would be okay once he got back to his normal life.

Keith clung to the belief that he would be okay back in Weymouth. If things did not get normal quickly, he did not know how he would deal with the unpredictable and frequent headaches.

When, at last, all the paperwork was done, his personal gear was packed, the awards and appreciation speeches were complete, and the mission of the 1058th was finished, Keith wanted to reflect on the year, but he could not do it. He was acutely aware of the fact that he had been to war, had been injured, had witnessed terrible things, and was leaving before the war was won or at least hostilities were suspended. In fact, to Keith, it looked like things were going to get worse before they got better.

The main body of the 1058th headed to LSA Anaconda in Balad on the fourteenth of April. Keith and the rest of the trailing party completed the Relief in Place and Transfer of Authority paperwork and flew home on the nineteenth. The 1058th returned to Hingham on the twenty-third, and the town celebrated their return on the twenty-seventh.

Keith marched unannounced into Academy Avenue Elementary School on Monday, April 26.

Sharon was in the gymnasium, the door to Natalia's office was closed, and the secretary, Shawna, had her back to the door. She sensed someone behind her and spun around in her chair. For a moment she looked confused, but then she gasped and let out a yelp of happy surprise.

"Hi," said Keith. He then put his finger to his lips and pursed his lips as if to say, *Shh.* Natalia's door opened, and she, too, let out a happy cry.

"Keith, you're back! Thank God," she cried.

"Hi. I wanted to surprise the kids," he said.

"You look great."

"Thanks." Keith saw her eyes go to the scars on his neck.

They both had moved toward him. He opened his arms and tightly hugged them.

After a minute, they stepped out of the hug, crying.

"Let me call Sharon. She'll be so happy to see you."

"Sure. Have her meet me in the classroom."

He turned back toward the door.

"Wait. I'll get the camera. We want to get a picture of this. The kids will be so happy to see you."

"Did most of them stay in the same class when they got into fifth grade?"

"Yes. They're in Lucy's class. Can I go in ahead of you and get a picture when you walk in? There's, like, nothing secret about you being here, so I can take a picture and it'll be okay?"

They had dated a couple of times. Keith remembered she liked military men and was intrigued by the military. She assumed everyone in the service had knowledge of supersecret information and had to guard their anonymity. He tried to tell her he was just a truck driver and didn't have a top secret clearance and that he was only told what he needed to know to accomplish the immediate mission. He was unable to convince her of his ordinariness and the fact that most people in the service were doing very ordinary work. The difference was that most military members were willing to do ordinary work in very challenging settings.

"Sure. I'll hang back a minute."

At that moment, Sharon walked through the door and dropped the papers she had been holding. She started crying.

"Keith," she choked. She walked over to him and hugged him for a long time. "I'm so happy you're back."

She pulled away and reached for a tissue to wipe her eyes.

"I was about to go and surprise the kids," he said.

"Yes. Of course. I'll get the rest of the fifth graders."

She picked up her papers from the floor and set them on the desk. Then they all left.

Keith drew in a deep breath and thought about the kids murdered in Iraq. He felt the familiar lump in his throat. Thoughts of the explosion immediately followed. *Vague, murky,* and *fractured* were the words he'd used with the counselor he was required to talk to one time at the hospital in Germany during his treatment following the IED explosion. The counselor said what he was feeling was normal for the type of injury he experienced, but over time the thoughts would dim and the feelings would diminish. Keith wondered when that process would begin. His thoughts of the explosion, however, were never as definable as his memories of the children. He talked with no one about the tremendous sadness and guilt he felt about the murders of Jumah, Lufti, and the children.

There in the school's office, a safe, very familiar, and ordinary place, his anxiety suddenly surfaced. The silence set his heart pounding. He rapidly scanned the area, looking for anything out of place, a place where something like a bomb could be concealed. His anxiety grew. He turned to run out of the room when he heard a door open down the hallway and the steps of a child moving in the direction of the bathroom.

It was enough to ground him. He drew a deep breath and reached for a tissue to wipe the sweat from his brow. As happened with his other moments of anxiety, a headache began.

He turned back and walked the hallway to Lucy's classroom.

TBI, PTSD, and Normalcy

May 2004

"What happened?" asked Keith.

"Doyle. DUI, with his kids and wife in the car," Lieutenant Egar replied.

"Crap."

"He's lucky he didn't get in a wreck and hurt someone. He was speeding on that curvy road near Wompatuck and blasted past a cop sitting there."

"I know the road; I ride my bike there. No room for error."

"What's worse, when the cops finally stopped him, he mouthed off and resisted."

"What happens now?"

"He's going to court and maybe getting some jail time."

"What about his guard career?"

"Done. He'll be ADSEP'ed."

"That's too bad. He's a good soldier."

"I know. That's why I called you. He's one of your guys. This is the fourth incident in two months with one of our guys coming back from deployment who has got himself in trouble. There's something going on. We don't have a unit full of deadbeats and losers. I think they're having trouble settling back into normal life. I want to see if we can get some help for these guys and anyone else who's having trouble. Tell me about him."

"Yes, sir. Can you tell me who else is in trouble?"

Egar listed off three other soldiers whom Keith thought were stable, regular guys. One had been arrested for DUI, another for disturbing the peace, and the third for assault. This last soldier was thrown out of a bar in Canton and went back in and beat the bouncer.

"LT, those guys aren't kids getting out of hand or guys who already had issues before deployment. They're guys with families and decent jobs."

"Yeah. I know they're good guys. I think the problem is being in the guard."

"What do you mean?" Keith asked.

"You know, I recently came off active duty and moved back home to Massachusetts," said the lieutenant. "I affiliated with the guard, and headquarters put me here in Hingham. It's a pretty good unit. While I was on active duty at Fort Lewis, if someone was having trouble, there were plenty of ways to get help. Of course hardly anyone ever willingly sought help. Usually a wife or a girlfriend dragged the soldier into the family support center, but help was there. A soldier could be ordered to attend anger management classes or get counseling or whatever. It helped, but here there's nothing. Even civilian resources that could help don't receive much funding."

"Yeah, there's little active duty military left in New England," agreed Keith.

"I know," Lieutenant Egar said. "I always thought it would be wise to spin Devens up into a big regional army reserve and guard center, like Fort Hunter Liggett in California, but the planners have decided New England doesn't matter enough anymore. But that's a different conversation that I want to have with some politicians."

"No one is going to come forward, sir. No one wants to admit to anything, and no one trusts Medical."

"What's the problem with Medical?"

"In the reserve and guard world, the perception is that they're all about separating people. Deployed, they're great. You walk in and they take care of you—eight hundred milligrams of Motrin fixes everything—but on the drill weekends no one tells them more than they absolutely have to. Like if you show up on crutches, you have to tell them what happened. Other than that, no one says anything."

"That's not been my experience with Medical on active duty."

"I'm not sure it's all that different on active duty, sir," said Keith.

"I've heard stories of how pilots don't tell Medical anything for fear of being grounded. And senior enlisted members pay for care out of their pocket, so there is no trail."

"Okay, I wasn't tuned into that, but I'll take your word for it. However, I still think the biggest problem is what you said earlier. No one wants to admit to being emotionally scarred."

"So what are you thinking, sir?"

"Not sure yet. I've got some ideas, but I want to know if I can use you as an example. I want to push this issue, the lack of resources, up the chain."

Keith went silent. He didn't view himself as wounded or as a victim or resentful because of his injury. He thought it was a consequence of the risk he agreed to when he enlisted. However, he wished the headaches would go away. The doctors told him they would subside over time, but they hadn't. Every day he had a headache. Sometimes his head was pounding all day, and other times the aches were fleeting. He'd convinced himself the frequency and ferocity were less.

"Morris? You still there?" Egar asked.

"Yeah." Keith refocused his attention to the phone conversation.

"Let me ask you, how are you? You took the worst injury of anyone in the unit. You've been back about four months now. Are you dealing all right with everything here back in the real world?"

"Sir, I appreciate you asking, but I'm fine. You can talk about my injury, since it's widely known, but I'm really doing okay."

"Yeah?"

"Yes, sir. You know I got partial disability because of the slight hearing loss in my left ear, but other than that I'm happy, getting ready to go back to school, teaching, seeing my friends, and getting back to being a regular weekend warrior with the guard."

"So, it's like nothing happened while you were over there?"

"Yes, sir. Well, you know. I did get some scars, but I came back intact. Lots of soldiers didn't. The army did help. I got plastic surgery for the scars and burns. Every once in a while I'll think of the kids who were murdered over there, and that makes me sad, but people pick up guns and kill kids here too."

"When do you start back teaching?"

"September. I'll be back at school getting set up at the end of August, and the kids will start right after Labor Day."

"Okay, Sergeant," said Lieutenant Egar. "Good luck. If you have any ideas about how we can help our soldiers until the army figures out something, let me know. This problem is not unique to the 1058th. All over the country, people are coming back from mobs and deployments with problems."

"Yes, sir."

Keith hung up the phone and stared at a blank spot on the wall for a few minutes. The lurking headache surged. It felt like someone was stabbing his brain from inside his skull. There was a grinding sensation and a burning ferocity. At the onset, he knew it was going to be a bad one.

He went to bed early. He was departing for Arizona in the morning to visit his mother. He hoped for a good night's sleep. During his first few weeks back, his sleep was deep and sustained. But during the last couple of weeks, his sleep was fitful, elusive, and frustrating.

Pit Stop

May 2004
Aztec, Arizona

During the course of his deployment, Keith had written, e-mailed, and spoken with his mother on a regular basis. Communication with his father was infrequent. He recognized his mom's concerns and worries as those of any mother. She had sincere pride and deep respect for his confidence and abilities, and she'd held the omnipresent fear that her son would be hurt or worse. He listed his mother as next of kin, and she was notified when he was injured. He called her from the hospital in Germany as soon as he was able and assured her that, according to the doctors, his injury wasn't bad. The rapid blood loss was the problem, but as soon as he received some transfusions and rested, he felt as good as new. He promised to visit her as soon as he redeployed.

After the parade and cookout in Hingham, his visit to the school, going through all his mail, reacquainting with Caisson, and searching for patterns of normalcy to grab onto, Keith made arrangements to visit his mother. She wanted to fly to Massachusetts to greet him when he returned, but as she explained on the phone one night, her claustrophobia forbade her from the confines of airplanes, and that fear evolved further into a fear of flying. He reassured her that he understood and would get to Arizona to see her. He just needed some time to reorient to a noncombat zone.

He spent a lot of time sleeping. At first it was restorative, but he quickly grew frustrated with himself. He was sleeping well into the afternoons and not going to sleep until dawn. Keith had always been an early riser. Even in college, after staying up late into the night, he still awoke and got out of bed early. However, back at his house in Weymouth after reorienting himself to home, he had taken to walking and riding his bike around town at all hours. He had even been questioned by the police a couple of times. He explained he was just back from deployment and readjusting to the time zone. They nodded, thanked him for his service, and drove off. The nights, the shadows, and the dark of a moonless night didn't bother him.

Several weeks after his return, Keith boarded a plane for Phoenix. He slept most of the way, waking only as the pilot dropped the plane onto the runway at Sky Harbor Airport. The plane taxied west and then turned, so Keith could see the sunset. The orange-colored light turned the sandy-colored earth and brown buildings into muted, unique colors. He felt the warmth of late May ease into the plane the moment the ramp agent opened the door. He stepped out of the plane and peered through the crack between the Jetway and the aircraft. The pleasant 95° temperature of the Valley of the Sun in May felt good. He had grown to love New England, but the sensation of pervasive desert heat was refreshing. He knew it wouldn't last. The oppressive heat was just around the corner, and he didn't miss that.

The visit with his mother was pleasant. The house in Chandler hadn't changed a bit. She cooked and was happy to see him. They walked a few of the easier trails in the Phoenix Mountain Preserve, went out to dinner, and visited with a few of her long-term acquaintances. They all were very curious about the war and what he had seen. Most did not support the president and his decision to go to war in Iraq. He was asked by several people to explain why the United States was fighting in Iraq instead of Afghanistan. He responded by saying that it wasn't his place to make policy. He said he followed orders and was glad he had had a chance to make a difference. He kept the story of Jumah, Lufti, and the murdered children to himself. All in all, he was satisfied with his trip to Arizona, until the second to last day, when he drove to Yuma to see an old friend.

His mother's car was a Lincoln, big, safe, and comfortable. He set the cruise control at eighty miles per hour, drove Interstate 10 South, and then went westbound on Interstate 8. He passed the turnoff to

Gila Bend and turned up the music when he rolled the window down. The road was etched across the mostly flat, forlorn terrain. Small, hearty, thorny scrub and brush peppered the desert. The coffee he had drunk in Casa Grande was filling his bladder. He exited the interstate at Aztec and turned north away from the interstate toward an abandoned building that was probably a gas station back in the day.

He stopped the car in what was one of the repair bays and went behind the building remains to relieve himself. Standing there, he thought, *Why am I being discreet? No one can see me.* He was more than a half mile from the interstate. The noise from the large long-haul trucks abated. The railroad tracks, south of the interstate, were unoccupied at the moment by the mile-long freight trains that paralleled the interstate. The sounds of the feedlot, also to the south of the interstate, faded away, but not the smell. It permeated the whole area. He zipped up and noticed the remains of a small structure on a little rise about a half mile away. He thought, *I'm in no rush. I can stretch my legs and see what's there.* Beyond the structure was a mountain range many miles in the distance.

No need to take compass bearings, he thought. He could see everything he needed to see. He walked toward the structure, glancing behind to orient himself with the horizon. The most noticeable structure was an old, abandoned steam-locomotive water tower.

It's quiet, he thought. In Iraq there was noise everywhere: generators going constantly, the heavy sounds of military aircraft, and random explosions off in the distance. It was hard to hear anything in Iraq. That day, back in Arizona, he noticed the sound of his steps crunching the desert gravel and also noticed the imbalance in his hearing. Purposefully, he shuffled his feet for a different sound to disturb the monotonous silence around him. He stopped. The breeze stopped. Sounds stopped. The mountains he'd noticed earlier seemed much farther away than when he'd started. They were barely discernible now. He turned his head back to reorient himself with the abandoned building where he had parked the car. It, too, was but a speck in the distance. The old railroad steam-locomotive water tower had diminished to a shape indistinguishable from the nearby cluster of tamarisk trees. He abruptly turned his whole body back, searching for another point of reference. He couldn't have walked that far. He looked at his watch; the time was 11:13. How long had he been walking? He tried to remember what time he'd left his mother's house. He kicked himself for not taking a look at the time when he left his car and for not picking a solid point on the horizon that he could use to orient himself. *Some soldier,* he thought. *My survival skills have dulled since I left Iraq.*

His mind raced between two thoughts: *I'm in Arizona in some kind of trance,* and *I'm in Iraq alone, evading. No, I'm in Arizona. Where is my car? Where's my Humvee?* His head spun around searching for the car or the former gas station. He started to sprint in the direction from which he thought he had come. Then, quickly he changed his mind and thought, *FOB Speicher is only a couple of miles away. No, I'm going the wrong way.* He lurched in another direction. Then he stopped running. *This is crazy; I'm in Arizona.* He searched the area and the horizon again for something. He started to feel as though someone was watching him. He started walking quickly toward the structure. His thoughts continued to alternate. He spun into a frenzy. *This is crazy. Where am I? Get a grip. I'm fucked out here by myself.* He heard the familiar roar of a fighter jet in the distance. He looked and saw three of them zip across the sky and then disappear. Two Apache helicopters materialized over the mountains. *What the hell?* he thought. *I am in Iraq. Where's my squad? What direction is Speicher? Why am I alone?*

He slowed as he neared the dilapidated structure. *Damn, I have little to conceal myself.* He dropped into an arroyo that curved around the small mound the building sat on. It wasn't much, but he felt it gave him some cover. Carefully he crawled, looking for any movement near the building. He stopped to catch his breath and sat up against a large rock that prevented anyone in the building from seeing him. He noticed the knees of his pants were dirty; one had a tear. He sat and studied his pants, wondering why he was in chinos and not ACUs. He put his hand in his pocket and pulled out his mother's key chain. The oversized Lincoln fob confounded him. His thoughts came back to calm and reason. *I'm in Arizona.* His heart was pounding. He let out a long, slow breath and stood.

My God, he thought. *Am I going to have a life of flashbacks?* When would they pounce on him? *No, this is temporary,* he reasoned. *I'm still readjusting. I can't live in fear of them.* He strode back to the car, telling himself he was okay. A tiny thought surfaced from deep in his subconscious: *But what if the flashbacks continue?*

Suddenly, a headache surged. It was so sudden that he lifted his hands to his head as though he had been shot. His frustration with frequent and severe headaches made him despair. *Is this the way it's going to be for the rest of my life?* he wondered. As the jagged sensations intensified, he thought, again, *If this is how it's going to be for the rest of my life, I don't want to live.* After six months of headaches, a tiny suicide thought had surfaced, and each subsequent headache amplified that thought. He feared the flashbacks, but the headaches and the fear of the headaches triggered thoughts of death-borne relief.

He refocused his thoughts and searched the horizon. He saw the abandoned gas station and his mother's car parked there. The objects were less than a mile away. The railroad water tower was the highest man-made point on the horizon. It, too, was less than a mile away.

Two more jets zipped across the sky, the pilots practicing their skills on the air force's Barry Goldwater Bombing Range located in southwestern Arizona.

School Bells

School started with a celebration of Mr. Morris's return. All the kids he had taught prior to his mob were now entering fifth grade. They all came by. The girls hugged him. The boys gave him high fives. He was very happy to see them growing. Anna had finally made a friend and had stepped out of her shell a little. Thanks to some intensive physical therapy and innovative medicine, Ramon was out of the wheelchair and getting around with forearm crutches. The wheelchair, however, remained a fixture in the school because he tired easily. Tony and Marie had moved away over the summer.

Teachers, parents, and administrators from all over Weymouth came to the cookout the school held for Keith the day before classes started. As he mingled and chatted and greeted many of the nearly two hundred people who showed up, thoughts of roadside mines, murder, and an ever-present threat were far from his mind. He was glad to be home.

During the two weeks of preparation prior to classes beginning, Sharon met with him and explained the resources the Weymouth School Department was willing to make available.

"If you need time off," she said, "you can take up to six months with pay."

"Really? Wow. I think I feel a really bad cold coming on," joked Keith. "It'll take several months to get over, I'm sure."

"Nice try, soldier boy," Sharon retorted without even looking up. "You can also get counseling paid for by the school system." She looked at him. "If you want it."

He looked away, shook his head, and said, "No. I'm doing okay."

"Okay. Well, it's there if you need it. You continued to accrue retirement points, but not seniority, while you were gone."

"Nice."

"Yeah. Do you know the superintendent, Dr. Monroe, at all?"

"No. He comes around and talks with everyone. He seems like a decent guy, but no, I don't know him."

"He has loved the Troops to Teachers he's met over the year. When he learned you were restarting teaching here, he stopped by last week. He wants to do right by you. He said if you need anything, just ask. Did you know that he's an old marine? He was in Vietnam."

"No, I didn't know that."

"Neither did any of the rest of us. No one remembers the last time someone in the system was sent off to fight. Might be as far back as World War Two. Anyway, so, are you ready to get back in the classroom?"

"Yes. It'll be good to have some normalcy, and if I do have some unknown readjustment issues, I think getting back to work will make them go away."

"Is there any chance you'll get called up again?"

"Yes, but I think it's very unlikely to happen anytime soon."

"Good. I don't want to go through that again. Tomorrow, there's an all-staff meeting. We'll be looking at the school year and talking about the kids who are advancing. You'll be getting an earful," said Sharon. "You've got some of the brightest kids in your class, but there are a couple who might be a challenge. Laura had five kids in her class, and they were just trouble. Nothing serious, but they were disruptive to the point that the other kids lost out. We broke them up, three for you and two for Leslie. Hopefully, we can rein them in."

The excitement of the first week of his return and the vigor of a new school year waned by the end of September. Keith remained an effective and well-liked educator, but he lost some of the patience he might have previously afforded a troublesome student. At the end of most days, he was frustrated with the two disrespectful boys, Ruben and Jerome, and one manipulative girl, Elise. The three of them constantly disrupted class and made him focus most of his attention on keeping them if not in line, then at least less disruptive.

Most days started well. He was in the classroom by seven thirty in the morning, but by nine thirty, one of the three had already created some measure of chaos. Ruben, lanky with dark hair and intense brown eyes, would get up and run around the room, or crawl or hop on one leg. Then he'd turn around and hop on his other leg until he got close to the door. When no one was looking, he would step out into the hallway and run up and down the corridor. At first, Keith would allow him one loop around the room, once in the morning and once in the afternoon, but Ruben knew no limit. If Keith told him to sit down, he'd sit, and then slide under the desk and crawl around the floor. If someone kicked him, he bit or punched back or screamed as though someone had stabbed him. Within twenty days of the beginning of school, Ruben had been sent to the principal's office three times and twice to the nurse. Keith made four calls and had two parent–teacher conferences.

He met with the nurse and wondered if there was undiagnosed ADHD or autism at work. The nurse had no information on Ruben. He had started school halfway through the previous year. There had been problems, she said, but to Keith, Ruben seemed to have deteriorated over the summer. His parents seemed nice enough and were concerned. When Keith mentioned the possibility of attention deficit, they both froze and stared at him. "How could you say that?" they asked. He laid out the facts, and they were shocked. He wasn't convinced they were sincere in their surprise, but they agreed to get an appointment with a doctor and were agreeable to the suggestions offered by Principal Sharon Wells, the nurse, Keith, and the social worker.

Once a week the star student of the week could come to the classroom early for breakfast with Mr. Morris. Every student was guaranteed to be the star of the week for at least one week of the year. The kids were always excited. He'd provide hot chocolate, danish, McDonald's, breakfast burritos—whatever was Mom approved. He even brought a waffle iron if the child wanted homemade waffles. They'd just talk about sports, school, dreams, pets, trouble, home, vacations, or anything the child wanted to address. The alone time with Mr. Morris also gave Keith the opportunity to find out what was going on at home if the particular student was struggling, disconnected, or disruptive. If a student was struggling, Keith could usually find a hook so that at least the child's perception of school was as a place where things were stable and safe.

"Hey, good morning, Ruben," Keith said when the boy showed up for breakfast. "Come on in. Sit down."

Ruben shuffled his way to his seat.

"No, come on up here," Keith said, pointing to a chair next to his desk.

When Ruben was seated, Keith asked what he would like first. The boy shrugged and then looked at the danish.

"Go ahead, help yourself."

Ruben reached over and took two.

"You did well on that math quiz Monday. I think you're starting to get it."

Ruben shrugged, fidgeted, and looked at the juice.

"Go ahead. Don't be shy, just take it."

Keith tried to get him to talk about the Patriots and the Red Sox. No luck.

"How come you're still here?" Keith asked. "You're so unsettled in class, but here you can talk and move around all you want and you're not. Anything wrong? Feeling okay? You having trouble here or at home?"

Ruben said nothing.

"What do you like to do, Ruben? Do you like to run or read or build things or play video games?"

"I like to run."

"Okay. Running is good. Do you go fast, or do you go for long distances?"

"Both." Ruben stood and started pacing.

"Does my asking you this make you nervous or worried?"

"Yes. I think you're going to yell at me again."

"No, I won't here," Keith replied. "I wonder if we can make a deal?"

"About what?"

"If I give you a chance to run every day, will you do your best to sit still in class and not crawl or hop around the room?"

"What do I have to do?"

"Just that. You get to run at morning recess, but that means no crawling, hopping, or walking around the hallways without permission. There's a path that goes all the way around the school. You run past the upper playground and the lower one and someone can keep an eye on you the whole time, so you're safe. I'll see what I can work out with Mrs. Wells. But you don't get to run if you're being all crazy in class and making it hard for me to teach the other kids. Deal?"

Ruben kept pacing. He lowered himself to the floor and crawled toward a desk.

"You want to go to the path now and take a run before school?"

"Really?"

"Yes. I run at the end of the day sometimes. I've got some running shoes under my desk. Deal?" Keith put out his hand.

"Yeah." Ruben reached up from under the desk and shook Keith's hand.

"Let's go."

It worked, most days.

Elise was sneaky. She'd put her hand up to go to the bathroom, and after she got permission, she'd walk past another girl's desk and bump into it. Whatever project the girl was working on would be marred. If the desk was vacant, Elise would steal the pens or break the pencils or push the papers onto the floor. If the victim said anything, Elise would attack, with insults and comments like, "Oh, you're such a baby," "It was an accident," and "Are you going to cry like a baby?" If one of the girls left her journal out, Elise read it or tore out pages or scribbled all over the pages, and otherwise damaged or exposed the benign secrets of the young girl.

It took about two weeks for Keith to see Elise's treachery. At first Keith thought that some of the girls, and infrequently a boy, who'd had something sabotaged by her were unfairly blaming Elise or overreacting. He'd work with the student to recover or restore the project he or she was working on. He'd caution Elise to be more careful. Then one day he saw it. Elise was clever. Usually, she struck when there was a hubbub of activity in the room, when there was free time, or when the class broke into groups for projects. One day Keith was reading papers and happened to look up as Elise stood. She looked around the room and saw a table vacated by its occupants; they had gone to the bathroom. Some of the other pupils were busy moving items in and out of their cubbies and were walking back and forth to their seats. Keith turned his back to the room, but he watched Elise in the reflection of a mirror installed in the room near the coatrack. She assessed the room, glanced in Keith's direction, and then moved to a table next to the empty one. She struck up a conversation and leaned in to help. When the kids left to go to the bathroom, she grabbed a pile papers off the vacant table, tore them in half, and then shuffled them into one big pile. She glanced around the room, walked up to Keith, and asked to go to the bathroom.

"No," he replied. "I saw what you did. Why did you do that?"

She stiffened and was unresponsive.

The kids returned from the bathroom. When they got to their table, their happy chattering turned into wails of despair and tears.

"Go back and apologize."

She did not budge.

He raised his voice and told her again.

She trembled a little.

"Go," he demanded. His voice was loud enough for the whole class to turn and watch.

She lowered her head, turned, and ran for the door.

He went to grab her, but he stopped himself and instead got in front of her and blocked her escape.

"We're going to take a walk to Mrs. Wells's office and call your parents. I can't believe what you did."

As they walked down the hallway, he wondered what was going

on at home for the child to be acting in such a malicious way. *Could be anything*, he thought: divorce, abuse. Or maybe the family had fallen on hard times and Elise was angry at the other students who, she thought, had things she wanted.

At Sharon's office, Elise remained as unresponsive as she had been when Keith thwarted her escape. The only reaction came when Sharon called her mother and requested both parents to come in for a meeting.

"Okay," Sharon Wells said. "She's not going back to class. As soon as you and your husband get here, we'll discuss a plan that will help Elise get back into the classroom." She nodded. "Okay, we'll see you then."

She turned her attention to Elise. "Your mother is calling your father, and they'll both be here in an hour. Until then, you can work on your homework and any projects you have here in my office.

"Mr. Morris, please send someone back here with Elise's backpack and any homework you have for her. She won't be returning to the classroom today." She turned to look at Elise. "This is not the first time she has been in my office and sent home. We had set some rules before summer about what was expected. I think we need to go over the rules again."

Elise's parents arrived right at the end of the school day. They seemed as ordinary as could be. The mother worked in the marketing department at the Quincy Hospital, and the father was a dispatcher for the Massachusetts Bay Transportation Authority. Neither was trim nor fat, stylish nor wearing the look of a previous decade. There was no swearing, aggression, or accusations that the was not school doing its job correctly. No threats of a lawsuit or letters to the mayor and superintendent were leveled. They nodded and agreed, promising to work with Keith and Sharon so Elise could have a great year.

Keith was struck by how attentive Elise was to her father. She stood close and watched him closely every time he responded. She and her mother were very agreeable to everything he said and seemed as though they did not want anyone in the meeting to lose their patience. The dad promised that Elise would be nicer or else she would lose some privileges. In spite of the nods to the suggestions from

Sharon, saying the right words, and reassuring Sharon and Keith that he would work to get Elise in line, the father's manner did not match the seriousness of the meeting. It seemed as though he knew he had to say the right things but that he still would handle the matter in his way.

"What do you think, Keith?" asked Sharon as the family exited the building.

"I don't know. I'm hopeful."

"Do you know the nine-out-of-ten observation?"

"No."

"Nine times out of ten, a child will stand next to the abuser in order to try to keep him or her calm."

"I didn't notice. But now that I think about it, she was standing next to her father and holding his hand."

"He pulled his hand away several times, and she kept reinserting it."

"Do you think he's beating or molesting her, or something else?"

"I don't know. There are no obvious signs. I called our social worker last year, but he found nothing to go on."

Elise was back in school two days later. She was better, but it didn't last. Before Keith had to take a leave of absence, there were two more parent meetings. Talk of expelling Elise surfaced.

Keith had heard Jerome say several times, "The best defense is an aggressive offense." At the first parent–teacher meeting with Jerome's stepmother and ex-marine father, it was clear why the boy thought that way. Jerome was the spitting image of his father and identical in deportment. Like his son, Jerome's father had a very short fuse.

Even at ten years old, when Keith asked him to be quiet or take his seat, Jerome reacted slowly after a pause, during which he seemed to decide whether it was to his advantage to go along with the request. His irritation at being told what to do was obvious, and his tone was aggressive when he responded.

Whenever the class had to go to another room, to the gym, or anywhere else, Jerome was always the slowest, making everyone succumb to his pace. He wasn't special-needs or underperforming. He just controlled as much as he could. One day he was moving so slowly that the class was going to miss the start of a performance. The high school band had come to the school for a concert. Keith was herding the class down the hall when he noticed that Jerome had disappeared. He stopped the class and walked back to the classroom. No Jerome. He scanned the playground in case Jerome had decided it was time for him to go outside, which he had done previously. Nothing. Finally Keith looked in the bathroom—and there was Jerome wiping his sneakers with a paper towel.

"Come on, Jerome," Keith yelled. "You're holding everyone up."

"I had to go the bathroom," he yelled in response.

"You're supposed to ask before you disappear. I spent the last five minutes looking for you. Let's go before we miss the concert."

"I'm not done," he replied as he turned on the water and started washing his hands.

"Let's go!" Keith yelled.

"I'll get there," Jerome yelled back.

"Now," Keith said as sternly as he could.

Jerome turned back to the sink and pushed the plunger for soap to come out of the dispenser. Keith reached over to turn the water off and bumped Jerome's hand in the process.

"Don't touch me," said Jerome.

"I didn't touch you."

"You hit me."

"I didn't hit you. I barely touched your hand."

Jerome walked out of the bathroom and yelled, "Mr. Morris hit me."

The kids were milling in line. When Jerome yelled, they stopped and stared.

"Stop yelling and get over here," said Keith.

"I'm not going near you," Jerome said as he started to run down the hall.

Keith took off after him. "Stop," he yelled again.

Sharon stepped out of the office to see what the commotion was all about. She stood in Jerome's way and stopped him.

"What's going on?" she asked Jerome.

"Mr. Morris hit me."

"I did not. He was stalling in the bathroom. I reached over to turn the water off and touched his hand."

"Is that what happened?" she asked.

"I want my father."

"Come into the office," Sharon ordered.

"I want to call my father."

"We'll call your father. Keith, take the rest of the kids to the auditorium. I'll call Jerome's family."

"I didn't hit him," Keith replied, barely holding his anger in check.

"Let's let things calm down. We'll sort it out." She said to the rest of the class, "Kids, go with Mr. Morris. Everything is okay. Keith, get the kids settled, and then come back here."

She turned to Jerome and gestured for him to step into her office. He stood still.

"Come on."

He slowly strode toward the office.

Keith escorted the other children to the auditorium, his head splitting. He stopped in the empty hallway to rub his temples. He was hurting and angry. He cussed Jerome silently and continued his walk to Sharon's office.

She met him in the hallway. "Let's take a walk."

"What kind of shit is that little punk saying?"

"Keith! You know my rules. No cussing in school, and the kids are referred to with respect."

"I know. I'm sorry, but he's a pain and I've got a killer headache."

"I'm sure he is, and I'm sure you didn't hit him. The problem is going to be his father."

"Why?"

"When I called, he asked to speak to his son and Jerome said you hit him. When I got back on the phone, he said he was going to get you fired and sue the school."

"You're kidding."

"No, I'm not. I got him to calm down. He'll be here in about twenty minutes. He said he was going to call his lawyer first."

"Fuck."

"Keith!"

"Sorry, but you know this is bullcrap."

"I'm sure it is, but I had to call the superintendent and let him know."

"Great."

"Tell me what happened."

Keith explained the chain of events.

"All right. First off, I know you've got three troublesome students."

"Yeah, that's for sure. Ruben is okay as long as he gets to burn his energy."

"You've told me, and you've said it works most days. But I think they're getting to you."

"I can handle my kids."

"I know you can, but you've got a lot going on."

"What's that mean?"

"It means I want you to take the rest of the week off."

"No."

"Yes. Step back from this and let me handle it."

"Tell me what you mean, that I've 'got a lot going on.'"

"You came back from the war, you were injured, and you've got a few challenging students. Those are not insignificant issues."

"I'm fine."

"Yes, but have you dealt with all those forces?"

"Yes."

"Really?"

"So? What? You think I'm going to climb up the bell tower at the city hall with a rifle and start picking off people as they walk past."

"No, I don't think that, but I don't know what's going on inside. You've changed. You're still a great teacher, but there are changes. Your patience, your enthusiasm, your humor, it's all … I don't know. I'm not a psychologist, but there are changes, understandably so."

As Keith listened to her, a rage erupted inside. He wanted to yell and hit, kick, punch, do something. He held it back. If he could make sense of what he was feeling, he might have understood she only wanted to help, but the thoughts were rapid and furious.

"Keith, you're one of the best teachers I've ever worked with. I want you to continue teaching. God knows we need strong, decent male teachers in the school system. I am on your side." She reached out, took his hand, and looked him straight in the eyes. "I'm on your side," she repeated. "I care for you like you're my own son. But you have to step away for a moment."

The second pass of the phrase *I'm on your side* penetrated his fury. He took a deep breath and pulled his hand back.

"Fine. You're the boss. I'm going for a run."

"Good. I'll call you as soon as the meeting with Jerome's father is over. Let's meet for coffee. Better yet, let's go for a walk. I know you like to run at Bare Cove Park. I'll meet you there and we can walk. I'll tell you how it went and what happened. Okay?" she said.

"Okay?" she repeated into his sullen silence.

"Yeah, fine."

"You're a good man, Keith. You're a teacher and a soldier. You serve your country and, just as importantly, you teach. It's sounds corny, but it's true: what you do is noble."

The rage abated a little more.

"So, I'm likely to be suspended."

"I doubt that very much." A tone emanated from the cell phone in her hand. "What did you have planned for the rest of the day?" she asked.

"Not much. It's art today. After that, I was going to have them read some, and I had an easy history quiz planned."

"I'll take care of it." She looked at the message on her phone and then said to Keith, "He's here. Are you going to be okay for a few hours?"

"I'm fine."

"I don't think you are. And I don't know how to help you."

"I'm annoyed as can be right now, but it'll pass."

Sharon stared at him.

Keith looked away and then stepped away from her. "I'll be all right. I appreciate your concern. This is about a difficult student and a family that is clearly the source of the aggravation. It has nothing to do with my deployment. You've got to go to your meeting. I'm going for a run. We'll meet later."

"All right."

Point Allerton

March 2005
Hull, Massachusetts

The school year progressed. Keith's headaches did not subside. The weather seemed to affect them. Sunny days were the days when the headaches felt less intense or dissipated sooner. A good day was when he felt his head was not splitting, just being beaten with a hammer and on fire.

Jerome did not change. Ruben ran and got Bs. Elise met with a school counselor every week.

By March, everyone was tired of winter and snow and ice and gloomy days.

All week the weather had been miserable. There was no snow and, therefore, no sledding. It was not cold enough to freeze the ponds, so there was no ice skating either. The days were overcast with a cold drizzle, dank, and dark. Shoes, socks, jackets, and sweaters were wet and unable to dry out enough without going into a dryer. Everyone was in a foul mood.

Elise had torn up another girl's intricate art project a couple of weeks earlier. Jerome had been in a fight with a boy from another class. It was unclear exactly who started it. Keith and Sharon were convinced it was Jerome, but there were no witnesses. Both boys were in school but on detention. Ruben had not run in a week.

It was Thursday, March 3. All the kids were dreading the weekend because the forecast called for more of the same. Keith's headaches were particularly bad.

"Okay, kids," Keith announced, "pop quiz time. Math. Division tables." He handed a stack of paper to each one of the tables. "Leave them facedown, and no peeking."

He had given his students a math quiz every day that week, allotting thirty minutes for them to complete it. He used the time to give his brain a break from the weather-weary din of the kids and his headaches.

He sat in his chair and watched. The only sound were pencils scratching paper, an occasional huff and puff of breath, an infrequent murmur of someone sounding out the problem, and the shuffle of small bodies shifting in their seats.

It had been a long day. The girls were chattier than usual, but instead of the usual giggles and whispers, little squabbles and low-level bickering broke out among even the best-behaved students. Keith had to hush them several times and even move one of the students to another table for a couple of hours. The boys were just as vocal, aggressive, and twitching and squirming in their seats too. Ruben had stood and walked around the class several times. Fortunately, he wasn't crawling anymore. Keith told him to sit down. Jerome was antagonizing another boy with monkey bites in the fleshy area below his biceps because the boy would not let Jerome copy some answers off his paper. Earlier in the day, Elise was sent to the office for taking one of the other girls' journal out of her backpack and licking and spitting on the pages. She had done her time at the office and was back in the class.

Ruben suddenly stood and started walking again.

"Sit down, Ruben. You're disturbing everyone else."

He dropped to the floor and started crawling.

"Get up and get back in your seat." Keith stood and walked toward him.

At that same moment, Jerome locked another monkey bite onto the same boy, who screamed.

"Jerome, that's it," Keith yelled.

Two boys and one of the girls started crying. Mr. Morris had frightened them with his fierce yell.

"Stop it," he yelled again.

The boy receiving the monkey bites punched Jerome, who tackled his assailant in return. They crashed to the floor, which startled the crawling Ruben, who stood and knocked the table over. He bolted for the door. Elise ran out the door too.

"Get back here!" Keith yelled as he ran out the door after them.

The other children cried even more.

Keith yelled as he ran down the hallway, his head pounding as the blood sped faster through his veins. Ruben and Elise ducked into the nurse's office.

He shook the door and yelled, "Get back to class."

Natalia came out her office door. "Keith! Stop yelling."

"Don't let them hide in there. They are completely destroying the class. Those little shits need to get back in class, sit down, and behave."

He reached for the door. Shawna stood in his way. She was a small woman, and he towered over her. He flexed all his mass to intimidate her. He invaded her space and pressed his face in close to hers.

"No, Keith. Calm down."

"Keith," Sharon said from behind him. "Step back."

"Sharon, we've talked. You know how those three are." Keith seethed as he responded.

"I do. But right now, what you're doing is not helping."

"I don't care." He reached around Shawna and started beating his fists on the door. "Come out of there."

"Keith. Stop it. Don't make me call the police."

His headache surged. His hands rose to his temples, and he tipped his head forward.

"What's wrong, Keith?" Shawna asked.

"I have a headache."

"If you step back, I can get you something to help."

"No, nothing helps. Not prescriptions or over the counter; it's been going on for more than a year now."

"Come sit down," said Sharon.

"No." He unclenched his muscles. "I'm going to leave. My career is over." He moved toward the doorway.

"No, your career is not over. You might have to take some time off, but it'll be good. You can deal with whatever it is and come back as good as always."

"I don't think so."

"I do," said Sharon. "You're not the first teacher to have a meltdown."

"Yeah," Keith replied slowly. "I don't want to go into the classroom. Can one of you get my coat and things?"

"Sure. I can give you a lift home."

"No. I walked to work today."

Sharon went to the classroom and returned with Keith's jacket and backpack.

"How are the kids doing?" Keith asked.

"They're fine. I said you have a headache and that I'll be in the classroom for the rest of the day. We'll attend to Ruben and Elise," said Sharon. "Don't worry. The kids know who the troublemakers are. This will pass."

"And Keith," she added, "you've got to find a way to come to peace with what happened and whatever you saw or did while you were over there, or it will continue to eat at you."

"Yeah."

Keith turned and walked down the stairs and out the front door, finding himself in the gray, cool, damp afternoon.

He wondered, *How did the men of World War II come home and slide back into normalcy so easily?* He could not recall a single story of the men of the greatest generation coming home and being as troubled as the soldiers of Vietnam or the Gulf War or Iraqi Freedom. Nor could he think of one story of a World War I or Korean War soldier having troubles readjusting. He knew some of them were labeled shell-shocked, but he assumed they got over it and fell back into their normal lives once they got home.

Was there something different about boomer and Gen X men because of the hard times they had settling back in? His thoughts were not clear and linear; rather, the theme was one of unmanliness, because he did not see himself like the stoic soldiers of other generations who fought and came back and kept their stories and their troubles to themselves. He felt he should be smarter and more able to deal with all the residual junk in his head because he was more educated than many soldiers. Plus, guard and reserve members tended to be older, more mature, and more educated than those in the active force. What was wrong? The headache was one thing. It was a physical reaction to an injury. That was easy to process. Why couldn't he get the other thoughts into a similarly neat little box? Was it the fear of another flashback? Would reality warp profoundly for him? How would he know if it did? Sometimes he wanted to grab and shake the troublemakers in the class. Would he someday lose control and actually grab one of them? The fears and confusion bounced around. Did he somehow, in a way he couldn't grasp, cause the murder of Jumah and the children? Had he not been a teacher, would the colonel have created the schoolhouse and outreach program? If he hadn't gone to Iraq, would those children be alive?

How can I put these thoughts aside? he wondered.

He had wandered as far as Jackson Square. He turned on Commercial Street to go back to his house, but then he turned again toward the Lower Square and the Dunkin' Donuts. He sat and drank a coffee. His thoughts settled into a cycle of dread about a life of headaches, concern about outbursts like the one he had earlier, a sense of isolation, and a desire to force himself back into normalcy. He could talk to the women he worked with, but there was not a woman in his life whom he felt he could confide in. As he sat, he saw the sign flash, announcing a train arriving at the station in two minutes. He stood, finished his coffee, and bought a ticket.

The train was mostly empty, as rush hour had not begun. He rode it to Greenbush, where he bought another ticket, and rode it back as far as West Hingham. He thought a walk through Bare Cove Park might make him feel better.

He walked past the building that was once the guardhouse to the Naval Ammunition Depot—Hingham. Now it was a credit union branch. The 1058th stored its trucks on the property, so the place still had a military purpose. Two trucks were in the lot. The rest had been left in Iraq for the replacement unit at Speicher to use. He continued his walk to the park entrance. There were a couple of cars there. As he approached the gate, one of the doors swung open.

"Keith, wait a minute."

Keith stopped and looked at the old overweight man struggling out of the car.

"Dr. Monroe," Keith said.

"Yes. Call me Troy. Good to see you."

"How did you know I was here?" Keith asked.

"Sharon called and told me about what happened."

"So?"

"So she was worried about you," Dr. Monroe replied. "She said you might come here. So I waited. I want to talk to you. Okay?"

Keith considered saying he wanted to be alone. He wanted to find a spot and sit. He didn't want to listen to anyone, least of all someone who was going to go on about how important it is to have a positive mental attitude. Instead he said, "I don't care."

"You want to walk, or can I take you for a ride?"

"I don't care."

"Good. I'm not in fighting shape anymore. Hop in." He started the car, reached for his cell phone, sent a text message, put the car in gear, and drove toward the exit.

"Where are we going?" Keith asked.

Dr. Monroe waited a long time before he responded. He did not answer Keith's question directly. He said, "I grew up here. Born in Quincy, raised in Weymouth, and attended college in Boston. After graduation I took a trip to Southeast Asia, courtesy of Uncle Sam."

Keith did not respond. He just stared out the window, glancing at the 1058th trucks as they drove past.

"When I got back, I spent a lot of time here too. Before it was a park, it was excess government property. Nice. Quiet. No aggravations."

Keith was thinking he did not want to listen to some old marine's story of how hard it was coming back from Vietnam, how bad they'd had it, and how easy and welcoming the country is now for returning service members.

"Where are we going, and why are you taking me along?" asked Keith.

"There are some people I want you to meet."

"I'm not going to a fucking clinic or group therapy. If that's where we're going, then let me out."

"I get it, and that's not where we're going. Give me an hour, and I'll drive you home," he replied.

"You know, I'm fine. I'm not some PTSD victim here," said Keith. "I get headaches 'cause my brain got sloshed around a little."

"Got it. I've still got shrapnel in my leg that makes my knee ache on rainy days, and the ringing in my ears took eight years to go away. An hour, Keith. That's all I ask," said Dr. Monroe.

They drove through Hingham and on through Hull out to Point Allerton. They stopped at a big old house that had a grand view of Hull Gut and Boston Harbor.

"Who lives here?" Keith asked as they got out of the car.

"It belongs to an old veteran."

A police car pulled up. Dr. Monroe waved at the car. When the door opened and illuminated the driver, Keith thought he looked familiar. The officer stepped out of the car and walked over to Monroe.

"How you doing today, Troy?" the cop asked as he extended his hand.

Keith knew the cop, but he couldn't recall how or when they'd met.

"This is Keith Morris," Dr. Monroe said by way of introduction. "Keith, this is Joe Donahue."

"We've met," said Joe as he extended his hand. "Iraq."

Their meeting came rushing back to Keith. Joe was mobilized to Iraq with the 772nd MP Company of the Massachusetts National Guard. Several members of the 772nd spent a few days at Speicher. At a burger burn, members from the two Massachusetts units talked. Keith and Joe spoke briefly about their connection, the South Shore.

"Now I remember, Joe. Good to see you. Glad you made it back okay."

"Likewise."

They walked around back and went through a door and into the basement.

Keith stopped as the other two men stepped down the cinder block stairs to the door. "What's going on here? Is this some fucking group therapy place for veterans? If it is, I'm not interested in sitting in a circle and talking about how I feel."

"It's not."

155

"Then what is this?"

"Just come in. Sit on the couch and watch TV. Take a nap, read the paper, whatever. Leave whenever you want."

Keith nodded toward the door.

Joe opened the door and stepped in. Dr. Monroe stopped and held the door for Keith. Keith stepped in.

It was an ordinary cellar. There was some 1960s-looking paneling on the wall. The stairwell was enclosed, and the door to access the stairs up to the first floor was closed. There was a door in the paneling. Keith guessed it was where the furnace, oil tank, and electrical box were. There were a half dozen couches scattered around, a few easy chairs, a refrigerator, a shelf with snacks, a stove, and a sign on another door reading, Smoking Allowed Here. The American flag and flags from each of the five armed services were draped on the wall. Alongside the US flag was a long sheet of seamless paper, with handwriting covering about half the sheet.

There were six men already in the basement. There was one really old guy—in his eighties, Keith guessed. Then there were four other older guys, probably about the same age as Dr. Monroe, Keith guessed, and one other guy, probably in his fifties. One was reading, two were watching TV, two were talking, and the youngest of the group was sleeping on a cot in the corner.

"Gentlemen, this is Keith. Soldier and one of my teachers," said Monroe.

"Welcome, Keith" reverberated around the room as each man spoke. "Write your name on the wall, and make yourself at home."

Joe and Dr. Monroe left Keith alone. Joe opened the fridge, grabbed a beer, tossed it toward Monroe, and pulled out a piece of cake for himself. They settled into the couch and watched a rerun of *Law and Order* already on the screen.

Keith stood there wondering what was going to happen. He looked around the room for posters or something encouraging veterans to talk, to share, to cry, and to do other things he did not want to do. Nothing. It was a little confusing. He walked over to the wall and looked at the signatures. The first name was John Anderson. Beside his name it read, "US Army, 1944, Ardennes." The next read, "Harris

Johnson, US Navy, 1944, Leyte Gulf." The list continued with at least five hundred names from World War II, Korea, Vietnam, and the first Gulf War, and only one name for Operation Iraqi Freedom, Joe Donahue. Also, there were two clearly female names, and numerous other names that could go either way. Keith reached for a marker and wrote, "Keith Morris, US Army, 2003, Tikrit, Iraq." He set the pen down and stared at his name. In a small and unnoticed way, when he saw his name with all the other veterans', he felt okay for a moment.

He walked over to the couch. "What is this place? An extension of the VA, or VFW or American Legion post?"

"No," one of the other men answered.

"Most of us are members of the Legion or VFW or DAV, but this has nothing to do with them," said another, not looking up from his book.

Keith's head started pounding again.

"Keith," said Dr. Monroe. "There's no agenda here, there aren't membership requirements, and there are no expectations. All of us and others over the years come here to be around people who have had a similar experience, war. You don't have to talk. You can come here as often as you want or never again."

"So you guys swap war stories."

"Nope, but if you've got stories to tell, this is the place to do it," the man reading the book said. "Usually, though, if anyone says something about what they saw or did, it's in response to seeing something on TV or reading the paper, usually saying how much bullshit it is or, once in a while, saying how they saw something similar."

"Who's here?"

"If you mean who's welcome here, it's pretty open. There is an expectation that anyone who comes is connected to the service in some way. Wives, a husband in one case, sisters, brothers, children, friends, veterans, whomever. Although, over the years, it tends to be combat vets who come here more often. Female vets don't come back much."

"Why?"

"Don't know. Maybe it's the lack of conversation or the lack of other females here."

"It's all the farting and burping that drives them away," a voice from one of the cots said.

"Yeah, could be," someone else said, laughing.

"I was in Vietnam," said Monroe. "An intel guy. I was in one firefight."

"Korea," said someone else.

"Vietnam," said another voice.

"Desert Storm One," said a third voice.

"Iraq," said Joe.

Keith sat down in one of the large chairs.

"John Anderson started this place after World War Two. He had made some money before the war and bought this house. After the war, he and some of his veteran friends would hang out here. Ya know, shared experience. Those World War Two vets never talked about what they saw and did. Anderson said he didn't have to. He really didn't even want to talk about his role in the war. He'd answer questions if someone asked, but, you know, the details, he didn't talk about that. This was his way of dealing with it, and that's how it is now.

"John died twenty years ago, but he left a trust fund to have a housekeeper who lives here, and more than enough money to keep this place going for a long time. Mona stocks the refrigerator. She also calls the police if someone gets out of hand. It's happened, but not often. She keeps the place clean. If someone is being a leech, she gets in touch with a number of us and we steer that person in another direction. This isn't a homeless shelter. She locks the door to the upstairs at night when she's sleeping, but the door to the cellar is never locked.

"Her husband killed himself years after Vietnam. She says this is her way of looking out for other veterans."

"So, Keith," said Joe, "you can leave. I'll drive you home. You can stay, you can come back, or you can never step foot in here again. But I guarantee you this: this is the most uncomplicated place you'll ever be. I tried the VA and they're good, but I didn't want to sit around in a circle with someone who never even served telling us to talk about what we saw. It worked for many of the guys there, but not me. This place—no emoting, no talking about it, no nothing—works for me."

The men went back to whatever they were doing, while Keith stood there.

"I can't shake the headaches."

"Sit down, Keith. Take a load off," said Monroe.

"I saw the pictures," Keith said. "I saw the pictures of the murdered students. I was friends with one of the Combat Camera guys. He had to photograph the scene. He should be here."

"Invite him."

"He should be here. I drove a truck and got a little banged up. He's the one who had to see that. So why can't I get past it?" Keith asked.

"Everyone reacts differently."

"Keith, you need to take a load off, and not just off your feet," said Joe.

"It all sucks. Stop beating yourself up," someone said.

Keith walked to one of the cots in the corner and lay down.

Following his meltdown at the school, Keith found that it took time for him to reestablish his rhythm. After he'd spent a fitful night on the couch in the basement of the Hull house, Joe Donahue drove him home the following afternoon. The next week Keith stayed at home. He never left his house. Sharon called to check on him every day. His responses to her questions were little more than grunts.

His only physical effort was to put food out for Caisson once a day. A fog settled over his brain, and a miasma permeated his soul. Most days he was just waking up at two o'clock in the afternoon. He'd walk to the refrigerator and drink soda and beer for breakfast. Then, with a bag of chips, he went to the living room, lay on the couch, changed the channels with the remote, and watched reruns of *Friends*, *M*A*S*H*, and *Home Improvement*. Although he hadn't had a skull-busting headache all week, the furious edge of it loitered, waiting to strike. After a week of too much sleep, too little food, and crappy television, he was mentally and emotionally spent. He felt bloated, lethargic, meaningless, irrelevant, and empty.

Hearing a truck stop in front of his house, he thought, *I hope it's not for me.* The doorbell rang. *Shit.* He rolled over and peered out the window. It was the mail truck. He heard an aggressive knock on the door. He didn't move. Eventually he heard the truck leave. Then he walked to the door, cracked it open, and peered out to confirm that whomever it was had left. Stuck to the door was a notice with instructions for him to pick up a registered letter at the East Weymouth Post Office. He would have to go to the post office before nine in the morning within the next three days or else the letter would be returned. The sender was Headquarters, National Guard Bureau, Washington, DC. He let the delivery notice drop to the ground. *Probably another form letter telling me I have six months to claim benefits,* he thought. He went back to the couch and fell back asleep.

The next day, there was a knock at the door and a voice calling his name. The sounds penetrated his sleep. Eventually he recognized the voice as one of his neighbors, Sara, a stay-at-home soccer mom. He considered not answering the door.

"I know you're in there, Keith. Open the door," she said.

He ignored her.

"I know where you keep the outside key. I'll let myself in."

She's not going to go away, he thought. He struggled to get off the couch and made his way to the door. Standing in the shadow of the hallway, he opened the door.

"Yes, Sara," he said without even looking at her.

Sara was short, barely five feet tall. She was still in shape but had to work harder at it each year, she told him. She was a lawyer but decided to stay home while her sons were young.

"I found a notice for some registered mail for you in my yard," she said. "Did you already pick this up, or did the wind blow it into my yard?"

"No, I didn't go to the post office."

"Well, here's the ticket."

"Just throw it away."

"No. It might be important."

"I doubt it. Just leave it. I'll get it later."

"No. Take it." She reached her hand out and opened the screen door. Then she pressed her hand against the wood door. It opened enough for her to thrust the slip at him.

"Fine." He stopped resisting her pressure on the door. It swung open, hitting his foot.

Sara stepped toward him. "I haven't seen you for a while. How's things?" she asked.

"Okay."

"Will you invite me in or at least come out here so we can visit for a minute?"

"I'm busy," said Keith.

"No, you're not. I can tell."

"Oh, are you my mother?"

"Don't be a jerk, Keith," said Sara.

"I'm not. I'm just not feeling well."

"Do you need anything?" she asked.

"I'm fine. Thanks."

"I don't think you are. I've never seen you unshaven." She paused for a moment. "I heard about what happened at school, so I know you're not yourself. That's not you. Can I come in?" she said.

"I don't think that's a good idea," Keith replied.

"Why?"

"You know why."

There was a long pause.

"All I'm trying to do is help you. I don't need you to throw that up into my face."

"I'm not throwing anything in your face. What happened was unexpected, and it happened while we were alone in the house during the day. If you come in, we'll be in the same situation again."

"That will never happen again."

"If I promise to go to the post office, will you leave me alone?" asked Keith.

"No, I won't. I'm worried about you," Sara replied, "And I'm not the only one who's worried about you."

"For Christ's sake. Wait a minute." He pulled on some shorts and a T-shirt and opened the door fully. He stared at Sara. "You happy now?" he snarled.

"You look terrible, Keith."

"Good to see you too."

"Here's the notice."

"Thanks. Sorry for being a jerk."

"You've lost weight."

Keith shrugged.

"Come on over and have a bite to eat."

"Thank you. No."

"You know," she added, "you're the only soldier I know. If you won't let me help you as a friend, or as a neighbor, or as the teacher of my son, then at least let me do something for you as a veteran."

"You really don't know anyone else in the service?"

"I dated a guy in the air force, like, two times—years ago. I'm sure there are veterans in the neighborhood, but I don't know who they are."

The sun was feeling good to Keith. It was a pleasant spring day. Trees were budding and the early flowers were blooming.

"I appreciate your concern."

"And now you're going to politely tell me to leave you alone, like when someone breaks up with someone and says they want to be friends."

"Actually, I was going to take you up on your offer of a bite to eat."

"Really?"

"Really. I've been sitting around feeling sorry for myself, and, I don't know, the sun or talking to you or just being vertical makes me think I need to get my ass in gear."

"Keith, I'm so happy to hear that. What do you want?"

"Oh, I don't know. I'm easy."

"All I have in the house is kid food—mac and cheese, hot dogs, peanut butter and jelly, things like that."

"Kid food? Those are standard bachelor staples. I'll take a shower, shave, and clean up. I'll be over in about fifteen minutes."

"Takes me an hour to clean up." She gave him a hug. Keith accepted it.

Keith's slog out of his depression began with lunch with Sara and accelerated each day. He went to the post office and signed for the certified letter. The army had put resources in place for active duty, guard, and reserve soldiers, and the letter detailed what was available and where. He did not act immediately, but between the sunshine, motion, and being outdoors, he found some motivation again.

Dr. Monroe and Sharon Wells had arranged a five-month convalescent leave for Keith following his tirade at his students. To return to teaching he would have to meet with Dr. Monroe, Sharon, the union rep, and the PTA chairman in July. If they determined he was emotionally fit, then he could return to school in August and prep for the school year. Teaching and the kids would lead him back to normalcy.

It was what he needed—a purpose.

At first he took short runs in the neighborhood. Initially his head pounded after each run, but gradually the severity of the headaches diminished. He signed up for a softball team and registered for an online NCO leadership course with the army. Then he added day and evening courses at Northeastern University. His momentum swung far, his runs became longer, he pushed through several more online army courses, and he added rugby to his twice-weekly softball games. But the pendulum of his momentum did not swing back. He started working out at a manic pace. Every day, he lifted weights in the gym and ran for as much as three hours at a time. The routine of study, workout, and sleep defined his life for a month, regardless of rain or sun, dry cold or humid heat. A weekend or break between the conclusion of one course and the beginning of another simply meant more time to work out or to read about working out.

If a conflict surfaced that appeared to interfere with the manic pace he had set, he grew stubborn and almost intractable; a stronger headache followed.

A dinner party one evening, hosted by one of his coworkers with a thinly concealed agenda of wanting to introduce him to a friend of hers, ended poorly when he excused himself to leave early. His eagerness to leave the dinner to get to the gym made the hostess angry and made her friend pity him. He was completely unaware of his rudeness and obsessiveness. That night he worked out until well past midnight, thinking he needed to compensate for the rich food and inattention to his routines.

The next day his coworker called and told him how much of a jerk he had been.

It was a knee injury during a late-night basketball game at the gym that sent Keith to the doctor. The doctor said that Keith had to stop everything except minimal walking for two weeks, unless he wanted to turn his injury into significant damage and surgery.

After a cortisone shot in the knee, ice, and aspirin for a week, Keith felt that his knee was fine. He was eager to resume his workout routine. He was edgy the whole time he recuperated. The doctor's order to rest and give his knee time to recover gave Keith just enough justification not to condemn himself for being physically weak, or lacking in discipline or a measure of fortitude. However, as soon as he felt well enough, and in spite of the doctor's advice to resume activity slowly, he went for a five-mile run. He had to call a friend to drive him home when his knee gave out at the mile-and-a-half point.

He was forced into surgery and idleness—a week of rest, and six weeks of physical therapy. The mania departed and mild depression set in. He kept going to therapy and did some of the self-directed exercises the therapist prescribed.

Slowly and steadily he found his rhythm again. It presented a different beat. He even dated some.

LOVE

2009-10

Fossil Creek, Arizona

August 2009

"Keith!"

He recognized the voice, but it wasn't exactly as his memory told him it should be. He turned his head and saw the woman who had called his name. She was on the other side of the river, away from the rest of a group gathered near the tents and table.

He saw the strawberry blonde hair and knew who she was. It was Allison, his high school girlfriend. She seemed taller than he remembered. She was standing on a large rock up on the embankment. It was her face; it certainly was her smile. Wearing a loose-fitting T-shirt and shorts, her body looked about the same. Then the doubt surfaced. Was it really her? What were the chances? Fifteen years had passed since he last saw her.

"Allison?"

"It is you. I knew it," she said. Her arms had been at her side. Now they were akimbo. She nodded.

Keith stepped to the edge of the water on his side of the creek. She stepped off the rock and moved toward her edge. She was smiling, the expression taking up most of her face. It was her eyes that completed the fullness of her smile, and that was exactly as he remembered.

"What are you doing here?" she asked. "I know you moved to Massachusetts, but I never heard anything about you moving back."

"I didn't move back. After I graduated Corona, I went to college there. Then I graduated, got a job, and stayed there. My mother is still here, so I come back and visit at least a couple of times a year."

"But what are you doing here?" she asked again. Her arms and eyes swept the area surrounding the creek. The late afternoon shadows were darkening the forest. Only in places, the sun still broke through the trees and highlighted the gently moving water.

"I try to get here at least once a year during one of my visits. I really like this area. It's like a pilgrimage."

"Are you here with anyone?" she asked. Her arms and hands, her head tilts, and her weight shifting from foot to foot emphasized every word she spoke. Her arms dropped to her sides now.

"No. Not this time. I almost always come here by myself and spend a night or two alone in the woods." Keith stood very still, hands close to his sides. It was as though he were almost at attention. It was his usual stance.

"Really? You've come a long way from that first time you camped here. Remember that trip? I think it was the first time you'd ever been camping." Her arms started moving again. She took a small step when she shifted her weight and slipped on the muddy embankment toward the water.

"Oh yeah, you and your parents had a good time busting my chops on that trip." Keith feigned a look of despair. "It took a long time to recover from your father putting that rubber snake in my sleeping bag. And you, you were no help either, telling me that a piece of bark floating in the water toward me was a rarely seen amphibious Gila monster."

"That was hysterical. You were thrashing around in your sleeping bag. I think you broke the zipper trying to get out of it. You were so mad when you saw all of us laughing." Her smile grew bigger.

"How did your father do that?"

"He said he saw some guys do it when he was in the army. I think he used some fishing line tied to a rubber snake, and he pulled on it once you had settled into the sleeping bag." She paused for a moment and then added, "He's pulled that trick on a number people over the years, but I think you were the first."

"At least your mother didn't pull any pranks on me."

"That you know about."

"Your sister was nice to me."

"Annie had such a crush on you. She was so mad at us for teasing you."

The conversation dipped for a moment. Keith shifted his feet a little, while his hands remained firmly at his sides. His eyes wandered from Allison to a point just beyond her, and then back.

"You must have gotten over it. Otherwise you wouldn't be here," she said.

"That was oh so much fun." Keith shrugged, smiled, and continued. "In spite of you and your father, that trip really changed me—you and me walking around the woods here, swimming in the creek, and, well, you know, the stuff we did the other time just you and me went camping here." He grinned at her and then looked away.

Allison blushed, smiled, twirled a lock of her hair around her finger, and then smoothed it out.

"Anyway, yes, I've done a lot of hiking and camping all over since then. I really enjoy the mountains of New Hampshire and Alaska. What about you? What's your story? It's been, what, fifteen years since we were hanging out together."

"We weren't just hanging out. We went out for almost a year and half. You were my first serious boyfriend, and I know I was your first girlfriend," Allison reminded him. "I graduated NAU and did some odd jobs for a couple of years. Now my work is in pharmaceutical sales."

"You happy?"

"Yeah. I guess. It's a lot of pressure and paperwork, but the money is good. What about you?"

"Teacher."

"Really? I know you went to Boston, but I thought you wanted to study engineering; you wanted to do something with transportation planning. What became of that?"

Out of the corner of his eye, Keith saw a large man stand up and look at Allison. The man stepped away from the group and walked toward them.

Allison saw Keith look away and turned her head. She saw the large man moving toward them too. She sighed, and her shoulders dropped.

"I did get a degree in engineering," Keith said. "But there were no jobs, so I did substitute teaching to get some cash and discovered I really liked it. I joined the Massachusetts National Guard as a truck driver. When I got back from basic training, I went back to school and got my teaching certificate. Been teaching ever since."

The large male arrived and stood next to Allison. He stared at Keith. Their eyes met. Keith sensed the threat.

In one second, Keith assessed him. He was with Allison and he did not like her talking with someone he didn't know. He was a big guy, bulky, probably a weight lifter, maybe doing steroids, but not quick. He had a flattop haircut, which meant he might be military, but, Keith guessed, probably ex-military or a wannabe. When he spoke, his voice was high-pitched and not as loud as Keith anticipated.

"Who's your friend, Allison?" he squeaked. There was an agitation in his voice.

"As a matter of fact, Frank, he is an old friend. We knew each other in high school." She turned her attention to Keith and continued. "Keith, this is Frank."

"Nice to meet you. I'd shake your hand, but there's twenty feet of water between us."

Frank didn't immediately respond. He stared at Allison and then at Keith. Eventually he spoke, saying, "Yeah, good to meet you too." He turned back to Allison and grabbed her hand. "Come on back to the group. The food is just about ready, and we're having a few drinks."

Allison turned to Keith and said, "Come and join us for happy hour and dinner."

Keith saw Frank shudder and felt the glare. For a fraction of a second their eyes met again. Without saying a word, Frank communicated "don't come."

Keith thought, *I don't want to deal with this kind of crap.* He said, "I appreciate the offer, but I'm going to pass."

"Are you sure? It would be great to catch up more."

"I would, but I've been hiking around all day. I'm beat. I'm going to jump in the water and clean up, and then bust open the MRE I brought with me and relax. I head back to Boston tomorrow night. I want to spend a little more time with my mother before I take off, so I'll be hiking out of here very early tomorrow morning."

Frank's shoulders dropped a little.

"Okay. Well, say hi to your parents for me. It was really good to see you. Look me up. I'm on Facebook."

"Uh, I'm not the most connected guy in the world. I have a minimal Facebook presence. I'm an infrequent lurker on Facebook. I'm not some Luddite; I just don't spend a lot of time sitting in front of a computer," Keith explained. "Can you give me your e-mail address?" he asked.

"Sure," she replied. Then she told him what her e-mail address was.

He repeated it aloud and hoped he'd remember it long enough to write it down in his notepad when he went back to his camp.

"What are you driving?" she asked. "I'll put my card on the windshield."

"That'd help. The green Suburban. It's my mother's. It's up the road about a mile and a half. The right-side rear bumper is damaged."

"It's unusual to find someone under fifty who isn't on Facebook," Allison said.

"It's not that I don't see the value of it; it's just me. I like disconnecting."

"Okay. Well, it was really good to see you. Will you e-mail me?"

"I will. It was good to see you too."

They turned to leave. Frank was still holding Allison's hand. As he started walking back toward camp, he tugged her. She lurched into motion and stumbled. Keith turned and started walking in the opposite direction. He looked back in time to see Allison removing her hand from Frank's.

Keith walked the short distance upstream back to where he had dropped his pack, and set up camp. He unfolded a small camp chair, spread out his ground cloth, being careful to not place it on an anthill, set up single-person tent, and unrolled his sleeping bag into the tent. He dug deeper into his backpack; the MRE came out first. He broke open the package, activated the heating element, put the main course against the heater, and folded the heater and meal back into the box to heat while he washed in the creek.

He unwrapped a bar of biodegradable soap and carefully looked around. He had picked this spot to set up camp because the water flowing in the creek pooled into a deep water hole and it was fairly well concealed by the brush and trees. Removing all his clothes and dropping them on the bank, he scrambled up a large rock and jumped into the water. His feet touched bottom. He recoiled off the bottom, and two feet later his head broke the surface.

Keith had camped along Fossil Creek dozens of times since the auspicious camping trip he experienced with Allison and her family. The course of the creek changed slightly year to year, depending on the rains. A couple of years ago the meandering path of the water changed dramatically when the power company decommissioned the dam upstream. Places he had camped were now under water or far removed from the water, but Fossil Creek remained a deeply personal and treasured place for him.

He had driven through Strawberry, Arizona, at dusk the night before and slept in the back of the Suburban. The next day he'd hiked several miles along the banks of the creek and discovered the deep water spot. He decided to spend the night there. It was only about a mile and a half from the truck. He'd be up before dawn and back in Chandler by midmorning.

He soaped up, rinsed, and swam around for fifteen minutes or so. Before he got out of the water he looked around again to make sure no one was close by. He put his clothes back on, sprayed on a heavy dose of bug repellent, and sat down to eat.

It was such a pleasant surprise running into Allison. She was right: Allison was his first girlfriend, and they did do so much together. The only other girl he had any interaction with prior to Allison was the one he had taken on a group date to the movies, and Allison was part of the group. After the movie, a friend of Allison's told one of Keith's friends that Allison thought he was cute. Keith wasn't quite sure what to do with that piece of information.

They had been friends since eighth grade and had first met on a plane flying back to Arizona from Massachusetts. She had gone to summer camp on Cape Cod, and he had spent a week with relatives in Rhode Island. They were both in middle school. It took several years before they had their first date. They wrote letters, and when instant messaging and e-mailing became mainstream, they swapped e-mails occasionally. Finally, halfway through his junior year in high school, he got up the courage to ask her out.

Allison's voice broke his thoughts.

"Hi again. It's me," she said.

Keith looked up from his camp chair. When he saw it was Allison, he stood up. "Hi. You surprised me again. I didn't see you coming."

"I watched you leave earlier, and thought I saw you stop. I had to go to the bathroom, so I walked into the woods a little farther than I needed to. I saw you here and wanted to talk with you more."

"I'm glad you did. I wanted to catch up more too, but Frank didn't seem thrilled with us talking earlier. Is he your husband or boyfriend or date or …?" Keith's voice faded out. He scanned the forest for movement while he asked the question.

"He's a friend." Allison shrugged. "He wants more of a relationship with me than I want with him, but I don't want to talk about him. I want to hear more about you and how things have gone for you. I've wondered about you from time to time. So you were saying you're a teacher and a soldier. I can see you as a teacher. I'm having trouble picturing you as a soldier, though. What grade do you teach?"

"I'm a rarity. I'm a male teacher, and I teach fourth grade in Weymouth. It's a city just south of Boston."

"I think that's great."

"I like what I do. I think I make a difference. All the other teachers, plus the secretaries, administrators, nurse, and principal, are female. The building maintenance guy and I are the only males."

"Really? Even the gym teacher is female?" asked Allison.

"Yup. Sometimes I think some of the parents assume I'm some kind of pedophile when they first meet me, but I work hard to win their trust. And usually by the end of the year they trust me and appreciate the fact that I bring some maleness to the school," replied Keith.

"How's your family? I really liked them," Keith said.

"Good. Annie graduated ASU," said Allison. "She got married a couple of years later and moved to Minnesota. We talk every few days. She will be excited to hear about you. Mom's good. After the two of us left home, she went back to work full time when Dad got sick. She's an accountant."

"What happened to your father?" Keith asked.

"He's okay now, but he got really sick about ten years ago."

"What happened?"

"He got cancer. Lymphoma. The doctors at the VA thought it was related to the whole Agent Orange thing from his time in Vietnam. Eventually he went back to work, but it took a long time."

"I'm glad he's okay now," said Keith.

"It was a very difficult time," Allison added. "While he was getting treatment his insurance company canceled his policy. He was self-employed and there were caps on how much they would cover. My parents didn't know about the limits. He had never been sick a day in his life. It was so sad to see him get so sick. He'd always been so vibrant."

Allison continued, "Annie was in her senior year and my parents couldn't help pay her tuition. They almost lost their house covering the medical bills. I couldn't help because I was waiting tables. And Dad wouldn't declare bankruptcy or seek help from the state. He is so stubborn."

"I can understand his desire to do the right thing. I admire his sense of integrity."

"Yes, I know, but it can be frustrating and misapplied."

"Yeah, but a man either has integrity or he doesn't," said Keith. "And I think many men don't."

"I agree, but I don't want to get into a discussion about personal values now."

"Got it."

"Anyway. The worst thing of all was, while he was getting treated, he lost his carpentry business. Dad turned the business over to his foreman while he got chemo, and the foreman took off with all of Dad's tools and most of our money. But they worked it out. Dad's back at work now as a facilities maintenance guy, and he does some carpentry on the side. Best of all, he hasn't had a relapse."

"That's a terrible run of bad luck. I'm glad he's okay now. Please tell them I said hello," said Keith.

"I will. What else has been going on in your life? Have you been called up?"

"Yes. Already been to the sandbox for a year," replied Keith. "And it's looking like we're going again soon."

"What was it like? You must have seen some unbelievable stuff. Were you scared?"

"Most of our work was running resupply convoys. We just wanted to complete our route and get back without any problems, so I didn't have a chance to take in the sights. What I did see was crappy. All of it was either run down and shabby or rubble. Everywhere we went in that part of the world was a dump. There was some interesting architecture, but even if it wasn't a war zone, it's not a place you'd ever want to go." He paused. "And, yes. I saw some bad stuff," he added.

"How did your wife handle your deployment?"

"I'm not married. Got close one time, though."

"Girlfriend?"

"Not at the moment. Just dates. The women I work with, though, seem to be on a mission to set me up with somebody. They say since I'm in my early thirties I should start looking for someone.

"I was seeing someone for a long time. It was hard on her when I deployed. She wanted me to quit the guard, but I didn't want to, because it's important to me. Within a few weeks of my deployment, we broke up. She sent me a Dear John letter. She ended up with a guy who isn't in the military and who probably doesn't even travel with work."

"That's sad. She must have been terribly worried about you."

"I don't think so. She never said anything like that."

"She was probably worried that you were going to get hurt or worse."

"She never said that. Before September 11, mostly all she said was that she didn't like my being gone. After the attacks and with the country at war, she said she knew I would be mobilized. After I was deployed, she sent me a letter saying she couldn't deal with my being a soldier, and that was it. We broke up. She was a very practical person, and kinda emotionally stingy."

"Believe me, Keith, she was worried about you. And maybe she couldn't deal with the worry too well."

"Yeah, I suppose. I hadn't thought about it that way, but it doesn't make any difference now."

There was a pause while Keith considered the possibility that his old girlfriend had indeed been worried about him and not just annoyed that his drill weekends and deployment got in the way of the kind of life she wanted with him. She had a funny way of showing her concern, he thought. It looked a lot like irritation, overreaction, and anger.

"What about you?" Keith asked. "I'm guessing Frank's not the guy."

"No, he isn't. I was married one time, but for the most part now I just go on dates."

"You were married?"

"Yes. I regret it. I was stubborn and headstrong. I didn't go straight to college after I finished high school. I met someone older. I thought the whole 'love can conquer all' thing would work, but he had a lot of stuff going on behind my back. After about seven months, I left and moved back in with my folks. I got divorced a few months later."

"Hard lesson to learn."

"Yeah. Tell me about it."

There was another lull. Keith wondered how their conversation had gotten so intense so quickly. He usually held back and didn't open up too much; he usually steered the conversation so the other person did most of the talking. But this was Allison, and she was unique.

"I've always been curious about why you broke up with me, Keith. Did you meet another girl when you got to Boston?" She looked him right in the eyes.

"No, I didn't. When I called you and said I wanted to break up, it was because we lived three thousand miles apart. You had to finish your senior year, and I wasn't going to be back to Arizona until the following summer. Just like I said at the time."

"You're serious? You're telling me the truth? You got to college and didn't end up in bed with some girl?"

"I'm telling you the truth. I didn't get close to a girl or even go on a date until almost the end of my freshman year. What about you? How quickly did you start going out with someone?"

"I was in high school, so, you know," Allison answered. Her voiced faded as she shuffled her feet and looked away.

The conversation hit its endpoint. They both looked away. Keith looked toward the river and then up at the stars. She looked toward the forest and her camp. The glow from the campfire interrupted the dark woods.

"I should get back," Allison said.

"Yeah. Frank's probably looking for you."

"No. He's stoned by now."

"Allison, it was really good to see you. I hope we do stay in touch."

"Me too."

Keith stood up and opened his arms toward Allison. "You were and are a very special person to me."

"You, too, Keith." Allison stood and walked into his arms. "You too."

They hugged for a long time.

Allison finally broke the hug. She stepped back to start walking back toward her camp. "You've stayed in shape," she said.

"Um, thanks," Keith said, thinking she had noticed while they hugged that he worked out.

"I saw your scars."

"When?"

"I was here when you came out of the water. What happened?"

"Oh, Allison," he groaned.

"You were very modest when we were together," she said. "It's refreshing to know that you still are."

"What happened?" she asked again.

"Roadside bomb."

"Can you tell me about it?"

"No."

"If you want to, I can be a good listener."

He didn't reply.

"Okay. I don't understand why you won't talk about it, but I won't push it. It makes me sad to know you were hurt, Keith."

Keith stood still.

"Okay. Please look me up when you're in the Valley again." She kissed him on the cheek and disappeared into the Arizona forest.

Camping Trip

May 1996
Fossil Creek

"They'll never know. They're going to Tucson for the weekend. They'll be home midday on Sunday. I told them I'd stay with Misty for the weekend," Allison said quietly into the phone.

"Your father will kill me if he finds out."

"No, he won't, Keith. He likes you, and besides, he's a lot of talk. He lets me get away with a lot of stuff that my mother doesn't. My mother is the one who would be mad if we got caught. Dad would pretend to be mad only because my mother would be mad. He doesn't want her yelling at him too."

"Where do you want to go? I liked that place we went the other time, Fossil Creek," Keith suggested.

"Yeah, that would be good. I know how to get there."

"I don't have any camping supplies."

"We'll use our stuff," said Allison. "We'll just have to clean it and put it away before my folks get home."

"All right, I'll pick you up Saturday morning."

Saturday morning, as Keith drove from his house to Allison's, he tried to think about all the things they should bring for a camping trip: a tent, sleeping bags, and some snacks. Water, too, of course. It's July in Arizona. Even though they were going to camp next to the creek, he had heard that they shouldn't drink the water. It could make them sick. He had an uneasy feeling that he should be more prepared. When he had camped with Allison and her family, they had lots of gear in the car. There was barely enough room for the five of them. He had never gone camping before, and it seemed like a lot of stuff. But after they set up camp, the car was almost empty. It was unclear if it was all used or not.

It was a fun time.

Allison's family was easygoing, not like his. At the campsite, her family spent all day in bathing suits. They made minimal efforts to conceal themselves when they were changing. At night the girls were in long T-shirts and underwear while they sat around the campfire eating s'mores. Her father shared a little bit of his alcohol with Keith and offered him a cigar. They were clearly welcoming and very comfortable outdoors. Keith's mother, on the other hand, wouldn't even let Keith see her without her hair done, makeup applied, and dressed as though she were going for a day at the country club. She didn't work. She volunteered at the hospital, the library, and an animal shelter. They had a comfortable life; his father was diligent about paying child support and alimony. Keith wished his father wanted to spend more time with him, but he lived in Seattle and was very busy with work.

Allison waved him into the garage when he drove up. She shut the garage door behind him and ran to open his door. She planted a deep, passionate, and long-lasting kiss on him and then said, "I'm so excited. This is going to be great."

"Why'd you close the garage door?" Keith asked.

"We've got busybody neighbors and I don't think what we're doing is any of their business. Come on. I've got most of the gear ready."

She led him into the house, stopping to kiss him again in the kitchen. "Do you want some breakfast? I can cook you something, or you can help yourself to whatever you want," she offered.

"Thanks. I just want some juice."

It was strange for Allison to offer to cook him something. She said she hated to cook. In fact, she told him that when her mother forced her to help with the cooking, she sabotaged it by using too much spice, or undercooking or overcooking the dish, no matter what was being served. Her mother stopped tasking her with cooking and left her to do the dishes.

"I thought you hated to cook," Keith said.

"I do, but it would be okay to do it today." She looked out the window. "Hurry up. I want to get out of here before Mrs. Spooner gets back. She'll rat me out."

They went to the shed and started shuttling the gear to his truck. Keith kept a mental list: tent, sleeping bag, flashlight, matches, and a cooler with a six-pack of Coke.

"What are we going to do for food?" he asked.

"We'll stop at the store in Payson and get some snacks."

Allison disappeared into the house and returned with a small overnight bag. "Can't forget my retainer or toothbrush," she said.

"Crap. I forgot my toothbrush. Do you have an extra?" Keith started wondering what else he forgot. A change of clothes? Soap?

"Yeah, I've got an extra toothbrush," Allison replied.

"All right. I think we're all set. Can you think of anything else?" Allison asked.

Not wanting to appear foolish or unknowledgeable, Keith said, "We're good. Let's go."

"Guess what I have?" she asked, holding up a midsize paper bag.

"Food?"

"No. I asked Kelli to see if her older sister would get us some beer, and she got me like a dozen wine coolers."

"Cool."

The ride up the Beeline Highway to Payson was uneventful. It was midmorning and the sun was shining bright. The temperature did not drop as much as they'd hoped when they rolled into town. The Valley was 105° when they left, and Payson was at 92°. They stocked up on supplies there: cookies, chips, soda, canned beef stew, marshmallows, and a couple of submarine sandwiches. They tried to buy alcohol, but no luck. They pushed farther north on Highway 87 until they got to Strawberry, where they turned west.

They never ran out of things to talk about on the two-hour drive: friends, dreams, teachers, past crushes and loves. Every topic was deconstructed, analyzed, and then shrugged off as a new topic surfaced.

The pavement ended and they began the descent into the valley.

The steep mountain road dropped nearly two thousand feet into the Fossil Creek Basin. The road was narrow with blind corners and no guardrails. At one point, a large modified pickup truck sprang on them on one of the blind horseshoe turns. Keith got as close as he dared to the edge of the road. He felt the right rear end of his pickup slip and dip a little as the gravel under his well-worn tires gave way. The other truck continued its upward assault without slowing or even acknowledging the near miss. Finally, they reached the bottom. There the road flattened and straightened.

They drove past the Childs power plant and turned left off the road several times until they found a secluded camping spot close to the creek. Stepping out of the truck, Allison took her shoes off, and then her T-shirt and shorts, revealing the bikini she wore underneath. She waded right into the creek.

"Come on, Keith. The water's great," she said.

Allison had swum down to the bottom of a large close-by boulder. The water was well over her head. By the time Keith finished undressing, she was on top of the boulder.

He walked to the edge of the water and sat down. Slowly he took his shirt and shoes off and waded into the water.

Keith was watching the fish swim in the clear water when he heard her yell. He looked up in time to see her leap off the boulder and splash into the water. He ran up the same path to the top of the boulder and leapt in.

"This is going to be great," he said as he swam over to her.

"Yes, it is," she said as she threw her arms around him.

After swimming, diving, and kissing and hugging under water for nearly an hour, Keith said he was hungry.

"This is great," he said again, as he unwrapped his gigantic roast beef sub sandwich.

"We forgot to bring camp chairs," Allison said.

"That won't stop me. I'm famished," Keith said as he and Allison sat on large rocks and ate lunch. After lunch, Keith excused himself and stepped away.

"We're in the outdoors, Keith. You don't have to step away to fart."

"My mother is really uptight about that," replied Keith. *And a whole lot of other things,* he thought as he walked back toward Allison.

"I appreciate it, but when we're outdoors it doesn't make a difference. My dad says the flatubeast runs wild in the woods and stalks people camping, men in particular."

"The what?"

"Flatubeast. Flatulence. Beast. Get it?"

"That's funny," Keith replied, laughing. "I never heard that word before."

"I think he made it up. Even my mother smiles when he says it, and she is really tired of his jokes."

Quiet settled over the camp. Keith sat down next to Allison and put his arm around her shoulder. She leaned her head on his shoulder and sighed. Around them the sounds eased into their ears. The birds and insects at first seemed cacophonous, but eventually the entomological noise smoothed into an appropriate harmony with the rest of the woodland sounds. The water rolled easily in the travertine pool in front of them. The slight rush of water tumbling down a small waterfall two hundred feet away added a flourish to the symphony playing for them. The leaves being brushed by the wind added their sounds. In the distance, a barely audible thunder roll added a percussive element.

"What time is it?" Allison asked.

"It's almost four o'clock."

"I think it's happy hour now. Do you want a wine cooler?"

"Yup." He took one and finished it: one big pull on the bottle.

"Do you like it?" she asked, sipping hers.

"Yeah, kinda sweet, but not much of a taste."

"We should set up the tent. It'll get dark and it's clouding up," said Allison. "I hope we get some rain."

Keith looked skyward. He saw several anvil-topped clouds in view just over the rim. He looked up again a few minutes after they had set up the tent. The wind had quickly pushed the clouds into sight, and now they were almost directly overhead. Lightning popped behind the clouds like a camera flash. He couldn't see any lightning bolts, but the thunder growled louder.

"If we get a monsoon, are we in a safe place here? I mean, does the creek rise?" he asked.

"I don't remember being here during any strong rainstorms. I think we're okay," she replied.

Their camp was only ten feet from the water's edge and was only inches above the water. The tops of the trees were bending from the strong wind, but fifty feet below, Keith and Allison felt only a breeze.

Keith walked around and gathered small twigs and branches for a fire. The area was picked clean of any wood that would suffice as logs. He rummaged around the floor of his truck. He found some wrappers, old school papers, and fast-food bags, which he crumpled up to start the fire.

"We forgot pillows, too," Allison said. "We can put our clothes in the stuff sacks for pillows."

"Does that mean we're going to be naked?" Keith asked hopefully. Another erection started.

"I've only brought my bikini, a towel, and the clothes I wore here," Allison answered, smiling. She tipped her hips forward slightly, put the wine cooler to her lips, tilted her head, and finished the bottle. She went into the tent, rustled around for a minute, and then stuck her head out the flap. "Come here."

Keith had just put a match to a piece of paper, an English test he had failed his junior year. It burst into flames as he walked toward the tent. He stuck his head inside the small two-man backpacking tent Allison had brought. The sky had darkened more, but there was more than enough light for him to see Allison. She was wearing only a T-shirt and bikini bottoms. He crawled into the tent and lay down next to her. She leaned over and kissed him.

He put his hand on her back. While they kissed, he slowly moved toward her breasts. She stopped kissing him, sat up, and took off her T-shirt. He kicked off his shoes and his shirt. Their skin-to-skin contact intensified the kissing. He slowly worked his hand toward her panties.

The first few gentle raindrops hit the tent. Keith broke the lip-lock and laid his head back. She put her head on his chest. They listened to the rain. The raindrops came faster. The wind picked up, and small branches bounced off the tent. Allison moved her hand and wrapped it around his already hard penis. It got harder, so hard that, for Keith, it felt as if the muscles were going to burst through the skin.

The rain came faster.

He sat up and slid her panties off and then removed his own briefs. He leaned over to her and started kissing her again. The temperature outside had dropped fifteen degrees as the rain and wind grew stronger. It blew the rain and forest debris around like a tempest. Inside the tent it was hot. He was sweating. He moved on top of her, careful not to drop all his weight on her, holding himself up on his forearms.

"Wait," Allison said suddenly. She squirmed out from under him.

"What?"

"I'm the rain baby." With that, she crawled out of the tent.

Keith watched her go. A moment later he stuck his head out of the tent. The thick cloud cover made the late afternoon seem like twilight. Flashes of lightning created a stop-action effect to her movements.

Allison was running, dancing, and jumping in the pouring rain.

"Allison, you're crazy. Get back in here before you get hit by lightning," Keith yelled over the ferocious wind.

"No. You come out here," she yelled back.

Keith was reserved. He had always been that way. Ever since he was a small child he carefully studied every situation before he jumped in. He seldom missed out on anything, but he was methodical in his participation. However, Allison had a way of compelling him to chuck his careful manner without saying a word. He looked around very briefly, bolted out of the tent, and ran to her.

He hugged her soaked body and sensed her nipples under her wet T-shirt. He felt even more rising fullness in his groin. She seemed content and stayed in his arms. Suddenly, she slipped out of his arms and ran away. In the rain, they played tag. He ran after her. She let him catch her, but only for a few teasing moments. Then she bolted again, laughing the whole time. They were lost in themselves and each other, oblivious to the storm around them. He finally stopped chasing her, out of breath but excited and aroused. She met his eyes and slowly came close, this time to stay. She held his warm body close, and their kiss seemed to last forever. The rain and wind and thunder and lightning grew more intense. This time, she stayed in his arms, kissing and squirming and caressing.

They hurried to the shelter of the tent and huddled together, giggling and shivering. The sleeping bags acted as blankets. Their hearts slowed as the warmth took over and their naked bodies joined.

Lying together with Allison, Keith listened to the rain. He had been through monsoons every summer of his life. Summer monsoons are normal for Arizonians. But this storm was vicious. *Maybe it's just being in a tent that makes it sound so powerful,* he thought. He certainly didn't want to say anything to Allison. She seemed so confident in the woods. He still had a lot to learn before he was comfortable out of doors.

He stuck his head out of the tent door flap and quickly pulled it back. It felt like he had been shot. He and the other boys in the neighborhood used to play a game with a BB gun. They would shoot each other and take a step closer to the gun after each shot until it was too painful. There, in the storm at Fossil Creek, it felt like he had his head pressed against the barrel and that hundreds of BBs came out at once. In the dim light of Allison's flashlight, he saw hail on the floor of the tent.

Putting on a ball cap, he stuck his head out of the flap again. This time he saw water from the creek spilling over the embankment and rivulets forming where the water ran down off the hill. He looked over to his truck and saw that the water was already up to the rim on one of the tires.

"Allison, are you awake?" he asked.

"Yes. I'm listening to the rain," she replied.

"The water's overflowing the creek. It's hailing too, and it's looking pretty bad out there. I think we need to get out of here."

"Let me see." She stuck her head out the flap. A few seconds later she pulled it back in and said, "Yeah, it looks pretty bad."

"I don't want to get stuck here," Keith said. "The tires on my truck are almost bald, and we've got to go up that hill to get out of here. I say we throw everything in the back of the truck. Tomorrow, in Phoenix, we can clean it up."

He moved to put his clothes back on. Allison did too.

The storm attacked the little tent harder as they scrambled to get out of there. The storm was aggressive and getting bolder. At times, they couldn't hear each other speak over the bombardment against the flimsy fabric of the tent. The tent gave up its water-repellent feature in the face of the torrent. Water seeped through everywhere and soaked the inside of the tent, but the rain didn't pierce the material. The sleeping bags resisted the water, but if Keith and Allison were in a survival situation and needed the tent and sleeping bags to withstand the weather in order to survive the next day, they would be in trouble. Their gear failed. Lightning burst with such frequency that they didn't need a flashlight. Allison dropped the one she had anyway. It was quickly lost in the ankle-deep mud.

Allison dressed quickly. Keith was able to find only his shoes and pants.

"Have you seen my shirt?" Keith yelled over the wind and rain and thunder as he grabbed a couple of bags and prepared to run to the truck.

"No," Allison yelled back. "We'll find it later."

Keith scrambled out of the tent and ran to the truck. Allison followed right behind him. They put the sleeping bags and whatever else they could fit—and thought needed to stay as dry as possible—into the cab of the pickup. Everything else went in the bed. They went back to the tent, collapsed it, pulled it up by its stakes, and ran back to the truck.

Keith made one last loop around the campsite looking for anything they might be leaving behind. Shirtless, he climbed into the driver's seat, soaking wet. They both were panting by the time they got in the truck. Allison leaned back in her seat, let go a big sigh, and looked at Keith as he pulled the keys out of his pocket.

Keith knew his truck well, so he knew it was not reliable. On the rare damp mornings in Phoenix, his truck struggled to start. There, at Fossil Creek, in the middle of downpour, he jammed the key in the ignition, and this time the engine started right away. Usually when he started his truck, he let it idle for a couple of minutes while the engine found its rhythm. Not this time. The truck started, he put it into gear, and then he hit the gas. He turned the steering wheel over hard, and the truck spun out into a doughnut.

"Easy, Keith," Allison said.

"I just want to get up out of this low spot," he replied. He got the truck back under control and lined up for a straight shot up the road and away from the overflowing riverbank.

The side road they had taken to get close to the creek was rough with rocks and deep ruts when they drove down it. Now it was exponentially worse. Keith gunned it and headed straight up the road. They hadn't gone twenty feet when the truck hit a big rock and dropped into a sudden unseen rut. Keith's chest smashed into the steering wheel, and Allison almost smacked her head against the dashboard, but the truck lurched up and out of the rut and kept moving forward. With three more hard hits on rocks and ruts, they made it up the short incline and out onto the slightly more improved road.

"Okay. We made it out of there," Keith said. "We should be good the rest of the way."

The headlights on the truck barely shone ten feet ahead. In the beams, the rain appeared as though it were coming down in long lines instead of a dashed line of drops. The rain etched small crevices in the road as the water worked its way into the drainage ditch. Keith's truck handled this part of the drive easily, but he took a couple of corners too fast and the rear end slid out. The ascent back up the hill toward Strawberry was going to be the next challenge.

At first, all it required was concentration. His wipers worked mightily but pointlessly against the rain. He stayed in first or second gear all the way up. Even in those low gears, the truck slid on the mud and rocks. He tried to stay in the middle of the road, but any break in his concentration made the truck drift toward one side or the other. Being trapped against the canyon wall was better than the alternative, the cliff and a drop of hundreds of feet.

When they were near the top with less than a mile to go, the water rushing down the road took control of the truck and slid it in a lateral move across the slippery rocks toward the lethal edge.

"What are you doing?" Allison screamed.

"I can't get control of the truck," he yelled back. "Open your door a little and be ready to jump out if we start heading off the cliff." He unbuckled his seat belt and unlatched his door. He could push and be out of the truck in a second. But he was on the cliff side. One misstep and he would go over the edge or be crushed by the truck, which would probably take him over the cliff regardless of his escape effort.

Allison was unbuckled and ready to fling her door open too.

The truck slid sideways and backward, closer to the edge. Allison couldn't see the road anymore and bailed out. Keith turned the wheels as much as he could. He felt the truck start to tip when one of the front wheels slid into a large rock. The rock acted as a wheel chock, and the truck stopped its treacherous slide.

Keith put the transmission in neutral. He slowly took his foot off the brake. The truck didn't move. Carefully, Keith opened the door. He stepped away from the truck, looked under it, and studied the situation. He saw that he could cut the wheels the other way and back away from the precipice, but to do that he had to go forward a foot or so toward the edge to give the wheel enough room to clear the rock that had stopped the slide. He had less than three feet between where the truck was and where the road gave way to the canyon.

Allison ran over to him.

"Are you okay?" he asked as he pulled her close.

"Yes, but I was so scared when I saw you sliding toward the edge."

Her face was soaking wet from the rain, but Keith saw a tear drop from her eye and quickly disappear into the wetness.

"What are we going to do?" Allison asked.

"I think I can get the truck unstuck, but it'll be tricky."

"What can I do?" she asked.

"Stand uphill of the truck and let me know when I'm about a foot away from that rock." He lowered himself to the road and pointed to the lifesaving rock.

"What are you going to do?"

"I'm going to go forward a little, cut the wheels hard, and then let the truck slide backward, back toward the middle of the road."

"Shouldn't we wait for someone to come along?" Allison asked.

"I think I can do it." Keith got back in the truck and nodded toward Allison. He put the truck back in gear and let out the clutch as slowly as possible. The vehicle started to move forward, but it hit another rock and the tires spun like they were on ice.

"Watch out. I'm going to give it some gas and see if I can lurch it forward. Then I'll hope it slides backward."

"Be careful," Allison yelled back as loud as she could.

Keith feathered the gas pedal. He held the door open with his left elbow. His left hand was on the steering wheel, and his right hand was on the gearshift. He pressed the clutch against the floor and gunned the engine a couple of times, and then he let the clutch pop up as quickly as it could while staying within its won't-stall ratio.

Allison heard the engine and saw the truck jump. She screamed out Keith's name.

His plan went exactly as he thought it would. He backed off the gas and pushed the clutch in after he felt the truck break free. He cranked the steering wheel over as far as it would go. The truck slid backward and away from the edge. In the middle of the road, he applied the brake and the truck stopped, idling quietly and perfectly.

Allison ran to the truck and climbed back into the passenger seat.

"You were awesome," she said as she wiped moisture off her face. She leaned over and kissed him, full force.

Keith let out the clutch and they continued their climb up the hill, never getting out of first gear. Three-quarters of the way out of the valley, the rain slowed. At the top of the hill they broke through the clouds. There were only occasional drops. Keith stopped the truck and looked back at what he had done. The clouds were below, in the valley. The adrenaline rush was leaving both of them. They had come up out of the dark storm into a mellow, dim dusk.

Keith lowered the gate on the back of the truck and sat. Allison joined him.

"Well, that was pretty scary, and really cool, too," he said.

"Yeah. It was spectacular and terrifying at the same time," she said.

"What did you mean when you ran out of the tent saying you were the rain baby?" Keith asked.

"I was born during a monsoon. I always like the rain."

"Oh. Did this storm change your mind?"

"No. Rain is my element."

They sat and watched the storm clouds below move toward the southeast. The sun broke through the thin layer of clouds above them just before it sank below the west canyon wall.

"Do we have anything to eat?" Keith asked.

Allison looked at him. She nodded her head once and smiled at him. "Yeah. I think I have a candy bar in my bag."

"Can I have it? I'm starving," Keith said.

"Sure."

"What do you think we should do now, head back to the valley or see if we can find a place in Payson?" Keith asked.

"I don't know. I don't think we can get a room in Payson. Neither one of us is eighteen."

"You're right. And it'll probably cost, like, a hundred bucks even if we could get a room. I've only got ten bucks on me. Let's head back to Phoenix."

Keith stood up, turned, and opened his arms toward Allison. She stood and stepped into his hug. It was a long, quiet hug, accented only by a couple of long sighs. They broke apart and started a slow drive back to Strawberry, and then on down to the Valley.

Back at Allison's house, they showered first, and then they sorted, washed, dried, and stowed the camping gear.

Allison invited Keith to spend the night. He did.

Midday Sunday, Allison's parents were exiting the freeway, when her mother thought she recognized Keith's truck entering the highway.

"Is that Keith's truck?" she asked.

"Where?"

"Over there," she said, pointing. "On the on-ramp."

"No. That's not his truck. There are a thousand trucks like that.

Besides, Allison knows the rules: Keith is not supposed to be there unless one of us is home," he answered.

The mother and wife watched the truck disappear down the freeway, and then she looked at her husband. She decided there was no point in disappointing him and explaining the possible actions of the teenage daughter he adored so much.

Nor'easter

Fall-Winter 2009
South Shore, Massachusetts

Keith called Private Christine Hamblin earlier in the week and left a message for her to report to the Hingham armory fifteen minutes early. Ten minutes before muster, he was getting annoyed. The soldiers were forming up in the drill hall and she was nowhere to be found. He looked out to the parking lot when he heard a car squeal as it turned into the lot. From the window he saw it drive to the farthest corner. *Hamblin is not off to a strong start,* he thought. He looked toward the straggler's car and saw the trunk open. A uniform top was lying on the roof. *Whoever it is, is cutting it close,* he thought.

From a window in the NCO office inside the old castle-shaped armory made of red brick, Keith watched the trunk slam close and a female soldier run toward the building. She had a large uncovered cup of coffee teetering in one hand and her backpack as a counterweight in her other hand. At the front door he heard a soldier ask for her ID, and the unknown female asked the soldier on duty where she was to go for muster. He heard her running, alternately swearing and apologizing to the people she almost ran into. He thought, *That better not be Hamblin.* He looked at his watch and then left the office for the drill hall. He saw the hurrying soldier ask something of the corporal at the drill hall door. He pointed to Sergeant Morris's squad.

"Hamblin," Keith called.

The banging door closed behind her. Keith stepped through the door and did not see her. She was small and could have slid behind the ranks of soldiers.

He stood in front of his squad and called them to attention. He saw the new face in the last row and her name tape—Hamblin—squared away and at attention.

"Hamblin?" he said as he called out names of the soldiers in his squad for the muster.

"Here," she replied.

Keith looked out the corner of his eye at her. *Big voice for a small girl,* he thought. Her brown hair was tucked up according to regulation. It looked like she had taken in the uniform blouse so it was more flattering like many of the women in the unit did, and she had a slightly mischievous smile.

At every following drill weekend, she was the last one in ranks. The other soldiers who came later were late. She was the last one to be on time.

Sunday mornings were the same ritual with different clothes: parking in the farthest corner of the parking lot and quickly changing out of her nightclub clothes and into uniform. Sometimes she reclined the driver's seat; other times she stood behind her car to change with the trunk up and the trees and brush behind her. Still other times she stood in the back of one of the trucks and changed out of her dance-party clothes into her uniform.

The young males in the unit had a bet to see who would be the first one to get a photo of her changing clothes.

In spite of her chaotic arrival and seeming disorder, Hamblin was always squared away. Her uniform was pressed, her hair bunned according to regulations, and any excessive makeup or jewelry removed. She marched smartly, completed PT well out in front of her gender peers (and in front of most of the males and part of the pack of males leading the unit run), followed orders promptly, and was eager to learn how to operate the trucks.

"What's your story, Hamblin?" Keith asked when he met with her during that first drill weekend with the unit.

"What do you mean, Sergeant?" she asked.

"Why'd you transfer to this unit? I've heard you were doing okay at your other unit, no problems."

"I wanted to be something other than a clerk."

"Okay. That's a good reason. What else? Where do you work? You going to school? Got family here? You know this unit has been mobilized once already in support of OIF, and we're heading out the door again and you're coming. You got any questions about mobilization?"

"I work as a cashier at a pharmacy in Whitman, and I live with my parents in Taunton. But I want to get an apartment closer to Boston, 'cause I'm bored in Taunton and Whitman. I looked at a place in South Weymouth, but with all the deposits it's more than I can afford. Maybe I can get a roommate."

"You might want to hold off on getting an apartment. By the time we get mobilized, get our training done, head to the sandbox, and get back, it'll be close to a year. Plus, you'll make a ton of money, and it's all tax-free."

"What's it like in Iraq?" she asked.

"Learn to embrace the suck."

"What's that mean?"

"It's a third world country. It's dirty. There's litter everywhere. Every one of them could use a toothbrush and dental floss. The men don't know what deodorant is, and it smells like burning shit wherever you go. It sucks, and the ones who come back with their head intact are the ones who learned to embrace the suck. It's an expression I heard one of the chaplains use when we were getting our briefs right after we got in country. And he's right. Don't expect anything to be comfortable or easy."

"I can handle it."

"Yes, I'm sure you can. When we were there the first time, things were very rudimentary, almost spartan. A friend of mine recently returned from Iraq and described it this way: 'No one is living large, but no one is suffering either.' It has to be better than what we experienced, and we're probably going to be stationed in Kuwait this time.

"However, to be fair to the decent Iraqi men and women there, the place is fascinating. The architecture, the history, and most of the people there just want to have meaningful work, have a few friends, raise children, and be married to someone who doesn't drive them crazy all the time. At least that's my opinion of the noncombatant Iraqis I met."

"I heard you got hurt."

Keith paused before he spoke. "Yes, I did." He stared at her, waiting for the all too common question about his injuries.

She didn't ask.

He gave his head a barely perceptible nod and then continued. "You've been trained. No one is going to set you up to fail. You'll do fine with all the stuff you learned in boot camp—weapons, body armor, and so on. And you'll get lots more training here about the unit and its mission and how to do what it is we do over the next few months, but it's the other stuff that'll get ya."

"Like what?"

"Like, right after we got to Kuwait, the whole camp was infested with body lice and some other tiny bugs. Everyone was miserable itching and scratching. Medical didn't have enough supplies on hand. It was about ten days before delousing spray made it to us. It was easier for the males. We all shaved our heads. A couple of the females shaved their heads too, but the rest of the girls were miserable for a couple of weeks. The mass of flies on your food in the DFAC, the burning garbage—it's that kind of stuff that can really throw people."

"Is there any extra work I can do around here to make some money?"

"We keep a list of people who can come in on short notice. Whenever a hurricane or blizzard is forecast, we always need people to be on standby to help residents or the police, if the storms are really bad."

"How can I get my name on that list?"

"I'll put your name forward."

The mobilization date moved closer. The soldiers trained more specifically for the task ahead of them. It was specialized hauling, taking the army and Marine Corps' tanks and other heavy fighting vehicles out of Iraq. Weekend drills at Camp Edwards consisted of maneuvering similarly weighted objects around muddy and narrow roads and tying the loads down properly. One particularly cold weekend was spent working with a navy reserve stevedore unit on a pier in Boston Harbor practicing getting tanks onto a cargo ship.

During a break, Hamblin found Keith.

"Sergeant Morris?" she asked.

"Yeah?"

"I want to go to college."

"Good. Go. What do you want to study?"

"I don't know. That's the problem. You're a teacher, right? How do you help your students know what it is they want to study?"

"I teach third and fourth graders. Talking about what they want to study in college is not part of the curriculum."

"I'm sorry to bother you," Hamblin said as she turned to walk away.

"Hamblin, get back here. I didn't say I wouldn't help you. Don't get so pissy every time someone doesn't instantly answer you the way you want them to."

"I don't get pissy."

"Oh, yes, you do, and you need to start getting over it."

"Yes, Sergeant," she said as she turned to leave.

"Do you want my help or not?"

"No, Sergeant. I'll figure it out myself."

"That's your choice, but I think you'd be a really good teacher."

"Thanks for your input, Sergeant. Am I dismissed?"

"Not yet. I want you to wash all the trucks. Lose the attitude while you're at it. Now you're dismissed."

By the time winter arrived, the 1058th was ready to deploy. When they left Iraq in 2004, they left all their vehicles and other equipment there. Most of their gear was well worn. It would have been expensive and inefficient to ship it all back to the Hingham armory. This created a problem when the unit returned to Hingham. Prior to the 2003 deployment, the 1058th had three trucks left in its storage lot. New equipment was sent straight to Iraq. However, used and out-of-date equipment from other units was gradually transferred to the 1058th. Over the years, the unit received new and upgraded equipment and vehicles. For the impending deployment they would leave their equipment in Hingham. When winter rolled in, at least they would be able to help if a storm slammed the South Shore.

And one did.

Master Sergeant Jarvis called on the phone. "Sergeant Morris."

"Give me a break, Des. Call me Keith."

"I know. We just keep getting reminded that we need to be formal so you guys have more military bearing when you show up for drill."

"I know, I get it, but I'm okay with the informality. After all, I've crashed on your couch plenty of times over the years, and you've crashed here enough."

"Okay … Keith, your name popped up on the list. We need a dozen or so soldiers to stay at the armory. The storm is supposed to be a bad one. We're going to put a few trucks in Quincy and a couple in Boston, and we might need to get a few trucks out here on the South Shore to help the cops if some residents get stuck."

"Fine with me. I'm on winter break anyway. Who else?"

"From your squad, it's Hamblin."

"Good. She's smart and works hard."

"Bring four days of clothes and whatever else you need to the armory. We got MREs, plus you'll get some bonus pay when it's all said and done."

"Okay. When am I supposed to report?"

"Hamblin's on her way here. Can you be here tonight?"

"Yeah. You going to be around, or do you get to miss this one?"

"I'm here. I'll pick up a little something so we can stay warm on the inside too."

"Good. Hey, did the quartermasters refill their cold-weather and rain-gear stores? It sucked a whole lot last winter in the snow that weekend."

"Yup, they're all set. You'll get what you want."

"Good. Thanks. I'll see you there in a couple of hours."

When detail arrived at the armory, the lieutenant read off a list of dos and don'ts and gave everyone their assignments.

"Morris?"

"Yes, sir?"

"Town of Scituate is getting some flooding in the Fourth Cliff area. You and Hamblin head down there. There are some residents choosing to stay. The tide is coming in, and it's projected to be twenty feet higher than normal. They might need something to go into the water to check on the residents. Their fire trucks are positioned around town, but the Fourth Cliff is kinda isolated."

"I know the area. There's the rec site there."

"When you get there, make a pass. Let the residents see you so they know you're there. Then wait on the west side of the bridge. Scituate will let you know if they need you to go back across and get anyone. Make sure you have your cell and the radio. Check in here every couple of hours."

"Yes, sir. Any idea how many residents are riding it out?"

"I think there's about a dozen. Be careful."

"Hamblin," Keith said, yelling her name in the drill hall. "Let's go."

They left the building. Other soldiers had shuttled the trucks from the storage yard to the armory. Their truck was idling and it was warm. The cab had several cases of water and MREs. In the back there were blankets, ponchos, stretchers, rope, powerful battery-operated lights, extra first aid supplies, and heavy-duty waders.

"We'll swap out the driving," Keith said. "You begin."

"Okay, Sergeant," she replied. "You know I've never driven these trucks in the snow."

"I know. Think of this as training. You'll do fine."

"Can we swing by Dunk's and get some coffee?" she asked.

"Sure."

Hamblin eased the truck into gear and let up on the clutch. The truck eased forward, no slipping or spinning. The knobs on the tires packed and shaped the snow into easy little hills for the knobs to grab onto. She turned out of the parking lot and expertly drove down the little hill that emptied into Hingham Square, where she turned right and made her way to Route 3A. The square was mostly empty, except for an elderly couple walking hand in hand, enjoying the snow. At first, the old man waved at Keith and Christine as they drove past. Then he stopped and lifted his hand farther, saluting the two soldiers. His wife waved too.

The two soldiers waved and saluted in return.

"That's sweet," Hamblin said as she watched them in her rearview mirror.

"They should be home out of the cold," said Keith.

"Uh, Sergeant, if they're out walking in the storm today, I think they probably have a lifetime of being outdoors."

"Winters here can be tough. Plus, those people are old. They could slip and fall, break a hip, or catch pneumonia or something. Unless they have to be outside, they should be home."

"Sergeant, you sound like an old woman. I know you grew up in Arizona, but we have an expression here in New England: 'There's no such thing as bad weather, just bad clothing.' I think they'll be fine," Hamblin said, as she turned onto Route 3A, southbound.

There was not a car in sight. The view out to Hingham Harbor was an odd mixture of bright and gray light. The snow fell from the dark gray clouds. As each flake settled on the ground, it reflected any nearby luminance. As more and more snow gathered, the light brightened. Streetlights, the truck's headlights, and lights from storefronts added spikes of light to the scene. Inside the warm, slow-moving truck, there was a sense of safety that Keith had not felt since the explosion in Iraq five years earlier.

They neared the rotary and got a look at the harbor. The waves were just breaking over the seawall.

"That's not a good sign," said Keith.

"What makes you say that?"

"Hingham Harbor is double protected. It's inside Boston Harbor, and geographically it's in the armpit of Hull."

"The snobs of Hingham hate to think they are even attached to Hull. They'd have a conniption if they heard anyone describe Hingham as being in the armpit of Hull," Hamblin added.

"I know, I've met a couple of those types. Fortunately, most of the residents are great. Anyway, if the waves are breaking over the road here and it's not even high tide, it's going to be intense where we're going in Scituate. It's not protected. It faces Massachusetts Bay. The shore there is probably getting pounded, and there's a good chance of it getting flooded."

"I've never been there."

"It's nice in the summer. The unit has had a couple of picnics at the rec site there."

When Hamblin signaled to turn onto Route 3A at the rotary, Keith spoke up and told her they were going to go the coastal route.

"It's a good chance to let the community see us. Head toward Hull, and then follow Atlantic Avenue to Jerusalem Road into Cohasset Harbor. We'll go as far as we can in Scituate before we pick up 3A and go into Marshfield and back to Scituate."

"I thought you said we're going to Scituate. Why do we need to go to Marshfield?"

"Where we're going in Scituate, you can't get to from Scituate."

"Huh?"

"A hundred years ago during a storm, the ocean punched a new opening to the North River. When it did, it severed the Fourth Cliff section of Scituate from the rest of the town. We can only get there through Marshfield. I'll show you on the map. Let's stop at Dunk's for coffee. We'll look at the map, and switch off driving too."

They drove George Washington Boulevard to Hull. There was more traffic on the road heading toward Hull.

"Where's everyone going?"

"My guess is they're heading to Nantasket to look at the ocean and the storm surge."

A police car was going in the opposite direction. It slowed and did a U-turn in the road after the army truck passed. It pulled up behind Morris and Hamblin and turned on its lights.

"Uh-oh," Hamblin said as Keith maneuvered the vehicle to the side of the road. "What do you think they want with us?"

"Probably nothing. Maybe they just want to share some of their doughnuts," Keith replied with a smirk.

"Really?"

"No. I'm sure they want to know where we are going to be positioned."

"Shouldn't Sergeant Jarvis and Ramirez be here already?"

"I don't know. Relax. We've done nothing wrong. Why are you so nervous about them?"

"I've been pulled over two times in my life, and both times I don't think I did anything wrong. And both times the cop was hinting that if I gave him sex I wouldn't get a ticket," she said.

"You're kidding."

"No, I'm not. I'm not stupid. I know when someone is coming onto me."

"Okay, let me do the talking."

Keith rolled the window down. The cop stepped up onto the running board.

"Hell of a day to be working," he said. "How you doing, Keith?"

"Not bad, Joe. How you doing?"

"I'm doing great. Are you two being stationed here in Hull?"

"No," Keith replied. "We're heading to Fourth Cliff."

"Got it. You got any idea where the guys for Hull are? The storm is kicking up."

"I can call and find out." Keith reached for his cell and called Desmond.

"Tell him to hurry up and get his sorry fat ass here. You can also tell Des to not be afraid, and to try not to cry and wet himself this time."

"Hey, Des," Keith said as he spoke into the phone. "Joe's here and he's saying you're a wuss, that you're hiding under the blankets at your house looking for a big mammary to nuzzle 'cause you're scared of a little rain and snow."

Keith started smiling. "Okay, I'll tell him. Hey, Joe, Des says you better say you're sorry, 'cause he's about a hundred feet away in a truck, targeting your doughnut-enhanced ass that's only slightly smaller than his truck."

They all heard the horn and turned as Sergeant Jarvis rolled to a stop behind the police car. Joe waved.

"How you doing, Corporal?" asked the policeman. "I'm Joe, Joe Donahue." He stuck his arm and half his body in the window across Keith's body, rubbing his cold, wet sleeve against Keith's face as he offered a handshake to Hamblin.

"What's your name?"

"Christine Hamblin," she said as she shook his hand.

"Listen, we appreciate your help on a day like this. Chances are, everything will be fine, but I'll betcha there's gonna be at least a couple of times we're going to need your truck and its clearance to reach someone."

"We're here to help. Whatever you need," said Hamblin.

"Are you new to the unit?"

"Yes."

"I met most of the guys in the ten-five-eight in Iraq. I still know a lot of the soldiers there. You're in a good unit. They'll take care of you. For today, if you need anything, there's lots of cops around here that are veterans or members of the MP unit. Whatever you want, you got. Plus, if you get hungry or cold, they'll open their homes to you and let you know which restaurants are open during the storm to serve the cops and firefighters and paramedics."

Desmond walked up. Joe turned and shook his hand.

"I gotta go." Joe shook her hand again.

He spoke to Keith, "You got another one, huh?" He turned to leave. "See you guys," he yelled as he slid back into his cruiser. Slowly, Joe disappeared into the gray storm.

The storm was growing more intense. Visibility dropped. Hamblin let up on the clutch, and the heavy truck rolled toward Hull and onto Atlantic Avenue, which would connect them to other roads and eventually lead them down the coast to Scituate's Fourth Cliff and Marshfield Hills.

"What did Joe mean when he said, 'You got another one'?" she asked.

"I'm not sure. Probably because I seem to get a lot of the new soldiers, or because I seem to get a lot of the female soldiers cycling through my squad."

"Why?"

"My guess is because I'm a teacher I can help people new to the unit assimilate better than some of the other squad leaders can."

"Do you like that?"

"It's okay. I'm not one of the best squad leaders in the unit, but the CO told me one time that the soldiers who come through my squad tend to do better."

"Who do you think is a good squad leader?"

"The best squad leader is Master Sergeant Jarvis. He's really good. This unit was sloppy until he got on staff. Now it's one of the best-run units in the state."

"Yeah, he's nice." She paused a moment. "You two seem like you're friends."

She then said, "There aren't many females in this unit. "Why?"

"The military is a male environment, and this unit is truck drivers and mechanics. Females don't tend to seek jobs as drivers and mechanics. This is a particularly testosterone-saturated unit."

"Yeah, I've noticed. Most of the guys are pretty good, but there's a few I wouldn't trust."

"What do you mean?"

"It's not the endless come-ons. That's okay. But some of these guys, I wouldn't want to be alone with."

"Why? You gotta expect some crap. Everyone, male and female, has to take some shit and ball-busting. I know the way guys speak to each other is different from how women speak to each other. Like, a guy can go up to another guy and say, 'Whoa, looks like you fell off your diet,' and everyone knows it's just a way of saying, 'It's good to see you.' You'd never see females greet each other like that. If they did, there would be bloodshed."

"I know. And I kinda like it when the guys tease me like I'm one of the guys. I think they like me and accept me when they do that.

But there's a couple who hate me and the other females just because we're in the service."

"Have you been threatened, or are they being inappropriate?"

"No, it's not that clear. Forget about it. It's okay."

"Okay, but everyone deserves to be treated with respect. You won't be liked by everyone, but I won't tolerate disrespect."

They turned onto Jerusalem Road in Cohasset and had their first glimpse of the ocean roiling in the storm. Keith stopped the truck and watched the surf. Every few seconds another wave would crash on the rocks. He heard Christine catch her breath a couple of times.

"This is amazing," she said.

"Yeah. Could you imagine being in the navy or coast guard and being out in this? No, thanks," Keith said.

Although the worst of the storm was still miles away, the air and water pressure demonstrated their effect on the coast with waves breaking over the seawall. Sometimes it was only a spray; other times it was a wall of water soaring past and settling back to earth fifty feet beyond the road.

He put the truck in gear and followed the coastal road as it turned inland.

"We need to get on 3A and make tracks to Marshfield. The storm is picking up."

They continued their drive to Marshfield. After crossing the North River, they turned east and reached the Sea Street Bridge.

"All right, we're here. Let's cross the bridge into Humarock. Take the first left, and we'll head to Fourth Cliff. We'll knock on doors if we see lights on or cars in the driveway, and then we'll head down to Brant Rock."

They turned north on the narrow road. At first the road was wide enough for houses on both sides and for small streets that jutted toward the ocean. As the road got closer to the Fourth Cliff, it narrowed, leaving barely enough room for the truck to stay in its lane. The marsh lay to the west and a single row of homes lay to the east, facing the ocean. The houses along the beach were empty and up on stilts. Porches and decks were elevated ten feet, and latticework enclosed the gap. Boats on trailers waited for summer, as did various floats and rafts, lobster pots, and fishing rods. Boxes held summer clothes and extra blankets for guests, and grills stored out of the weather also waited for summer. Regardless of thoughtful preparation and the careful storing of summer memories, the storm surge lapped the ocean-facing beach-access stairways, and the frequent supercharged waves tossed the packages easier than baggage handlers at the airport moved luggage.

"Look at that. It's not even high tide, the storm's not here yet, and look at the water. It's already reaching the houses," said Keith. "Some of these homes are going to get whacked hard. It may go across the road."

"Looks pretty empty here."

"Yeah, I think most of the homes on the beach are summer homes, but there are a few people here. See those cars?" Keith asked, pointing toward a row of houses.

"Yeah."

"They wouldn't be here if they didn't belong to someone."

"It feels like it's almost nighttime. What time is it?" asked Christine.

"Ten o'clock in the morning."

They made one pass and headed back toward the bridge. When they reached the end of the road, they found that the gate to the Fourth Cliff military recreation site was closed but not locked.

"Let's loop through here," Keith said.

Christine stepped out of the truck and opened the gate.

The place was empty. Caretakers had put plywood over the windows and door. Picnic tables had been turned over with their legs pointing skyward. It looked like massive beetles had died there. The elevation was about thirty feet higher than the road. A hill on the site rose to nearly sixty feet above sea level.

"It's eerie," Keith said. "Have you ever been here?"

"No. It's like a ghost town."

"In the summer this place is always busy," said Keith. "It's prime real estate."

"What's that?" Christine asked, pointing to a cement tower at the outermost point of the reservation.

"It's a fire control tower built during World War Two to guide artillery from the various emplacements and forts in the area to blow up German submarines."

"Really? That's interesting."

"Yeah, it is. There's another one in Brant Rock. I think there used to be lots of them along the coast, from Maine to Rhode Island."

The dark sky, drizzle, and isolation made it feel like it was dusk. The cloud cover had not settled all the way down to the ocean. There was a gap of a couple hundred feet between the water and sky, with an unexpectedly clear view. The ocean roiled, not just at the shore, but for as far as they could see.

They stopped to close the gate. "I'll get the gate this time. We'll switch driving," said Keith.

They drove back toward the Sea Street Bridge.

"Let's stop there," said Keith as he pointed to a particular house. "I see a light on inside."

Christine eased the truck to a stop and set the brake. "Do we want to turn it off?"

"No. We've got plenty of gas. I'd rather let it idle." Keith opened the door. The cold air blasted into the cab.

"Strong wind. Not too cold, though," said Christine.

"Let's go."

They stepped down from the truck and moved toward the front door. No one had shoveled the walkway or made footprints in the snow. An elderly woman peered cautiously out the window at them. When Keith looked at her, she pulled the drape back across the window. They heard commotion inside. A moment later the front door opened. An old man spoke to someone unseen inside the house.

"It's okay. They're soldiers, probably here to check on us," he said. His voice was strong, but despite the calm manner with which he spoke, there was a tiredness to his mien.

The drape over the front window parted slightly again. The old woman looked out again and screamed, "They're here. They will take everything. Don't let them in, Wallace. We'll be beat and robbed again." She screamed and fled down a hallway. Wearing a faded bathrobe and sneakers, she looked significantly younger than the man. She was small and moved with a peculiar gait, like one leg was longer than the other. Her gray hair flashed as she ran under the hallway lights.

The old man held the storm door open. It was easy to see that at one time he was a big, muscular, trim man. His face was weathered, but not with the craggy lines of a smoker. Nor was his nose colored with the blue vascular veins of poor circulation. And he had none of the enormous liver spots of age. His face was gentle. The lines were laugh lines, and his ruddy skin was the gift of enjoying years of sun and weather. But his eyes were tired and dull.

"My wife, Pearl," he explained. "She has dementia, probably Alzheimer's. She gets scared around strangers and anything out of the ordinary. But please come in."

"Sir, thank you, no. We don't want to upset her any more. We just want to let you know we're in the area. If things get bad, we can help," Keith said.

"Please come in," he said, as he pushed the door open farther. "Pearl will calm down. In fact, she does better when there are people around. And I would appreciate some diversion from the disease." His eyes pleaded.

Keith looked at Christine.

"Sergeant," she said, "I think it's okay if we visit with them for a few minutes."

"Thank you. I'm Wallace Hodges. I think I mentioned that my wife's name is Pearl."

Keith and Christine stamped their feet to remove any snow and stepped into a small hallway.

The house was furnished with contemporary furniture and carpeting, a wide-screen TV, and a thoroughly modern home theater sound system.

"Wallace," his wife yelled from behind a doorway, out of sight. "I'm calling the police. I'll not have hoodlums in my house. Get your rifle and be ready when they try to take the safe."

Wallace looked at Keith.

"We don't have a rifle. No safe either. She doesn't know where the phone is and probably wouldn't remember how to use a cordless phone."

He spoke to Christine. "We've never been beaten, and the only things that have ever been stolen from us were our kids' bikes, thirty years ago."

"Why does she say the things she says?" Christine asked in a hushed voice.

"Have you been around someone with dementia?"

"No."

"It's a horrible disease. Pearl was brilliant: a reader, a researcher, quiet, a homebody, and the most true friend you'd ever have. Now, you never know what her state of mind is going to be, and that's the worst part. She might come out of hiding in a minute and be delightful or paranoid or inappropriate, or she might stay hidden."

"I'm so sorry, sir," she said.

"It's the way it is." He paused. "I just made some coffee. Would you like a cup?"

"No, thank you. We've got a thermos full in the truck."

"How about some fruit or a danish?"

"Sure," Keith said. "That would be nice."

Wallace went to the cupboard.

"How come you haven't left?" Keith asked. "The storm is going to hit hard here."

"We can't."

"The Red Cross opened a few shelters in the area."

"Having a place to go is not the issue. Our daughter lives in Bridgewater, and our son is in Shrewsbury. We just can't leave. One of the few things that can keep Pearl calm is familiarity. If we go somewhere, I fear she will be uncontrollable. The disease has made her aggressive. She has even lashed out and hit me a couple of times. I fear the chaos she might create if we went somewhere."

Keith, Christine, and Wallace stood in the kitchen and talked about the storm. Wallace gestured toward the living room, where they went and sat to continue chatting.

After ten minutes, Keith reached for his wallet. He pulled out one of his business cards and started writing on the back. He stood and handed it to Wallace.

"We've got to get going," said Keith. "We are going to be in the area for the duration of the storm. If you need help, call me or call the Hingham armory. That number is on the card too. They can radio us. We're going back and forth between here and Brant Rock."

"Wallace," Pearl said as she walked into the kitchen, "why didn't you tell me we had company?"

She walked and stood next to Wallace. She had changed out of her tattered bathrobe and into a red sweater and plum-colored wide-wale corduroy pants. She was wearing feminine boots. When she walked into the kitchen, she hung a heavy kirtle, scarf, and wool hat on the back of a chair. She was a small woman, no more than five feet tall and very slender, unhealthily so.

"Are you going to introduce me?"

Wallace looked at Keith and Christine.

"Pearl, this is Sergeant Morris and Corporal Hamblin. They're from the Hingham armory to check on us during the storm."

"You're calling this a storm." She swept her hand as though she were shooing a fly. "This is not much of storm. I can tell you about some weather. My mother and I lived here when the gale of 1945 struck. The whole town was under water."

Wallace was in the background shaking his head. "You didn't live here in 1945," he said. "You were nine years old and you lived in Indiana. You researched the 1945 storm for a professor at Northeastern who was writing a paper."

"Why must you interrupt me and tell me things I know are not true?" Pearl yelled at him.

Wallace looked at the soldiers and shrugged.

"I dated a boy who was in the army. He was very handsome and strong," she said. She looked at Keith. "Like you." She reached up, caressed his cheek, and moved very close. "He was fun. We met when I was touring with the USO. I traded my dance cards so I would have many dances with him." She leaned in as though she wanted to kiss.

Keith leaned away from her. When he felt he could no longer lean without falling, he stepped back.

"Thank you, ma'am," he said as he took her hand away from his face. "But, as your husband said, we're going to be in the area while this storm passes through." He stepped toward the door. "Sir, if you need us, please call." Turning to Christine, he said, "Hamblin, we should go."

Wallace stepped between the soldiers and Pearl. He guided the pair to the front door.

Wallace offered his hand to Keith. "I'm sorry. Sometimes she gets confused and acts inappropriate."

He turned to Christine. "I was in the navy," he said. "She's never even been to the USO at any airport, much less toured with them. And I had to chase her hard before she would even talk to me." He looked at Pearl and then back at Christine. "I love this person and I'll take care of her, but the heart and soul and mind of the woman I married left this being about a year ago."

"Is there any help for her?" Hamblin asked.

"No. I should put her in a home. Our children think she should go to a care center, but she loves her home, and there are moments when my Pearl is here. It would kill her to go to a home, and it may kill me to keep her here. Maybe in the spring. Anyway, thank you. Please stop by when you make your next pass by here."

Wallace opened the door. "You be careful."

Keith and Christine stepped out into the storm. The sky had grown darker, and the winds had increased. They could hear the surf pounding the beach, which seemed far away. A peculiar, almost restrained hush settled around the soldiers.

Christine broke the silence. "That's so sad."

"Yeah."

"She didn't seem that bad."

"I don't know what's bad or not with that disease. A father of one of the women at my school had dementia. She said it was horrible. She had to take a year off to help her mother with him before he died. She's scared the disease is in her genes."

They reached the truck. Keith removed his jacket and climbed back up in the cab. Hamblin followed, still bundled up.

"You're gonna want to take your jacket off. It's warm in here."

"I'll be okay," she replied, climbing into the truck.

"Can I ask you something else?" she asked as they got moving.

"Sure."

"A while ago you said I'd be a good teacher."

"Yeah."

"What made you say that? You've never seen me around kids or watched me teach anything."

"Not all teaching happens in school," he answered. "I am a teacher. I work with teachers. I've seen a few good ones, many average ones, and a couple of bad ones over the years. I see that you can be patient, and those couple of times when you've had to train someone in the unit to do something, the way you teach is good. For someone who's never had any kind of training, you have some natural ability."

"I still don't get how you think I'd be a good teacher."

"Do you remember last summer when we went to Camp Edwards for the weekend?"

"Yeah."

"You were practicing backing the truck around the obstacle course. To pass you had to complete the course and not hit any of the cones, and then land the plate on the kingpin in one shot and pull the trailer out, go back out, back it up again, and drop the trailer."

"Yes. I failed. I tried six times and I didn't pass that weekend."

"I know. I'm your squad leader and I wasn't happy about it. Even though you didn't pass, when Specialist Dearborn was getting ready to run the course, he asked you what to watch out for."

"Yeah?"

"The way you explained it to him was very good. You told him how to do it very thoroughly. Then you showed him how you got fouled up, and he got it the first time."

"Yes. It made me mad 'cause he did it so easily."

"He was able to do it mostly because of how you prepared him."

"No. He was a better driver than me."

"No. Well, maybe. It's easy to regurgitate manuals, but I think your instruction helped him immeasurably. You probably don't think that what you told him made any difference, but the way you shared your knowledge with him made it easier for him. Your knowledge and insight gave him the confidence and knowledge he needed."

"Really?"

"Yes."

Corporal Hamblin was quiet. They drove the snowy, nearly empty roads to Brant Rock.

"Are we going to be here during the storm?" she asked.

"We'll go back and forth, but we'll stay near the Fourth Cliff and Humarock area most of the time. It's more isolated. This area has better access to the highway and stores than Humarock does. I want to stay up there most of the time."

"I see a couple of cop cars at the store. Let's go talk to them and let them know we're here if they need us."

"Are you worried about Wallace and Pearl?"

"A little."

They stopped and chatted with the cops for a few minutes, and then resumed their patrol.

The storm force increased by the time they were back to Humarock. The snow was getting deeper on the road, at least eight inches deep. Most of the waves reached all the way to the road. Some of the stronger ones crossed the road and cut a channel in the snow as they found their way back to water. The dark sky and streams of snow reduced visibility further. The headlights cut precise paths, the snow providing demarcation of the beam. High beams didn't help. They only brightened the field; they didn't expand the field of view.

"Someone's out walking," Christine observed.

"It's probably one of your crazy locals, like the couple back in Hingham who don't know enough to get out of the storm," Keith responded.

"It's Wallace," she yelled.

"That's not good."

"No, it isn't. He wouldn't leave his wife alone on a warm sunny day, let alone a dark stormy one."

"I hope he isn't out looking for her."

They rolled the truck alongside Wallace.

"Mr. Hodges?"

He slowed and looked at the soldiers. "She's gone," he yelled over the storm and engine noise. "She was really angry after you left, so I went down to the basement for a break. I was there for about ten minutes. When I went back upstairs, she wasn't there. The front door was open."

"How long have you been looking for her?" Keith asked.

"Ten, maybe fifteen, minutes."

"Did you call the police?"

"No. Not yet. She can't have gotten far. This is not the first time she's taken off. She's gotten lost a couple of times before. Our son got us cell phones, but she doesn't have hers with her."

"We'll help you look for her. Climb up in here."

"No. I think I need to stay on the road so I can look into carports and under porches."

"Hold up one minute, sir," Keith directed. "Hamblin, take over the wheel. Mr. Hodges, climb up here. I'll walk it. You stay in the cab where it's warmer."

He stopped the truck. Corporal Hamblin opened her door and slid to the driver's seat as Keith stepped out. Wallace climbed up.

"I can't thank you enough. There was a time when walking in a storm was a great, thrilling experience. Now I'm just tired. I'm worn out."

"No problem, sir. Always glad to help a veteran, even if you were navy," he replied with a smile, reaching behind the driver's seat for his jacket and cover.

"You army guys aren't too bad," Wallace said. "I had to deal with the army at Inchon."

"Oh, Inchon," Keith said. "Knowing that, I won't say anything about the easy life the navy has."

"That would be the air force."

Christine closed the door. Keith walked around to the other side. "We'll find her."

Wallace shook his head. "Sometimes—" He stopped. "Let's just find her," he said, sighing.

Keith stepped in front and to the right side of the truck. The houses on the street were mostly on the east side of the road, so his search would be easier as the truck drove north. He gestured forward with his hand. With his other hand, he called the police.

"Scituate Police, what's your emergency?" the operator answered.

"This is Sergeant Keith Morris with the ten-five-eight. One other soldier and I have been positioned here in Humarock."

"We know. Thanks for your help. What's up?"

"An elderly woman with dementia has wandered off, and we, along with her husband, are looking for her. Can you send anyone to help?"

"We're stretched really thin right now—two accidents and a number of medical calls. I'll put the word out, and we'll get someone there as soon as possible. Give me your cell number. As soon as I know someone is on the way, I'll call you."

"Okay." He gave her his number and told her, "I'm going to call and see if anyone else from the armory can get down here."

"Sure. Gather all the resources you can. Let me know how it goes."

"Okay. Bye." He hung up and dialed a number out of his contacts.

"Hello?"

"Des, it's Keith. What are you doing?"

"Parked at Nantasket Beach watching the waves. Big ones. There are people out there surfing. Makes me wish I knew how to surf."

"Can you get here?"

"Yeah. You okay?"

"Yeah. Hamblin and I are not the problem." Keith told Sergeant Jarvis about Pearl.

"Okay. Hang on a minute. I'm going to radio the mothership and see if I can get another team from the armory to cover us here."

Keith overheard Desmond call the armory on the radio and explain the situation.

"Keith?" Des asked. "You still there?"

"Yup."

"The LT and Murphy are rolling to cover us. As soon as they get close, they'll radio us and we'll head your way. Look for us in about twenty-five minutes. If anything changes, call me back."

"Who you riding with?" Keith asked.

"Groaning Jones."

"Must be a blast in that truck."

"You know it is, and you're jealous," said Des. "We're having some laughs for sure."

"Good. We'll keep searching. I hope I'll be calling you and telling you to stay away from me."

"You have a way with words. I feel the love."

"I appreciate it, buddy."

"Oh, now you're going to try and make up with me."

"No. I still think you're the worst excuse for a soldier I've ever seen. I'm scraping the bottom of the barrel, and you're it. You're like the burnt crud on the bottom of the grill that never comes off no matter how hard it's scrubbed."

"Got it. See you soon."

"Thanks."

As he moved to flip his cell phone off, Keith heard some loud classic rock music blare through his tiny, tinny cell phone speaker.

The window was open so Keith could talk to Wallace and Christine as needed.

"What was your wife like before she got sick?" Keith heard Hamblin ask. She had to speak loudly to overcome the growl of the engine.

Wallace paused a long time before he answered. "Well, I'm not going to be falsely cheerful about our relationship. It was work. I know I get very frustrated with her now because of the disease, and then I get mad at myself when I forget it's the disease taking control.

"She was a good woman. Our marriage was work, like all marriages are. We both made mistakes and got angry at each other for extended periods of time, but we made a commitment and toughed out the hard times. And we had some good times too."

"Oh," she replied.

"Don't get me wrong. It wasn't painful or bad, but I'm a dreamer, always have been, and she was a very practical woman, so we never jived for any length of time. You could say we clashed."

"I'm going to walk around each of the houses here and check the carports, decks, and so on to see if she is curled up somewhere. Or maybe she even got into one of these homes," said Keith.

"Do you want me to come with you?" Hamblin asked.

"No. I want you and Mr. Hodges to drive the length of the road and see if you spot her. I'll weave in and out between the houses. I've got a radio. I'll call you if I find her."

"Check in too, even if you don't find her," said Hamblin.

"Sure. Every five minutes I'll report."

Keith stepped away from the truck and onto the driveway of one of the homes. The truck continued slowly down the road, disappearing into the gray. Then it faded from sight. The sound of the engine grew dimmer until it was consumed by the rising peculiar acoustics of the storm. He faced the first house. It was up on stilts. The carport under the house looked empty, but there were closets and places where someone could stay out of sight. He stepped toward the house. No signs of anyone. He moved to the next house and the next.

Keith heard the muscular sound of the truck's engine before he saw its ghostly shape approach in the snow. He'd been alone for twenty minutes weaving in and out of the shuttered homes, shaking doors and peering under decks. He saw no sign of Pearl.

"Any luck?" Corporal Hamblin yelled.

Before he answered, he thought he should remember to give his father a call when he got home.

"No. You?" asked Keith.

"No. We went all the way to the gate at the rec site. Didn't see anything," said Wallace.

"Wallace," Keith said as he stepped up onto the running board, "could she have gone the other way?"

"I doubt it. That's the direction I went first."

Sergeant Jarvis's voice burst off the radio and into the cab. "Keith, you there?"

"Yeah. Where are you?"

"Just crossing the Sea Street Bridge."

"Turn north when you can, on Central. We're about halfway to the rec site."

"Roger. See you in a minute."

"Copy."

"It looks like such a small stretch of land," Keith said to Wallace and Christine. "There just aren't that many places where she could be, but she's in one of those places."

"Scituate Fire called," Hamblin said. "They're sending a truck and ambulance to join in the search."

"Good. We can use all the help we can get."

Sergeant Jarvis rolled out of the gloom and stopped alongside

Keith, Wallace, and Christine. The passenger window rolled down to reveal Desmond's smiling face and Sergeant Jones trying to sing along with the radio.

"Des, I'm at a loss. We've driven end to end here. I've gone up to every house and searched the outside and looked in to make sure no one was hiding inside. What do you think?"

"I was looking at the map as we drove here. You're right, there aren't many places to go. I'm sorry to ask this question, Mr. Hodges. Keith, have you searched the shoreline?"

"Yes."

"I think we need to dismount and walk the water's edge, on both sides."

"I was thinking that, too," Keith said. "Des, you and Jonesey take one more run down Central to River to where the road stops. I don't think she went that way 'cause we were driving that stretch and didn't see anyone, but I want you to double-check. Mr. Hodges, we're going to drop you back off at home. Hamblin will drive and I'll walk the river's edge, and we'll come down the shoreline.

"If we don't see her, then we hook up with Scituate Fire and expand the search area," added Keith. "Maybe she got across the bridge."

"Sergeant Morris?" Wallace asked.

"Yes, sir?"

"I'd like to stay with you. I can help. I'm another set of eyes."

"We can't be responsible for you, sir," said Keith. "We really should have returned you home when we first saw you."

"But you didn't, and that was the right thing. Also, you're not responsible for me. I'm aged, but I'm not feeble or incapable of knowing my limits—and I'm nowhere near my limits."

Keith looked toward Des. Des nodded his head ever so slightly.

"Okay, sure," Keith said.

"Thank you. Let's go," said Wallace as he slid to the middle of the seat.

The cloud cover kept the temperature from plunging. The forecasters called for temps in the single digits after the storm passed through. At that moment the wind blew, snow swirled and fell, and the surf howled a menacing roar. To Keith, it seemed foreboding.

"Wallace, I don't know how you navy guys do it, to be at sea in a storm with those waves crashing down." Keith shook his head. "I'm glad I joined the army."

"You're safe in a storm on a ship at sea," said Wallace. "With a good ship, a good skipper, and a good crew, you just roll, clean up the puke afterward, and sail on."

"No, thanks. I like dirt under my boots. I'm going to walk the river's edge now. I'll check in regularly. Stay close. There's a few places where I'm going to be out of sight."

Keith stepped off the road and moved onto the rocky river's edge. The map showed where the North River emptied into the Atlantic Ocean at the edge of the Fourth Cliff. The land wound around the point and continued south along the coast for miles, curving around Brant Rock and out onto Gurnet Road, where it ended in Plymouth Bay. One time, he had ridden his bicycle as far as he could go, ending at Fort Standish. He remembered that it was a long day and that the ride back exhausting.

He saw nothing. When he got to the old fire control tower at the rec site, he stepped up off the beach. He wanted to take a look at the cottages, perhaps discover Pearl in one them. When he walked past the tower, he noticed the door was ajar. He knew from the last unit picnic there that the tower was off limits. It had been built in 1942 to spot German submarines and track ships in Massachusetts Bay. It stood in the face of all the extremes of New England weather. Now it was unsafe. The question was whether to fund repairs or demolish it.

He walked across the snow to the tower. There were no footprints. He slowly swung the door open and saw a small boot print in the snow that had drifted past the door.

The narrow concrete stairs went up along the wall, stopping and turning on tiny landings. The stairs were cracked, in places separated as much as three inches. He looked up and saw light coming in through the narrow window at the top. He stepped on the first step. In addition to the crumbling concrete, there was ice. He went up the first six steps to the first landing and paused. So far, so good; the concrete held his two-hundred-plus pounds.

The structure was full of sounds; the wind was moving, faintly whistling, and sometimes howling through the various cracks and holes. Unidentifiable noises groaned, bouncing from top to bottom and side to side, presenting themselves from odd places and in unnerving sequences. Keith thought he heard a moan. He tried to concentrate his hearing, but the bizarre wind tunnel muted and changed all the sounds.

Wanting to get up and down as quickly as possible, he dashed up the crumbling stairs. The steps turned into a small stairwell, which leveled and emptied into the observation area.

Her boots were sticking out from under the shelf beneath the window. He went to her. She wasn't dressed inappropriately, but she certainly wasn't dressed for a New England blizzard. She stirred, moaned, and shivered. She wasn't wet.

"Mrs. Hodges," he said gently. "Can you hear me?"

She turned slightly toward the sound of his voice, but her eyes didn't open.

Keith took his jacket off and draped it over her. She was so small it almost fully covered her, like a blanket.

He reached for his radio. "Hamblin. Des. Over?"

"Hamblin, copy."

Keith paused a moment.

"Des, copy. Find her?"

"Affirmative. She's in the tower at the rec site. She's alive, but she's out of it. Copy?"

"Roger," Hamblin replied.

"Copy," Des responded. "What do you need?"

"Get here as soon as you can. Des, let Scituate Fire know. Tell them to get an ambulance as close as possible. Hamblin, get here. Be careful. The steps are old and not in good shape. I don't want to test the staircase with my, Mrs. Hodges', and Sergeant Jarvis's weight. Hamblin, you're a hundred pounds less than us. You and me will try and get her out of here. Copy?"

"Copy. We're rolling up to the gate now."

"The road hasn't been plowed, but you should have no trouble. Let me know when you're at the building. Out."

"Morris," Des's voice squawked. "We're a couple hundred yards behind Hamblin. Scituate Fire had to divert. Marshfield Fire is sending an ambulance, but it'll be a while before they get here. The snow is building up on the roads, and the plows are concentrating on the main streets. What do you need from us? Over."

"Get a stretcher and some rope ready. I don't know how this is going to play. If the stairs are too unstable, we may have to come up with plan B. Over."

"Roger. You thinking about that technical rescue training we went through a couple of years back? Over."

"Affirmative. Get here as soon as you can. Out."

Keith looked out the big bay window. It offered an expansive view of the ocean. If the storm hadn't reduced the visibility to a few hundred feet, he thought he would be able to see all the way to the tip of the Cape. It was a perfect spot to watch for enemy ships during the war. He saw Hamblin's truck roll up to the building.

Mrs. Hodges stirred, and pulled Keith's jacket closer around her shoulders.

"Sergeant Morris," he heard Corporal Hamblin call from the bottom of the stairs.

"Yeah. Hold on." He moved to the edge of the landing, lay on the floor, and reached out as far as he dared in order to talk with Hamblin. When he looked down he saw gradations of gray through the double-pane glass block, but there was enough light to illuminate the inside of the tower and stairwell all the way to the brighter doorway light behind Hamblin. "Get one of the wool blankets from the truck. We can use it as a litter to carry her down."

"Do you want to try the stretcher?"

"No. I think a stretcher will be too rigid and make it harder to maneuver the turns on the stairs."

"Be right back," Hamblin said as she ran out the door. She was back in less than a minute. "Sergeant, I'm coming up."

"Okay. Be careful. If the stairs feel like they're going to give way, stop and go back down. If they hold you, try and remember which ones are wobbly. We'll avoid as many of the really bad ones as we can on our way down."

"Yes, Sergeant." She started up the stairs. About halfway up she said, "So far, so good. Nothing is crumbling, and I only felt a couple that shifted a little."

"Good," Keith responded. *Crap*, he thought to himself. A number of the stairs shook and shed concrete as he ascended. His two hundred and ten pounds versus her one hundred and twenty pounds was the problem. Hamblin's head came into view as she rounded the steps to the office landing.

"How is she?"

"She's cold and semiconscious. If we can get her down and warm, I think she'll be okay, at least as far as her physical well-being is concerned."

"How do you think we should get her down?"

"Let's get her in the blanket. I'll go down first. That way the weight of her upper body will tilt toward me. You take the other end."

They folded the blanket in half and then spread it out next to Mrs. Hodges. Keith scooped her and lifted her a couple of inches off the floor, while Christine slid the blanket under her.

The office floor groaned under the concentrated weight and activity.

"Okay. Good. We'll slide her out to the middle of the floor on the blanket and then lift her. Make sure you get a good grip. Then we'll work our way down the stairs."

"Got it."

"If you get tired, we'll rest. The last thing we want to do is drop her."

"Okay. I'm ready."

"On three. One, two, three."

They lifted her easily. She shuffled in the blanket a little as her body conformed to the blanket's contour. Keith and Christine adjusted and strengthened their grip.

"Let's go." Keith walked backward to the steps, carefully stepping on the first stair. It shifted under his weight. He stopped and waited, assessing and waiting for the slightest tug of gravity. Nothing. Another step, and then another.

Hamblin stepped off the landing and onto the stairs. As soon as Pearl's and Hamblin's weight settled on the stair, Keith felt his step wobble. Bits of concrete fell from the underside. He heard the step crack open and felt it separate from the wall. A moment later, the step stopped moving as the crack stopped spreading. The concrete had found a pocket of still hard, intact concrete.

"Hurry," he said. "Back up the stairs. The steps won't hold the weight of the three of us."

Corporal Hamblin scrambled back up the steps. Pearl drew the blanket close to her chest as she stepped back onto the office landing. Keith followed close behind.

"What are we going to do?" Hamblin asked.

"I don't know. There's probably more than four hundred pounds between the three of us on those steps. They held my two hundred pounds going up, but it's too much going down." He reached for his radio. "Des, where are you?"

"We're here."

"I think we're going to have to do some kind of litter-out-the-window rope rescue."

"Really?"

"Yeah. Let me think about this for a minute."

"Okay. Wallace says he can come up there with you and try and talk to his wife."

"Tell him thanks, but no. The space is small, and the stairs are unstable. I don't want any more people inside the building than there has to be. Copy?"

"Copy,"

"Sergeant?" said Corporal Hamblin.

"Yeah?"

"I can do it."

"Do what?"

"Pearl and I together weigh less than two hundred and fifty pounds, probably less than two hundred and twenty five. You said the stairs held your weight going up. I can carry her in my arms or fireman-carry her down the stairs. I can do it."

"No. It's too unsafe."

"I can do it. I do more push-ups than all the other females during PT. I do more than many of the guys too."

"It's not about your strength, Corporal. I can't let you. It's too unsafe."

"I know it's risky, Sergeant, but if we wait to rig a litter, she's going to get worse. The storm is getting worse too. I can do it. If you help get her over my shoulder, I'll have her on the ground in less than a minute."

Keith stared at her. She was right. It was their best chance to get Pearl out of the building as quickly and safely as possible. He put the radio to his mouth. "Des, copy?"

"Here, bud. Over."

"Hamblin's going to carry her down to you. It's our best chance to get Pearl out of here quickly. Our combined weight is too much on the steps. I want you to be ready and waiting at the bottom. Over."

There was a pause. Keith knew Desmond was assessing the plan.

"Okay. You've got the SA. We're heading into the bottom of the stairwell now. The ambulance is rolling up. Out."

"Okay, Hamblin. Get downstairs as quickly and safely as possible. I'll wait here until you're outside the building." Keith squatted and carefully slid his hands under Pearl's shoulder blades and thighs, and easily scooped her up. She stirred. "She can't weigh more than a hundred pounds." He stood slowly. "As soon as I pass her off to you, I'll wrap the blanket around her."

"Are you ready?" he asked.

"Yes."

"Okay. Come in close so I can drape her on your shoulder." Keith lifted Pearl higher and rotated her so Hamblin could stand up. Then he transferred the tiny woman.

"Here she comes," Keith said as he gently lowered Pearl onto Christine's shoulder. "Got her?"

"Yeah. No problem." She shuffled to the top of the steps.

"Okay. Once you start down, you're committed. Be careful. The moisture formed a little coat of ice on the steps, and there are loose bits of concrete on some of the steps."

"Yeah. I noticed coming up," she acknowledged. "I'm going."

Keith watched as she stepped off the landing. She stopped on the top step and let all the weight she was carrying settle. Then she took off as fast as she dared while gingerly stepping on each step. He watched her disappear out of sight around the first turn in the stairs. He lay down on the floor and extended his head as far out over the stairs as he dared while he watched her as she emerged and disappeared around each turn.

"How you doing?" he yelled.

"Okay."

He stopped talking. She needed all her concentration now.

"Hamblin," Des yelled from the bottom of the steps. "You're halfway. Come on. You got this."

"I gotta stop," she cried. "She's squirming and slipping off my shoulder."

"I'm coming up," Sergeant Jarvis yelled. He stepped to the bottom of the stairs and ran up the first six steps.

"No!" Keith and Christine yelled at the same time.

"We don't want to add any more weight to the stairs," Keith said.

"I can shrug Mrs. Hodges back onto my shoulder," Christine added.

"Okay." Des backed down the stairs.

Keith watched Christine shift her weight and jostle Pearl into position. Christine resumed her march down the stairs. He saw her step onto the floor, and then Desmond reached out for Mrs. Hodges. He heard Des say, "I got her. I'll take her to the ambulance. Good job, Hamblin."

Des then asked Keith. "You need us to help get you down from there?"

"No. Go. Get her to the medics."

"Roger."

Sergeant Desmond Jarvis disappeared from Keith's sight.

Keith stepped onto the top step and heard a sound as though something was moving outside. The sound stopped at the window, making the weak gray light dimmer. The foghorn from a nearby lighthouse or buoy moaned. He felt the building sway when wind howled as it reared up the bluff from the beach and hit the building; a chill rose from the floorboards. The odd sound he heard outside the window moved again inside the observation area. He looked back at the decrepit work space when a groan emanated from somewhere in the building. *The building is settling,* he told himself. He stepped over three steps at a time and moved as fast as he could down the stairs.

At the bottom, he asked if Wallace and Pearl had gotten off okay.

"Yes, they took off a couple minutes after we got Pearl out of the building," Hamblin replied. "You okay? You were up there longer than I thought you would be."

"Yeah," he said, and then he paused and looked up at the old building. "Glad everything worked out okay. Let's see if we can get a hold of the ambulance. I want to know how Wallace is doing. Then let's see if we can find a place to eat. I'm hungry."

Boston Trip

January 2010

To: sgtmo@weymouth.ps.zyx
Sent: Tuesday, January 5, 2010, 09:28:17
From: allison23@alivepharm.zyx
Subject: Boston Trip

Hi, Keith. It's Allison. I'm going to be in Boston next week working a booth at a medical convention. It's short notice because the rep who works Boston got sick. I offered to cover for him.

I arrive on Saturday, but I don't have to set up until Monday. I'd love a tour of Boston. :-)

I hope it works out to see you.

To: allison23@alivepharm.zyx
Sent: Tuesday, January 5, 2010, 11:03:54
From: sgtmo@weymouth.ps.zyx
Subject: RE: Boston Trip

Hi, Allison. It'd be great to see you. My unit is getting ready to deploy and I'm supposed to report to the armory this weekend to help inventory gear, but my squad is done with our inventory. I can miss the drill.

Let me know where you're staying and when you're free. I've gotten to know Boston well. Can you give me an idea of what you would like to see? Heads up, bring warm clothes. It's not like Phoenix.

To: sgtmo@weymouth.ps.zyx
Sent: Tuesday, January 5, 2010, 11:06:13
From: allison23@alivepharm.zyx
Subject: RE: Re: Boston Trip

Are you deploying soon? If it's not a good time for us to meet, I completely understand. I'm sure you have a lot to do!

To: allison23@alivepharm.zyx
Sent: Tuesday, January 5, 2010, 15:44:37
From: sgtmo@weymouth.ps.zyx
Subject: RE: Re: Re: Boston Trip

It's not a problem at all. I'd love to show you around. Text me when you've arrived and are settled in. Unless you feel like you want to drive around, I suggest we take the T. Boston has great public transportation. We can take the subway everywhere. Plus, it's supposed to snow this weekend, so traffic will get even crazier.

Keith added his cell number to the e-mail and sent it. He thought it would be good to see Allison, for the second time in a year after not seeing her once in the previous fifteen years. She had looked in good shape when they met at Fossil Creek several months earlier. Soon after he returned to Massachusetts, she had e-mailed him.

The next Saturday afternoon he got a text from her saying she was staying at the Westin Hotel in Copley Square. She wrote that she would be ready to go whenever he got to the hotel, or she would be glad to meet him wherever. He responded, saying it would be an hour and half or so before he got there.

He decided it would be best to take the subway rather than commuter rail. He drove his car to the Braintree T station.

As he drove toward Braintree, the snow began to fall heavier. It had started as small light flakes early in the afternoon. It was enough to cover the dingy old snow and make it pretty again. Traffic was light; he got to the station quickly. The sun had been behind clouds all day, but as the storm grew and cloud cover thickened, the hidden sun lowered toward the horizon, taking its limited luminance with it. Soon the wattage of the streetlights overtook the timid strength of daylight. The snow fell through the streetlights, defining a cone of light from the streetlight as the larger, wetter flakes drifted down. It was one of his favorite sights. Standing on the loading platform in the comfort of warm clothing, and anticipating a pleasant visit with Allison, Keith felt good.

About a year earlier his headaches had finally ceased. Their frequency and intensity had been lessening over the previous five years. The VA doctor prescribed him new medicine that, when taken at the first sign of a headache, would stop the ache before it grew too strong. Knowing that he had a method to head off the headaches relieved the frustration and anger and despair he used to experience when he sensed one building. Also, with the help of Sharon Wells at the school, he developed some meditation discipline and yoga moves that helped lessen, and sometimes completely avert, the headaches.

Keith boarded the Red Line in Braintree and exited the T via the Green Line at Copley. Dusk was settling and snow fell at a leisurely pace. He texted Allison. She replied and told him her room number and to come on up, with a smile emoticon. The lobby of the hotel was warm and pleasingly bright for a midwinter's eve. He took the elevator to the eleventh floor. Her room was around the corner. As he walked there he felt a little nervousness surface. He concluded it was the combination of the impending deployment and seeing Allison again. Of the two, he thought, Allison should not be the worry.

She had slid the deadbolt out so the door was not sealed shut. *That's bold for a woman in a hotel in a strange city*, he thought.

He knocked and said hello.

She came to the door and opened it wide.

"Come on in, Keith."

He stared at her. She was beautiful. She was always pretty. In high school, during their surreptitious camping trip, and even with the unkempt look she had when they reacquainted at Fossil Creek, he knew that she was attractive. Whether it was the light in the room or her hair, dress, makeup, and jewelry, no matter: all the feminine accouterments served her well and she was stunning. It was her smile and its sincerity, though, that was most beautiful.

"My gosh, Allison, you're beautiful," he said, and immediately felt embarrassed. He thought he might have gushed like a teenage boy, unsure of what to say. He didn't think it was possible, but her smile grew more lovely.

"Thank you," she replied.

They stared at each other. He started smiling too. Soon it grew into lighthearted laughter. She opened her arms to hug him, and he gladly stepped toward her, opening his arms.

"Come in," she said. "Do you want something to drink?"

"Sure. What do you have?"

"I picked up a couple bottles of wine. I didn't know what you liked, so I got both white and red. Help yourself. Unless we have to rush out to dinner, I'd like to visit for a bit."

"No rush. I don't have to be anywhere until next Saturday at the armory."

"Have a seat." She sat on the sofa and gestured for him to join her.

He walked toward her. He stopped as he walked past the window. It was a beautiful view of Copley Square.

"Nice room. Nice view."

"Yes, it is. The guy I'm covering for has expensive tastes and manages to get the company to set him up in the nicest rooms. And he gets first-class airplane seats whenever he travels."

"He must be good at his job," said Keith as he sat down.

"Yes, he's very good."

"I imagine you do pretty well yourself."

"I do okay, but nothing like this, and quite honestly, I'm low maintenance. Even if I had the money, I don't think I'd ever splurge like this."

Keith was relieved. Even though Massachusetts was one of the best-paying states in the country for teachers, he couldn't compete with someone clearing six figures.

Allison raised her glass and said, "To old friends."

He raised his glass of wine and agreed. "To old friends."

They touched glasses.

"So can you tell me about your deployment, or is that confidential information?" Allison asked.

"Yes, it's supposed to be confidential, but in reality it isn't. Everyone in the head shed talks about OPSEC."

"What's *head shed* and *OPSEC* mean?" Allison interrupted.

"Oh, sorry, it's jargon. *Head shed* is a term meaning any place where the officer and senior enlisted leaders plan things. *OPSEC* means 'operational security.' Sometimes they say things about keeping our plans confidential, but they forget there have been press releases and news stories about our deployment. Anyone who knows anything about the Mass. Guard knows we're heading out the door and where we're going and what we're doing. If we really wanted to take OPSEC seriously, we'd leave in the middle of the night with no farewell celebration. It would be different if I were Special Forces, but I'm a truck driver."

"Have you met any SEALs?"

"Not SEALs, but, you know, every branch has Special Forces, and the army had the first Special Forces."

"Really?"

"Really, and yes, I have met several and worked with a few."

He looked at Allison. She seemed unsure what to ask next. "All the young females are very attracted to the Special Forces guys, and the SF guys know it," he said.

"Yeah, that doesn't surprise me. What are they like?"

"There are no Rambos. The young guys are full of themselves, but the older guys are just regular guys doing a job," he replied, thinking of Mark Gillespie, Miranda Diaz, and that dark night in the middle of nowhere in Iraq.

"You said there's a farewell celebration?" asked Allison.

"Yes, next Saturday at the armory. Too bad you're not here for that long. I'd bring you as my guest, if you wanted to go."

"Darn," Allison said, shaking her head. "I'm here through Wednesday."

"Well, maybe we can get together again while you're here. I'm off all week getting ready to go. The school is having a farewell party on Thursday. Other than that, I'll work out a few times. A couple of friends want to get together for dinner. I'll read, and maybe watch a little TV."

"No girlfriend?"

"No, not at the moment. What about you? Still with that guy you were with when I saw you at Fossil Creek?"

"No, and I wasn't really with him. He was just someone to hang out with sometimes."

"Oh."

"Since you told me about your deployment, I've been worried about you. A couple of my customers and coworkers were mobilized over the last few years, and I was concerned and hoped for the best, but I wasn't close enough to them to feel deeply about them going off to war. Yet I find myself very worried about you. Maybe it's because we have history or because you told me you'd been hurt the last time you were there."

She stood, went to the counter, and poured herself another glass of wine.

"Are you worried?" she asked as she sat down, closer to him.

"Yes and no. Yes, because I did get hurt and I know how abruptly it can happen. But it's different this time. The war is winding down. Our mission is different. We're being absorbed into another unit, and all we're doing is heavy lift work. It's important work, but we're way behind the front line." He thought for a moment and then added, "Though, there's never really been a real front line in this war."

231

"That sounds serious."

"We're loading the heavy equipment, like tanks and armored personnel carriers, and hauling them to ships at the port in Kuwait. So there will be a lot less opportunity for contact with the locals, and it's much better there now. Stuff still happens, but nowhere near as often. As controversial as the Iraq War was at the start, I think maybe we did some good. But whatever good we did wasn't worth the price."

"Are you all better?"

"Yeah. It took a while, but I am."

"Can you tell me about it?"

"Not much to say. I don't remember what I said when we met last summer, but my truck found an IED. I wasn't hurt badly, but I lost a lot of blood very quickly, and it gave me headaches for a while. And—" He paused. "I think the headaches and all made me difficult to be around for a while. But some veterans I met gave me a boost when I needed it, and the doctors at the VA got me a prescription that made the headaches go away. So, I'm good."

He paused again. "I guess it's okay to tell you this: sometimes I feel like I should have been hurt worse to justify the degree of my being difficult."

Allison looked Keith in the eyes. "I don't know what you went through or what you mean by being difficult, but whether you were wounded a little or a lot, you were hurt far, far from home and in a situation most of us can't even imagine. Whatever your being difficult was, you were entitled to it."

Keith nodded and said, "Thanks."

"Okay," said Keith after a moment, "now I'm getting hungry. You?"

"Yes. Let me finish this wine and we'll get going. Do you have any place in mind?"

"There's lots of places, but I like the North End when I'm in town. It's the Italian part of town: great food, always busy, lots of people."

"That sounds great."

She sipped her wine and asked about the school where he taught, how his mother was doing, and if he thought he would ever move back to Arizona.

To the last question, he answered no, saying he was happy in

Boston. Maybe he'd be a snowbird when he retired, but that was a long way off.

They left the hotel and walked into the cold, but it was not an uncomfortable Boston winter evening. She slipped her arm through his as they walked. He looked at her arm through his, and then looked at her and smiled. It was a two-mile walk from Copley Square to the North End. They crossed through the Public Garden and Boston Common. The Christmas lights were still up. They passed through Faneuil Hall, walked along the waterfront, and finished the walk on Hanover Street. It was the middle of winter in Boston, and still the streets and sidewalks were packed with locals and tourists. They put their name in at one place Allison said she had heard of. It was an hour's wait, so they walked the length of the North End. They visited Old North Church and stopped at a cafe for an irish coffee.

Dinner was perfect. The service was cordial and well timed, and the food was wonderful. The recommendations for wine, aperitif, meals, dessert, and cordial were spot-on. Keith had a mild buzz and enjoyed every moment with Allison. Things seemed to pick up right where they had left off years earlier. Allison laughed easily and kept the conversation going without focusing it back on her. When dinner ended and they were getting ready to leave, Keith helped her put her coat on. As they were leaving the restaurant, he opened the door for her. She stopped halfway through the door, tilted up on her tiptoes, and kissed him on the cheek. She smiled, turned, and walked through the door.

It released a tangible feeling of pleasure in Keith as she turned and walked through the door. She looked up at the falling snow. The light illuminating the entrance to the restaurant shone on her face, and again he was struck by how beautiful she looked to him. He wanted to say how pretty she looked again, but he didn't. He felt that somehow it would tarnish the moment. Outside they held each other's gloved hands. He turned toward her and cupped his other hand around the back of her neck. He gently pulled her close and kissed her softly. There was no resistance.

"Do you want to walk back or take a cab?"

"This has been such a lovely evening. Let's walk."

They started the walk back. However, unlike the walk to the North End, the walk back to Copley Square was less chatty, more contemplative, and comfortably peaceful in many ways. The city was beautiful with its fresh carpet of snow and the ambient night light brightening their entire walk.

"I feel very safe with you," Allison said at one point.

Those six little words made Keith swell. He felt strong, confident, and protective.

"It's like when we went on that weekend camping trip back in high school. Do you remember it?" she asked.

"Yes, I do. Every detail."

"When that storm came through and we had to drive out of the canyon and up that twisty road, do you remember how dangerous that road was when it was wet?"

"I thought it was dangerous even when it was dry."

"I wasn't scared at all because I was with you. Even when we almost spun off the road, it didn't frighten me."

"I was worried about it, but I was more worried about your father killing me if we didn't get back before they got back."

"My father always liked you. My mother, on the other hand, she was tough."

"Really? I thought she liked me."

"She did, but she was strict with me and tried to keep my relationship with you to a minimum. She wanted me to finish college and not get distracted by boys."

"Oh."

They had walked through the Public Garden and along Commonwealth Avenue. They turned onto Dartmouth Street, and the hotel came into view.

"I've really enjoyed seeing you. If you have time in your schedule, do you want to meet for dinner again or a drink or coffee before you leave?" he asked.

She took a long time to respond, so long that he wondered what was wrong. It seemed like the evening had gone well. He started searching his memory for a blunder. He could come up with nothing particularly egregious or even awkward he had done or said.

"I would love to. You tell me when, and I'll do my best to clear my calendar."

"Whew," he said. "You were taking so long to respond that I was starting to think I had blown it without even knowing. Usually, I know when I've blown it with a woman."

"Oh, I was just thinking about my schedule and thinking about the evening. I've enjoyed it so much. I am glad you asked to see me again."

They had reached the lobby of the hotel.

"If I'm going to catch the subway back, I've got to get going. Service is pretty light this time of night. I don't want to miss the last train."

"Do you have time to come up for a nightcap?"

Keith looked at his watch. It was eleven thirty. If he stayed no more than fifteen minutes, he felt he would be able to catch the last train. "Yeah, I'd like that. I've got time before the last subway leaves." He wondered for a moment if he would end up spending the night.

In the room, they had a drink. Keith sipped his slowly. He feared if he drank too much alcohol, a hangover might trigger a headache—something he never wanted to experience again. At a cookout or a party, he might have just one or two beers and sip water. Tonight he had already gone past his usual limit, but he felt no disturbances in his head.

They stood by the window in the darkened room and looked out over the city.

"It's beautiful," said Allison.

"Yeah."

She leaned against him and let go a long sigh. "This is so nice."

He turned toward her, leaned in, and lightly kissed her lips, and then her cheek, forehead, and near her ear before returning to her lips. He pulled her closer and held his lips against hers. He pulled back ever so slightly and she moved toward him, lightly touching his lips and his tongue with her tongue.

The kissing stopped. Keith moved two chairs toward the window. They sat down.

She was caressing his hand when she said, "I don't remember you having such big hands."

"Um, I'm not quite sure how to respond to that. Never gave my hands much thought." He looked at his hands, "But now that I'm thinking about them, I can open pickle jars without any trouble, so I guess they do the job."

She laughed, stood up, straddled him, and sat back down on his lap. She threw her arms around his shoulders. "So, are you going to leave and catch the train?"

He smiled. "My dog will be lonely if I'm not home."

"You're sure?" she said. Then she moved her head and started kissing and running her tongue around his ear.

She stopped kissing his ear and neck and faced him. "Well? Still want to catch your train?" she asked.

"I think Caisson will be okay, but what if I have to grade some papers on short notice? How will I fulfill that obligation?"

She pressed her lips against his and her body against his. She pressed her hands firmly against his shirt. Then she ran her hands down his chest. She squirmed to free herself to move her hands farther along his body. She moved her hands quickly toward his groin and averted touching him at the last moment. She retracted her hands, broke off the kiss, and stood up, her hair falling on her face. She pushed it back and said, "You should leave now if you want to catch the train."

"What train?" he said as he also stood.

She laughed again. "Give me a couple of minutes, okay?" she said as she stepped toward the bedroom.

"Sure. Not too long, though."

He took off his shoes and opened a bottle of water. His thoughts were mostly on the sex that was likely to come his way. Interspersed among the thoughts of sex, he thought how glad he was that they had reconnected. She was special, not just because they had history but also because her vivaciousness and humor remained.

"Keith?"

"Yes?"

"Are you coming in here, or do you want an invitation?"

He ran into the room, peeling off his sweater as he moved toward her.

The blinds were open. The lights of Boston reflected off the snow and threw a soft, dim light in the bedroom. She was in bed, wearing a white camisole. He couldn't see if she was wearing panties or not; she had the blankets pulled up to her waist. The room was cool. She had the window open a crack, but he felt warm. The radio was on and a candle burned on the dresser. He looked at the candle and thought it was odd. He'd never seen one in a hotel room before. Hotels undoubtedly discouraged them.

She noticed his gaze and said, "I like candles."

He sat on the bed next to her and looked at her face. Reaching out with his hand, he stroked her cheek. Running his hand along her jawline, he stopped at her neck and looked at her face again. If he had to describe her look, *sultry* was the word he'd use. She had a very pleased look, too, and a smile. His eyes scanned her features. His body twisted to follow his eyes as they moved along the camisole to the blanket covering her up to her hips. He looked around the room again and then back to her eyes.

"This is nice. This setting is very different from Fossil Creek and a tent." He looked out the window. "Maybe we have some kind of a storm theme going. It's snowing here, and we were in a monsoon all those years ago."

"I like that thought. Storms are passionate," replied Allison.

"Um, I hate asking this question, because I fear it might spoil the moment, but do I need to run out and buy some condoms?" Keith asked. He looked away from her and lowered his head while he waited for her response.

"No. We should be okay," she replied. "I'm glad you asked. It means you care. What about you? Anything I need to know about?"

"No. The army checks my blood every year for a bunch of things. I'm clean, unless you consider a slightly above-normal cholesterol level an STD."

She laughed. "Good. With my job I can get you some medicine to lower it, if you want."

Keith looked back at her as she spoke. He leaned in and kissed her. She responded and the fever released. She reached to remove his shirt. He pulled his body back but kept his lips in contact with hers.

He removed his shirt, dropped it on the floor, reached over and slid her camisole over her head, and dropped it on the floor. It landed on his shirt. Topless, they pressed their bodies together. Keith moved his hands along her body. His lips followed the same path. She responded similarly to his naked torso. He pushed the blankets away and continued moving his hands until he felt his fingers meet her panties. She lay on her back and lifted her hips. He slid her panties off and continued kissing her. Soon his pants were off. The kissing, touching, caressing, tasting, and stroking progressed.

"That was really nice," she said.

He was lying on his back; her head was on his shoulder. She had pulled the sheet up over the lower half of her body. Keith was feeling very relaxed and drowsy, and was nearly asleep.

"Yeah, I'll say," he responded, forcing himself to overcome his sleepiness.

"It was great. I was thinking how nice it is to be here with you, and I was thinking about the good times we had back in high school. That's what made it great."

"Oh, it wasn't me?"

"Yes, it was precisely because of you. It was great in ways I can't even explain. You were perfect, but all the other stuff I was thinking about, like your sounds and smells, made me think of all the fun we had. It brought back all the intensity and passion of young love."

"Smells? I do take showers once in a while."

"No, I don't mean body odor, silly. I mean all the other stuff that goes along with sex. What do you think about when you're having sex?" she said.

"Sex."

"That's it?"

"Yeah, that's about it."

"I've never asked someone what they're thinking about during sex. Really, that's it?"

"I guess I think a little about how I'm touching you, hoping it's pleasing for you. And I suppose that like most guys, I worry a little about finishing too fast, but mostly I'm thinking about your stuff and my stuff and how good it all feels. And, really, those thoughts aren't that clear."

"That's very interesting, but I'm not convinced many men spend much time thinking about those things."

"What do you think about?" Keith asked, hoping the answer wasn't going to be how he compared to other men and tales of her sexcapades.

"It was strange, but I remembered skinny-dipping with you on our camping trip and how exciting and carefree it was to be with you in that tent during the storm. I haven't thought about that in years. It's weird, but being with you now and hearing your sex sounds and how you feel and how you smell, even the sound of your voice, made this whole evening wonderful. Making love was over the top. Maybe it was because you were my first," she added. "Unless a woman marries her first guy, I don't think many women have a chance to fool around with their first again, fifteen years later."

Keith was pleased by what she said, but he wondered, too, if he'd missed something. Sex was fun. It felt good and was uncomplicated. But Allison had reactions on many levels. Sex with other women, and there had not been that many, was always enjoyable, but the women he had slept with never even hinted at the range of feelings Allison was describing. He was curious, but he was not going to ask if she experienced such visceral sensations and thoughts when she was having sex with other men.

"I'm glad it was so meaningful for you," said Keith. He turned to face her. "I'm really glad you let me know you were coming to Boston. It's been great to see you, and it is great to be here with you right now. I feel at ease in a way I haven't felt in a long time." He pulled her close and kissed her. He continued to hold her close as he settled back onto the sheets and pillows.

Allison smiled and drew a deep breath. "Keith," she said with hesitation. "I'm sorry, but I have to confess something."

His mind started racing. A husband? Herpes? Did she have a child? Terminal cancer? Was she a lesbian testing her sexual orientation?

"Okay," he replied, wary.

"I don't lie, but I lied to you and I'm so sorry."

He waited for her to say more, but she stopped and seemed to be waiting for him to say something. He said, "I can't imagine what you would have lied about."

"I kinda hinted to you that I haven't been to Boston before. Well, actually I've been here several times. It's such a premier place for schools and medicine and research, so I've been here at least a dozen times over the years. And the rep who I said was sick and I had to cover for him?"

"Yeah?"

"He's fine and in Hawaii covering a conference for me. I swapped with him so I could come here."

"So far that doesn't sound like the worst thing in the world."

"You don't understand. I don't lie. I don't always tell every detail of everything I've ever done, but I wanted to see you and I didn't want to come across as some desperate female trying to reconnect with an old boyfriend. So I swapped with Ron."

"Allison, don't worry about it. In the scheme of lies I've been told, yours doesn't even register."

"Really? I was dreading your reaction. I get very upset when someone lies to me."

"Everyone fibs and lies in some measure: my soldiers, even my students, and me. I just put everything in perspective. I, of course, encourage truth telling, but I don't get wound up about it. I get cagey with bits of information too sometimes, and some people think that is lying. I don't."

"But isn't it a reflection of character? It is for me."

"No. Well, it depends on the nature of the lie and the degree of dishonesty. And if it's a pattern, then it becomes a problem."

"I'll never lie to you again."

"I appreciate that."

They fell into a quiet moment. Keith looked at the clock on the radio: 1:13. Two hours had passed since he was thinking about the last subway to Braintree. He leaned over, kissed Allison, and moved to get out of the bed.

She reached out and took his hand. "What did you think when I e-mailed you?"

"I thought it would be good to see you, talk, get a bite to eat, and catch up."

"Did you think we'd end up like this?"

"I don't think so. If I did, it was momentary. I wasn't expecting it or even thinking about it. Just visiting with a good friend. You?"

She was slow to respond. "I'm not one who gets drunk in a hotel lounge and ends up in bed with clients or coworkers or strangers when I'm on the road. I know many people who do that a lot, and that's just not me, but the thought crossed my mind. I brought the candle because I like candles. Aromatherapy works for me. I didn't go and buy sexy lingerie, but I didn't wear the granny panties either."

"Ah, yes, the not-going-to-meet-anyone underwear."

She laughed again. "I'm so glad to be here with you."

"Yeah, I wish you were staying a little longer. As I mentioned, we've got a farewell party at the armory next Saturday. I'd like to bring you."

"Really?"

"Yeah. I'd like to show you where I live and teach, and maybe you could meet some of the guys in my unit."

"That's sweet."

"But right now you'll have to excuse me for a minute. I have to get up and get a drink of water, or else I'm going to fall asleep."

"On no, soldier boy, you're not going to sleep. I'm not done with you yet," she replied, smiling, lowering her hand so it brushed against his penis.

After a second round of intense, deliberate, slow lovemaking, Keith fell asleep.

He awoke to the sunlight brightening the room. Allison was asleep beside him. As he stirred to rise, she awoke.

"Good morning," she murmured in a sleepy voice.

"Hey. Good morning to you too." He leaned in and kissed her. "I'm sorry. Did I wake you?"

"It's okay. Are you going somewhere?"

"Yeah. I'm going to catch that train."

"Really?"

Keith saw a look of confusion and disappointment instantly appear in her eyes. "No. Sorry. I guess my attempt at humor failed. Being in the army and after years of getting up early and PT'ing, I became an early riser. I was going to get us some coffee at the shop in the lobby."

"That sounds suspicious."

"I was kidding. I'm not going anywhere. You're stuck with me. Would you like a cup of coffee?"

"No, thank you. I'm not awake yet. Go ahead. I'm usually not an early riser, but I'll get up and take a shower while you're gone."

"Okay. Do you want me to get you a muffin or anything?"

"No. Maybe we can get room service or go out for breakfast."

"That sounds great." He stood and moved to pick up his clothes from the floor.

"You exercise in the morning?" she asked.

"Yeah, most days."

"Are you a runner?"

"Yes, and I mix in weights and flexibility too."

"That's nice," she replied sleepily.

"However, I'm thinking there's a form of PT we could do this morning, right here, if you're interested," Keith said.

She smiled and pulled the blankets back.

"I was thinking about going for a run when I got home, but, hey, cardio is cardio." He lay back down on the bed.

She rolled on her side to face him and traced her fingers along the scars under his chin and along the base of his neck. Then she shifted and moved toward his waist.

Once they were finished, Keith said, "Well, that was a good workout."

"I'll say."

"So what were you thinking about that time?" he asked.

"Not much this time. Just kinda living in the moment."

"Good."

"You?"

"Pretty much the same as last night: your stuff, my stuff, and how it all feels."

"Men. You're so predictable."

"I think of it as being uncomplicated. However, continuing the theme of predictability of men, I'm hungry. How about breakfast?"

She laughed. "Yes. I'd like that. Do you want to get room service or go out?"

"I like going out."

"Okay. Me too. I'll take a shower, and we'll ask in the lobby for a suggestion."

She crawled over Keith, stopping on top to kiss him. "I saw your scars last summer and it made me sad. You have such a nice body and the scars don't look too bad, but still, I feel really bad for you right now. Do you think about it at all?"

Keith hesitated before he responded. "I don't think about it much anymore. At first I wore turtlenecks or extended crewneck long-sleeve T-shirts, but honestly, Allison, I talked about it a little last night, and really I don't like talking about it."

"Okay. I'm sorry." She kissed him again and lay on him for a minute before continuing on her way to the bathroom. He heard the shower come on. The toilet flushed, and the shower door opened and closed. Although anytime anyone pointed out his scars he felt uncomfortable, with Allison his discomfort was less. He stared at the candle and noticed its faint aroma.

After about ten minutes of lying in bed, he got up and walked into the bathroom. He opened the shower door and stepped in. "I just wanted to make sure that spot in the middle of your back got some soap."

"Oh, really? That's very chivalrous of you."

"Yes, my intentions are completely honorable."

"Really? Then what's that?" she said, pointing at his erection. "You recovered quick."

"That? Just think of it as a portable towel hook."

"You've become funnier and more lighthearted than I remember." She kissed him again and stepped out of the shower.

They left the hotel, stepped into the cold January morning, and walked toward Kenmore Square. In the shadow of Fenway Park, they found the little hole-in-the-wall basement restaurant the bellman at the hotel had suggested.

"You want to try this place?" he asked.

"Sure. I avoid chains whenever I can."

"Sometimes these little places are great. The problem is, I've bought into the myth that the little mom-and-pop shops are always undiscovered treasures. But they're not. I've eaten in many that were just gross."

They stepped inside and instantly noticed the strong coffee and cinnamon fragrance and the smell of bacon and toast.

"How's that aromatherapy for you?"

"Wonderful."

Once they were seated, they let the waiter's recommendations be their breakfast.

"So what are your plans for the rest of the day?" Keith asked.

"This afternoon is clear, but this evening we have dinner with all the clients," Allison replied. "Your day? What's in store for you?"

"I've got a few more things to tend to before I leave. I might work out or read or catch a movie. I don't have anything particular in mind."

"Who is going to take care of your dog while you're gone?"

"The family of one of the guys in the unit, Desmond, who's my best friend, will take care of Caisson. And Des's wife will check on my house every week or so."

"That's good," she responded. "I'd like to invite you to dinner this evening, but it's a closed event. If I can finagle you a seat, do you want to come?"

"Not if you're going to get in trouble. How's tomorrow night look for you?"

"Okay. Tuesday and Wednesday are full, and I'm supposed to leave Wednesday night."

"Plan to come to Weymouth tomorrow night. I can either drive in and pick you up or, if you're comfortable with it, meet you at the subway stop. Let me know. Also, I'd like to drive you to the airport Wednesday. Okay?"

"Yes, to both. I'd be game to take the subway."

Allison Redux

January 2010
Weymouth

It was dark by the time Allison got to Weymouth late Monday afternoon. Keith met her at the East Weymouth commuter rail station. It was a full moon and light reflected off the snow. Weymouth was bright. Christmas lights still shone in some of the trees and homes around the city.

"It's pretty here," said Allison.

"It can be. I like it here. But, you know, like in Arizona, everyone is tired of the heat when it is still 108 degrees in late September. By about the end of March, everyone around here is tired of winter."

They drove to his school. He still had his key to the building. He disarmed the alarm first and then opened the door for her. "This is work."

"Can I see your classroom?"

"Of course."

He led her down the hall a short distance. "This is it. The kids just started back at school today."

"You must really love what you do."

"I do. I do, indeed."

He unlocked the door and turned the lights on.

"Oh, Keith. It's just what a classroom should be. Lots of colors, oversized letters taped to the wall, and small chairs—and artwork on the walls." She went around and studied the essays and drawings and science posters on display, asking questions about the kids who created the artwork or wrote surprisingly detailed science reports.

"I'm envious. I don't ever get to interact with children in my job. All I get are office managers trying to keep me away from the doctors, while at the same time they try to get me to give them free product, and food for their staff."

"Oh, the kids can be a handful, believe me. And the pay, well, I'm sure you're making at least double what I make."

"Maybe. But money's not everything," she said. After looking around some more, she asked, "Do you want kids of your own?"

"Yeah, I guess. I don't think about it much, but I suppose it'll happen eventually. What about you?"

"I love kids, but finding a guy who wants kids and would be a good father, and then getting pregnant, is going to be difficult. Most of the men I've dated recently say they have no interest in kids. Plus, my dad, he was a good father. I have no doubts about my father loving me, like so many women I know do. That probably makes me pickier than I should be."

"You can always adopt or find a donor."

"Yeah, and I think about it, but I'm not ready to make that decision. I'd like there to be a father involved, not just a sperm donor."

"Oh."

She looked around the room some more and saw a large photo hanging on the wall. She walked over to it. "What's this?"

"We took a picture with the whole school and I hung it here so the kids would remember me."

"And this other one?" she asked, pointing to a smaller print.

"That's a photo from my first deployment."

She leaned in close to examine to it. "Was this before or after you got hurt?"

"Before."

She stepped back and said, "Thanks. I'm glad you showed me your classroom."

"Shall we go to my place now?"

"Yes."

It was a short drive to Keith's house. He had left his Christmas lights on.

"It's lovely, Keith."

"It's not much. It's small, but I like it. I've got a good-sized yard. I walk to work most days. Come on in. Watch out for Caisson. He's big, but he's a big cream puff. His nickname is Marshmallow."

They walked to the door and Caisson barked. "That's his way of saying, 'I'm glad you're home,'" said Keith.

He opened the door. Caisson looked at Keith and went up to Allison, stuck his nose in her crotch, and gave her the sniff test. She turned her waist away and squatted to pat him. She started talking to him too. Caisson sat down and leaned against her. He almost knocked her over.

"He likes you. That's means you're in."

"Well, good."

He showed her around the house. He had shopped for some premade gourmet food earlier in the day. Then it was dinner and talk and a news show. "Well, you're welcome to stay. In fact, I hope you will, but if you've got an early morning, I understand. I'll drive you back to the hotel."

"No. I was hoping for an invitation to stay."

He kissed her. "I'm ready for bed. This is truly way past my bedtime." He took her hand and led her to the bedroom. "It's a small bathroom. Please, you go first."

"No, you go ahead. It takes me a little longer."

In less than two minutes Keith was in bed. When Allison came out of the bathroom several minutes later, he said, "Those are definitely not granny panties."

"I went shopping today and bought these going-to-meet-someone undergarments."

"Come on over here and let me introduce myself."

He drove her back to the hotel early the next morning.

On Wednesday afternoon, Keith was fidgety around the house. He was thinking about Allison and wondering how to express what he was feeling. Even more than wanting to express his feelings, he wanted to better understand what he was feeling. She was wonderful. The last four days had been great. She was everything he remembered and so much more. However, he was also both frustrated by and resigned to the fact that he was deploying in seventy-two hours and she was heading back to Phoenix today. Still, she was terrific. He had to tell her that he hoped that when he got back from his deployment, she would want to see him. He felt that he couldn't ask her to wait for him. They had been reacquainted for barely four days. However, he hoped she would tone down her dating life while he was gone so he could at least have a chance when he got back.

He planned to leave at three o'clock to pick her up at four for her five-thirty flight. As he reached for his coat, he heard a car door shut and the car drive off. In the garage he pushed the button to open the garage door. As it lifted, it revealed Allison standing there with her luggage.

"I changed my flight plans. I want to go to the farewell party and ceremony with you on Saturday. Okay?"

Keith was instantly filled with a joyful rush and tingling in his stomach. He walked up to her, kissed her, took her luggage, and escorted her into his house. "This is the best going-away event I could ever hope for, and probably the worst one too. I'm going to miss you very much."

"I just couldn't leave. It's been so nice being with you. When I went online last night to confirm my seat and get the boarding pass, I found myself unable to click on the Go button. I was thinking about you so much. I postponed my flight until Sunday."

"I am very happy you did."

"So what happens now?"

"Well, I guess we talk some and just enjoy our time together."

"Yes, I do want to talk about us. But I meant, what's going to happen over the next seventy-two hours?"

"Tonight, my plan was, after I got back from dropping you off at the airport, for Des and me to catch a late movie and then grab a beer. Tomorrow, there's a get-together in the teachers' lounge. Tomorrow night, nothing. Friday, nothing. Then Saturday I report to the armory. There's the farewell party, and lockdown."

"Lockdown?"

"I'm officially mobilized as of Saturday. Once I report I can't leave. We stay, sleeping on cots if we have to, until the buses come. The last time they came quickly. No one wants to linger in the armory any longer than we have to. And that's it. We're gone until we roll back in."

"Oh. Whew. I couldn't imagine what you meant by lockdown. Well, don't change your plans for me. Go to the movies."

"Are you kidding? I'll have enough of Des over the next year or so. One less night will be good for me. I'll give him a call now."

"I'd like to go to the movies."

"That's okay too. Maybe he can find a babysitter and we can double-date with him and his wife." He stopped for a moment. "You're welcome to come to the get-together at the school tomorrow, but, you know, you're going to be the subject of conversation on Friday. I mean, I've seen how my coworkers slice and dice someone every time one of them gets a new boyfriend, gets divorced, gets new shoes, whatever. Everything is fair game."

"I know. It's how we are sometimes, and it's okay. I'm sure they're very nice."

"They're terrific."

The next day, holding hands, Keith and Allison walked into the school at noon. The assembly in the gym was at twelve thirty.

"How do you want me to introduce you? Old friend? Fellow Zoni?" he asked.

"Surprise me."

"Great. Thanks."

They went to Sharon Wells' office first. "Hi, Sharon," Keith said. She stood.

"This is my girlfriend, a girlfriend redux actually, Allison. Allison, this is Sharon Wells, my boss, the principal, and a really good friend."

"I'm very pleased and a little surprised to meet you. I had no idea

Keith was dating anyone," said Sharon as she extended her hand to Allison and gave Keith a friendly glare.

"It's a pleasure to meet you. We dated in high school and reacquainted over the last half year or so."

"I'm glad you're here, Keith. You made it just in time. Shall we go?"

"Yup."

"So, Allison, what do you do?"

They walked out the office door toward the gym. When Keith walked through the door, the din increased to a cacophony as many of the children tried to talk to him at the same time. The gym was decorated with red, white, and blue balloons. There were several large sheet cakes frosted with an American flag; these had been donated by one of the supermarket bakeries. In the background, a CD played John Philip Sousa brass marching music through the cheap gym speakers that were only used a couple of times a year, for the annual dance instruction and giggle festival. All the teachers hugged Keith and welcomed Allison. Dr. Monroe was there. He wished Keith the best and offered a firm and lengthy handshake. In his hand was a challenge coin from his unit in Vietnam. Their eyes met for a moment. There was a brief nod, and then they broke the grip.

The party lasted an hour, and then the kids went back to class. Sharon walked Keith and Allison to the parking lot. "Keith," she said, "no more deployments. I want a good night's sleep. You keep me awake at night like my own son used to." She hugged him again. "Come back as soon as you can."

"Thank you very much for everything, Sharon."

She let go of Keith and turned to Allison. "Here's my card. Please e-mail me so we can stay in touch while Keith goes and saves the world." They hugged. Keith and Allison walked back to his house.

"Thanks for taking me. Sharon is very nice."

"Yes, she is."

When they got back to his house, Keith announced he was going for a run. Then, like a married couple, they had dinner, watched some TV, and went to bed.

Saturday, Keith was up even earlier than usual. Report time was 1100. He was ready by 0600 and restless by 0630. Allison had hardly had any sleep. He prepared breakfast and ate heartily. Allison nibbled at a muffin and left most of it on the plate.

He put both duffel bags in his car.

"That's all you need for a year?" she asked.

"Yeah, I could probably get what I really need into one duffel, but I'm bringing some books and a few extra things. Every minute of deployment is not riveting and full of action. Lots of boredom."

Around 0800 Keith said, "Let's take a drive and then go for a walk. We'll go the long way to the armory."

"Okay."

They had made arrangements that Allison would drive Keith's car back to his house and spend the night there. The next day, Desmond's wife, Savanna, would take Allison to the airport.

Keith drove her to the site of the army's former Fort Revere in Hull. The old fort was located in the Point Allerton section of Hull, very close to the veteran gathering spot Dr. Monroe and Joe Donahue had taken him to. He did not tell Allison about that time in his life or the therapeutic cellar.

Keith explained that Hull was a town on some land that jutted into Boston Harbor. The old fort had been used during the Revolutionary War to bomb British ships as they left the harbor, and then it was used again during World War II as a coastal artillery base for the protection of Boston Harbor. It was cold, and the wind swept off the ocean. "I like the view from here," he said, gesturing toward the 360-degree view. Boston was in one compass point direction, and the tip of Cape Cod was in the opposite direction. He took several pictures of Allison by herself. Then he found a spot to set the camera for a picture of the two of them together. He set the timer and ran back to Allison, slipping on the ice and snow and almost tumbling down the hill. He ran to stand next to her three times before he got one good photo of the two of them together.

"I'm going to wait for you, Keith," said Allison.

"I was hoping you'd say that."

"Why didn't you ask me?"

"Didn't seem like it was my place to."

"I want to see what we have when you get back."

"And I want to see a lot of you when I get back."

"Be safe, Keith. I'm so very scared that something might happen."

"I will. I promise. I have a lot to come home to, and you're at the top of the list."

They stood in a silent embrace for a long time. Allison was the one who said it was time to go. They returned to the car and began a slow drive to the armory.

When they turned onto Central Street, they discovered a police car blocking the road. "Sorry, the road is closed. You'll have to go around on High Street to get by."

"I'm reporting to the armory."

"Okay. Then you get to go through." The officer held out his hand. "Thanks for your service, and be safe."

Keith shook his hand and said thank you.

"The road will open up again after the families have left. We'll escort you out of town when the buses show up."

They drove through the roadblock and weaved their way through the maze of cars, soldiers, family, friends, and well-wishers. Keith maneuvered the car to a place where Allison could easily get out and then return on a fairly direct course to his house. He gave her the keys and retrieved his duffel bags.

"I'm going to have to check in. All the other soldiers and I will be busy for the next hour or so. General Carter and a few others will say a few words while we are in formation. Then we break and the party begins. If you want to hang with Savanna and her family, I know she'd like the company."

"She and Des are very nice. I'm a big girl, but it would be good to sit with someone."

"Okay," Keith said. "Gotta go." He kissed her. "See you in a little bit. I love you." The last sentence fell out of his mouth.

"I love you too."

They stared at each other, neither quite sure what to say or do. Keith spoke again. "I, ah, I'm not sure where that came from, but it's true."

"I know. Me too. This is a very intense moment in both our lives, and I'm not going to question whether it's relationship love, or friendship love, or caring concern. I'm taking it for what it is," she said, and tenderly kissed him. "Go do your soldier thing."

Keith disappeared behind the building. Forty-five minutes later he was in formation in the drill hall. The hall was stuffed to capacity with a couple of hundred deploying soldiers at parade rest, at least three hundred family members and friends, several dozen dignitaries and media, other guard and reserve soldiers, and a few sailors from the nearby Quincy Navy Reserve Center who had friends in the 1058th. The speeches were brief, filled with many references to duty, honor, courage, and service. Then they fell out. The caterers put the food on display, music played, and the hugs and tears began. At 1700, the last guest left the armory and all the doors were locked from the outside. A special security detail from a Massachusetts Guard MP unit guarded each door, with orders to not open the doors until the unit deployed, except for a fire or an emergency.

At 0200 the buses rolled up. At 0251 the 1058th departed for Iraq—again.

Three days later, Keith arrived at Fort Sill for predeployment refresher training. It was the first chance he had to check his e-mail.

To: sgtmo@weymouth.ps.zyx
Sent: Sunday, January 10, 2010, 09:53:23
From: allison23@alivepharm.zyx
Subject: Miss You Already

Hi, Keith. I don't know when you'll be able to read this e-mail. I hope you are safe. Although I believe in God, I don't go to church often, but lately I've been praying for you and all of our service members. I actually stopped in the airport chapel here for a minute.

You looked so strong and proud standing there in your uniform in formation at the armory. I was and am proud of you.

I refused to cry until I was out of the building. All I can say is, I was not the only sobbing woman in the parking lot that day.

I spent the night with Savanna and her family. It would have been hard for me to be alone at your house that night. She knew it and insisted I stay with them. We talked for a long time. Des is a lucky guy. Say hi to him for me.

Your car is in the garage, and Caisson is with Savanna.

Well, they just called my zone for boarding, so I have to say good-bye for now. I can't tell you how happy I am to have spent the last week with you. Everything was wonderful. I don't look forward to my next trip to Boston, because you won't be here, but I'm already looking forward to your return celebration.

Write when you can. If you need anything, let me know and I'll get it for you. Be safe. Come back to me. I look forward to the future.

Love you.

P.S. Please e-mail me a copy of the photo you took of us at Fort Revere.

HOME

October 2010

Heavy Lift

October 2010
Iraq

Everything was muted, muffled, and unclear. When Des opened his eyes, he could sense light, dark, and nondescript shapes. Sounds were very small. It was as though noise were very far away. He thought he should be able to hear his breath and his heart beating inside his head, but no. There was no ambient noise. Then a lone sound moved slowly into and out of his perception. It seemed as though he should be hearing the sound of a metal tray clattering on the floor. There was no reason for him to think that, but that was what his mind said the sound should be associated with. But what should have been the sudden burst of that abrupt sound took a long time to arrive and move the tiny hair cells in his ears—and even longer for the hollow noise to dissipate.

There was nothing for him to taste either. His mouth wasn't dry and he wasn't thirsty, but he felt only the slightest contact when his tongue touched his lips. He couldn't tell if they were chapped or not. He pressed his teeth together. There was a hole. He knew he should have all his teeth. He pushed his tongue through the hole. The gap was on the left side, top and bottom.

His mind was aware of his body, but his thoughts and perceptions were unclear. He knew he was lying on his back. When he moved his hands to orient and brace himself, he felt his hand resting on something, but the sensation was a lethargic resistance emanating from his fingertips. He could not tell if he was feeling something flat or round, sharp or dull, coarse or fine. He thought he should be concerned about what he was not feeling, but the torpor of his senses also numbed his alarm.

Then he identified a smell. It was clear, pleasant, and not powerful. There were other smells too, but his muddled thinking prevented him from using the smells to help him figure out where he was. He thought he should be concerned about the daze, but he couldn't muster enough cognition to raise his unease to a level of concern. He formed the question *Where am I?* in his mind. And *How long have I been here?* crept into his limited thought stream.

Lavender, that was the smell. It came to him suddenly. It was nice. He drifted back to sleep.

He heard the distant voice say, "Sergeant," and he wondered if it was someone yelling for him from far away or if whoever was calling was trying to get the attention of another sergeant.

"Sergeant." He heard the voice again and turned toward the origin. It seemed to be coming from his right. He opened his eyes and found that things were clearer than they had been before. *How long ago was that?* he wondered.

"Hey, good. We've been worried about you," the voice said. He thought it might be a male talking to him. Whatever gender it was, it moved into his field of view. He discerned the shape of a body and a dark color. He remembered that he could not see the last time his eyes had opened. *Maybe I'm not blind,* he thought.

"How are you feeling?" asked the tiny voice.

He wanted to answer, but he was unsure of how or even what he was feeling, and the sound coming out of him was raspy, halting, and inconsistent.

"Good. Don't overdo it. Your body has had quite a shock. I'm going to go get the rest of the team. Be right back." The faint voice dissolved to nothing, and the disconcerting, isolating silence returned. His thinking was better than the last time he stirred. He tried to hear something. A distant indistinguishable noise murmured.

He saw the shape and color turn and disappear out of view. *I have to move,* he thought. *I have to make sure I can move.* Then the memory of what had happened launched. He remembered the explosion, the car with the Iraqi family being tossed onto its side, a

Humvee disintegrating, and a massive cloud of gravel, sand, dust, and rocks blocking out the daylight.

He struggled to move and could not. He tried to fathom why he could not. He released his muscles and panicked. *What if my legs are gone? Am I still a man? My arms? I have to move to see if I can. What if I can't?* The fear of his body being unable to respond if he tried to stand overwhelmed him. He heard sounds of people talking and saw more shapes and colors enter the field of view around him. It took an enormous effort, but he started to roll to his side in order to sit up. There was something restricting his left side from helping with the motion.

A distant female voice said, "Easy. Let me help you."

He felt a hand on his hip. It wasn't pushing him down; it was helping him roll.

"Good. You need to move a little. Get your blood circulating," said another female voice. This voice seemed closer. He noticed some background noise also, a hum like an air conditioner.

He released his exhausted muscles and flopped onto his back, panting. *I have to know what I still have,* he told himself. He forced his arms into action and sensed his right arm respond. He wondered if he was experiencing an ambulatory version of phantom limb pain. His right hand came in contact with his thigh. He bent his knee up and felt his lower leg follow. He was relieved that his calf and foot were intact.

"Good. Nice and easy. Gentle movements," spoke a kind male voice.

He tried to move his left hand toward his leg, but it would not go. He moved his right hand toward his left side. As he did, he felt his penis and scrotum react as he dragged his hand left, but the perception came though his hand. His groin processed no sensation. He pressed on toward his left leg. *Why is this so laborious?* he wondered. At the same time his hand arrived on his left inner thigh, the male voice said, "Your left side took a lot of the impact from the explosion. I know what you're thinking, and I can tell you that you've got your arms and legs and genitals. You came out of surgery about twenty-four hours ago. It's too early to say for sure, but things look good."

At the word *explosion*, he remembered seeing someone or something fall out of Keith and Hamblin's Humvee and drag itself on the dirt.

He fell back and tried to force his vision and hearing to be more acute. It hurt. He counted six people standing in his room. He thought the group might consist of four females and two males. He stopped forcing his senses and exhaled deeply.

"What happened?" he croaked. He sensed an awkward delay from the people in his room. Then he felt a hand on his shoulder.

"You were part of a convoy, an RPG hit one of the Humvees, and there was a firefight," said the kind male voice.

By his delicate tone and candid manner of speaking, Des thought the male speaking might be a chaplain. His mind flashed and replayed the gritty scene of Hamblin crawling toward the passenger side, opening the door, and reaching into the flames and pulling Keith out of the Humvee. They both dropped to the ground.

"What happened?" he croaked again, squirming to see the face of the speaking man.

"That's it for now. We'll talk more later. Rest. Your body needs rest."

"No. Tell me." He felt a subtle drowsiness quickly overwhelm him. It made him sleep. The next time he awoke, it was to the image of Keith and Christine on the ground next to the burning Humvee. There were bursts of gunshots and eruptions of dirt when bullets hit the ground. Hamblin struggled to drag Keith to safety. She tried to keep her weapon pointed at the source of the bullets while, with her other hand, she grabbed the handgrip on the back of Keith's body armor vest. A hail of bullets raked the soldiers from the ground up. Christine fell to the ground and then struggled to cover Keith with her body. Another burst of bullets stopped her effort.

"Hey, Sergeant Jarvis," said a different voice, "you awake?"

He heard the voice more clearly. It seemed closer too. He opened his eyes and the room came into view. He still smelled the lavender.

"Yeah. I'm awake."

"How are you feeling?"

"Been better."

"No doubt. Can I get you anything?"

He thought for a moment. "Yeah, ginger ale." *Odd,* he thought. *I never drink that stuff.*

"I'll get you some. Anything else? Your recovery is going well, and the doctors and everyone on the team wants you to get some food onboard and to start moving as much as you can with your casts."

"Crackers or whatever you can give me. Can you tell me what happened?"

"Yeah, when I come back we'll go over what happened since you got here and what's going to happen. And there are some people here who want to talk with you about what happened before you got here."

"I was in an explosion."

"Yes, you were."

"A couple of soldiers were hurt very badly."

"Yes. We know, Sergeant. Before we go down that path, I'm going to get you the ginger ale and something light to eat. We'll prop you up and talk. Your physical recovery is going very well, but we've got to address the other injuries. So, to begin, what do you prefer to be called? Master Sergeant? Sarge? Sergeant Jarvis or Desmond?"

"Des is fine."

"Okay, Des. Rank really doesn't matter here in the hospital. I'm Dennis. Be back in a couple of minutes."

Des relaxed his muscles and settled deeper into the mattress. A great emptiness rolled across his thoughts as, one by one, pieces of memory fell into place. The events of the explosion burst through the emptiness. Although the sequence of events that appeared in his thoughts was not linear, he knew what had happened.

"Des?"

"Yeah."

"I'm going to prop you up. Your left leg and arm are in casts, but we've got enough bend at your waist and room to sit you up. Eat a little, and then we'll transfer you over to the chair."

"You're going to have to speak louder. I can hear, but it's faint and not clear. It's like someone mumbling into a crappy cell phone."

"How's this?" said Dennis, louder.

"Better," Des replied. "Keith and Corporal Hamblin are dead, aren't they?"

"I don't know the names of the soldiers who died, but three people died as a result of the explosion. Two soldiers and a baby."

Des closed his eyes and saw the face of the Iraqi baby. The infant had reminded him of his own children and how much he was looking forward to getting home and seeing them. He closed his eyes and turned his face away from Dennis. Tears formed and seeped through his eyelashes and onto the pillow. He heard footsteps come into the room.

"Des," said the kind voice.

He turned to the voice but did not open his eyes. He raised his right arm and placed the crook of his elbow over his eyes.

"It is very sad about the soldiers and the baby. I know all of you were part of the same unit. I assume you were close in some way."

"Keith was my best friend. Corporal Hamblin was a very promising soldier—young, energetic, and just fun to have around."

"I'm very sorry that you lost your friend."

"Who are you?" Des asked.

"I'm Chaplain John. Most people call me Padre. You can call me whatever you want."

"I'm not very religious."

"You don't have to be. I'm here to listen, not to preach. We can pray if you want. Sometimes I guide conversations, but mostly I'm here to help people cope. We're in a shitty place, and the friggin' worst things in the world are happening to us and around us. I try to keep it from taking a bigger chunk out of our souls than it has to."

"You're the first preacher I've met who swears."

"I'm a priest, but I'm also a soldier. I have a wide-ranging vocabulary."

"How'd the baby die?"

"I don't have all the facts, but I'm told it was already sick. My guess is it was the sickness, the explosive concussion, and the bullets. Everyone in the car was hurt in the firefight. The Iraqi family was very close to the Humvee that took the hit."

Padre John was silent a moment and then asked. "Do you have children?"

"Yes, three. But what you don't know is that Keith has, had, a baby on the way."

"That's complicated news. A baby is always a wonderful gift, but in this case there's tragedy associated with it too."

"Keith didn't know he was going to be a dad."

"Oh."

"Dennis," said Des, "can I have that ginger ale now?"

"Yes, of course."

"Do you want to take a break?" asked Padre John.

"No. I'd rather get the dump of details now, so I can work on putting it to rest in my mind."

"It's going to be with you forever. It'll never go away."

"I know, but the sooner I get the whole picture, the sooner I can move it to a less destructive place in me."

"That's very wise thinking, Des, but be careful you don't take on too much too quickly. There's a guy from your unit and another from intel who want to talk with you. They have to complete a 15-6 investigation and get as much information as they can from you. You can stop or take a break whenever you want."

Dennis and a woman with a name tag that read "Felicity" stepped toward the bed, slowly moved him to a sitting position, and slid the rolling tray near his good arm.

"Keith reacquainted with an old girlfriend, Allison, just before we deployed. She came to the deployment farewell get-together and ended up becoming friends with my wife. Allison told my wife about the baby, and my wife told me. Allison didn't want Keith to know because she didn't want to put any pressure on him while he was here. I talked with her one time and she said that if Keith didn't want to know his child, a son actually, then Allison was going to keep the baby and never bother Keith. I told her that Keith loved kids—he was a teacher after all. He'd be a great dad and would be very happy at the news that he was going to be a father. She said that she, too, thought he would be a great father, but all she wanted was for him to come back. She made me promise that I wouldn't tell him, so I didn't."

"That's a pity."

"Yeah. Padre, do you know if she knows? For that matter, does my wife know I was hurt?"

"I don't know, but I have a staff of a half dozen people whose sole purpose is to get answers for wounded service members. We will look into it and find out."

"How long ago do you think you were hurt?" asked Felicity.

"I don't know. Feels like a long time ago. A week, maybe ten days."

"Less than four days ago."

"I've lost all sense of time."

"That's not unusual, and because of the mechanism of injury, you were sedated very heavily in order to give your neurological system a chance to rest. You weren't put in a coma, but we tried to significantly dull everything so your body had a chance to calm down."

"You were successful. I don't remember anything. Well, actually I remember one thing."

"What was that?"

"It's weird, but I smelled lavender a couple of times."

"You're not weird," said Dennis. "Felicity here is a big believer in aromatherapy and she puts lavender oil in the rooms of patients. You're one of the few who said they smelled it."

"Did it help?" asked Felicity.

"It was pleasant, so I guess it helped."

She smiled. "I'm glad to hear that. Are you doing okay now? You've been sitting up talking for several minutes now. We don't want you to overdo it."

"I'm okay. I can talk to the investigators, but then I'll want to lie down and take a nap." He turned to Padre John. "Can you let my wife know I'm okay?"

"Yes. I will."

"Can you find out about Allison, too?"

"Yes, of course."

"My gunner and the rest of the convoy?"

"Your gunner is okay. You were closest to the explosion. You took the worst of it. The gunner is okay. He's shaken up and upset about what happened, but he went home two days ago. The rest of the convoy, I really don't know about them, but no other injured came through here."

"Okay," said Dennis. "What's going to happen now is you'll talk to the investigators and rest, and then the surgeon will come by and see how you're doing. You'll get a PT eval, and then the medevac coordinator will be here to explain the process of going stateside. You'll stay at Walter Reed for a while. Then you'll be in the care of the VA and physicians back home." He looked at his notes. "You're from Massachusetts, right?"

"Yes. Just outside of Boston."

"Good. You'll get great care because Boston is such a medical mecca."

"Padre?" said Des. "One last thing. Please get in touch with my unit, the 1058th. I want to know what's going on. I'm sure there will be a memorial or something for Keith and Christine, and I am going to be there for it."

"I'll find out."

"Send in the investigators."

Des watched as Dennis went to the door and gestured for the two soldiers investigating the event to come in. They greeted Des, expressed their sympathy, and asked him to describe what he remembered about the day, urging him to provide as many details as possible about the stop and subsequent explosion.

Des relayed the story as best as he could remember. As he spoke, he recalled more and more detail. He asked the investigators questions and learned that about a quarter mile away a microbus had stopped and pulled onto the shoulder. After the RPG hit the Humvee, the microbus raced forward and started shooting at the convoy. There was some confusion, but within moments, the gunners in the convoy and all the soldiers retuned fire. The four men in the microbus were killed. Medevac helicopters were on scene very quickly and evacuated Des, his gunner, the Iraqi family, Sergeant Morris, and Corporal Hamblin to the hospital.

Padre John came back in and told Des that his wife knew that he was hurt.

"She knows I'll be okay, though, yes?" asked Des.

"Yes. She took the news hard, as you might expect, but was relieved to know you'll be okay."

"Where's Keith and Christine?"

"They were repatriated two days ago."

Stand Down

Des watched the fall New England landscape reveal itself through a window next to his head as he lay in a stretcher rack on an air force C-17 medevac plane approaching Otis Air Force Base on Cape Cod. Fall had reached southern New England. The trees were wearing color, but he knew that whatever climatic, geographical, and astronomical events had created the foliage display left the fall colors muted this year. In places, the gold, red, and green leaves intermixed in an indistinct display beneath the overcast sky.

He was grateful his recovery had gone well enough that he would be home for Keith and Christine's funeral. He, along with Padre John and the medical staff at the hospital, pushed hard for him to move through Walter Reed as quickly as possible and arrive in Massachusetts in time for the memorial service.

Savanna had traveled to Dover Air Force Base in Delaware to meet him when he first returned to the United States. She sat next to him on the flight to Otis. At the Cape Cod air base, numerous members of the 1058th and Massachusetts National Guard dignitaries greeted them when the tailgate lowered to the ground and a corpsman rolled Des's wheelchair down the ramp. An ambulance waited to transport Des to the South Shore Hospital in Weymouth, where he was to meet with the veteran services coordinator and, if he was not feeling strong enough, be admitted overnight.

He went home and spent the night with his family.

On the flight, Savanna told him about Keith and Christine's

return to Massachusetts. Des imagined how their aircraft looked as it landed at Otis and parked parallel to the solemn ranks of soldiers, airmen, coast guardsmen, sailors, and marines at attention amid the sad fall colors. Reserve and guard centers from throughout the state sent representatives to honor the fallen soldiers. Not since World War II had Massachusetts experienced the death of two of its resident military members on the same day.

Savanna told him she had stood with the 1058th commanding officer. The crew chief left the plane first and greeted the CO. She signed the documents to muster Sergeant First Class Keith Morris and Corporal Christine Hamblin. The ramp at the back of the aircraft then slowly lowered to the ground, and the pallbearers entered the plane and carried the flag-covered coffins off the plane and into two hearses. McDonald Funeral Home in Weymouth offered to hold onto the bodies until the details for the memorial service at the Hingham armory had been set.

The state police led the procession out of the base, off the Cape, and onto Route 3. Four motorcycles led the procession. The hearses were embedded between two trucks of the 1058th and Humvees driven by two soldiers. Farther back in the procession, more trucks belonging to the 1058th escorted their fallen comrades. TV news trucks set up on bridges spanning the highway, and a helicopter provided a live feed to all the local stations. Several more news agencies were set up at the armory. The convoy route was to carry the bodies past the armory and then on to the funeral home in Weymouth.

"There is an escort for you, too," Savanna said.

Des saw the yellow ribbons and well-wishers waving from bridges over Route 3 and on the surface streets as he returned to his home in South Weymouth. When at last the vehicle turned onto his street, he saw that in his neighborhood yellow ribbons adorned every streetlight, telephone pole, and bush in sight. A large banner hung over the street reading, Welcome Home.

His children, nieces, nephews, siblings, in-laws, friends, coworkers, and neighbors, and anyone with even a remote connection to Des, applauded and cheered as the ambulance rolled to a stop.

Savanna, his two brothers, and his oldest son lifted him out of the ambulance, and the swarm began: his children first, and then everyone else. He greeted and smiled at the crowd. Many in the crowd wanted to hug him, but he quickly fatigued. Savanna saw it and said he had had enough. She thanked everyone and ordered him into the house.

Savanna told him that a local carpenter had built a wheelchair ramp up to the side door closest to the driveway and the garage.

Neighbors had gathered around and continued applauding as he went into his home. People shouted, "As soon as you can, come on over for a cookout"; "If you need anything, just ask"; "You're our hero"; "God bless America"; and "God bless you." Reporters stayed a respectful distance away, and photographers used their longest lenses to get the shots of the reunion.

Savanna said all the neighbors had been very helpful while Des was gone and really poured on the helpfulness when they heard he had been hurt. She went outside and spoke with the neighbors. Once inside the house, Des asked her to go back out and thank everyone again.

Des settled into the living room and asked his son and brothers if he could have a few minutes. They stepped away. He sat there and looked around. Everything was the same, except for a few new pictures of the children, Keith, and himself on the mantel. Savanna came back into the house, settled onto the floor next to him, and laid her head against his thigh.

"How are you doing, lover?"

"A little overwhelmed." He reached his hand to her head and stroked her hair. "I'm sorry, babe."

"What are you sorry for?"

"I put you through a lot."

"I knew what I was getting into when you asked me to marry you fourteen years ago on that parade field at Fort Polk. I got used to the idea that all I had to deal with was your frequent absences, but when that stupid captain showed up on the doorstep, it scared me to death." Savanna started crying. "I know he is a close coworker of yours at the armory, but he should have known to not show up in uniform, without having called first, on the doorstep of anyone whose spouse is off to war.

"When I saw him standing there with those two other soldiers, a knife went into my heart. I thought you were dead. I couldn't open the door. Finally, Jesse from next door came over and talked with them. And then he told me you were alive but hurt. In a matter of seconds, I went from being so scared to being so concerned. Then the captain explained the nature of your injuries. When he said it looked like you were going to fully recover, I got so mad at you for scaring me so bad."

"I'm sorry."

"And now I'm even more upset 'cause you're hurt and you lost your best friend and I'm yelling at you."

"I understand." Then the lump in his throat and the tears in his eyes hit.

"And that scares me even more." Savanna continued, "If something were to happen to you and we couldn't be together anymore, I'd never find anyone who understands me the way you do. I require a lot of patience and understanding from a man, and you're the only man who was ever patient with me continuously." Her sobbing continued. "You scared me so bad."

They sat together. "I love you. I missed you. I'm sorry," Des said.

"You know what was the hardest part of when the casualty assistance officer and soldiers were here, after the initial terror?" asked Savanna.

"What?"

"When they told me about Keith and Christine. I had to tell them about Allison and the baby. They had no knowledge of her. I gave them her phone number and address in Phoenix. Then I called her."

"How'd she take it?"

"Hard."

"How's she doing now?"

"Okay. You can ask her yourself. She's here."

"Where?"

"She and Keith Jr. are close by. When you're ready, I'll let her know."

"Keith Jr., wow. She gave him Keith's name. Keith lives on."

"Last name too."

"It's going to be hard to see her and the baby. Keith talked a lot about her."

"Yes, it will hurt. She knows it too, but she's had a little more time to prepare."

Desmond sat in silence for a few minutes. Savanna held his good arm and gently touched his damaged one. "What do you need?"

"A little time."

"It's almost dark. Do you want to go out to your fire pit?"

"You know, that's a great idea. Wish I had a cigar."

"Honey, neighbors and complete strangers have been dropping off boxes of cigars, alcohol, desserts, and food. Everyone has been so generous. There's probably twenty-five boxes in the basement. I think I can find you one. I'll get your brothers to hoist you out there. I'll tell everyone to take off. The kids are staying at Andrew's tonight. I think you need some time to adjust."

"Before you do that, kiss me, babe. I need to have something to hold onto for a little while."

"You got me to hold on to for a long while, and all the kisses you want."

"The memorial tomorrow is going to hurt."

"Yes, it is. I'm at your side the whole time, but I need you beside me too. I loved Keith like a brother, and I'm very fond of Allison. The baby is precious. I need you as much as you'll need me."

She left and asked his brothers and a couple of the neighborhood men to take Des to the fire pit and start up a fire for him. They were happy to help. They started the fire and stacked wood close by his right side so he could feed the flames. Then they left. Savanna brought a cigar, his lighter, and a blanket. "I bet our crisp New England nights are a lot cooler than the scorching Iraqi ones."

"Yeah. I love New England. I missed it."

"I love it too. I guess I have the best of all worlds, the glory of being born and raised in the South and the privilege of living and loving in New England. Don't stay up too late."

"How am I going to get back in the house?"

"Every neighbor and family member, and probably just about everyone in town, is standing by waiting and hoping for a chance to help you. Here's my cell phone. Call the house number when you're ready to come back inside. Your brothers are staying at one of the neighbors'. I'll call them and they'll bring you back inside.

"Enjoy your cigar, babe."

The fire burned warm. He drew a deep puff on the cigar and slowly let the smoke out into the New England sky. His thoughts were scattered. He felt relief at being home, but he dreaded the memorial. He was appreciating Savanna. Their marriage was not any easier or necessarily harder than anyone else's. Right now it was good. Maybe this event would bring about a permanent change. He thought about Allison, and then she spoke.

"Des?"

"Allison. I was just thinking of you."

"Can I sit with you?"

"Please. Sit close, on my right-hand side."

She dragged a lawn chair over and sat close. Caisson was with her and sat next her. Des opened the blanket to welcome her to sit with him. She placed the blanket around her shoulders and settled in close to Des, resting her head on his shoulder. They stared into the fire. Every once in a while Des took a puff and released the smoke into the cool autumn night. He maneuvered the cigar into his left hand. By leaning his head forward and arcing his arm, he had enough range to smoke the cigar. Eventually, he tossed the nearly done cigar onto the coals. He leaned his head gently against hers, and she started crying. Des remained silent and stroked her head.

After a bit, he spoke again. "I'm going to miss him, Allison."

"Me too, and you have a much deeper history with him than I do."

"True, but he loved you."

"How do you know? I mean, we were together less than a week before you guys shipped out."

"He told me."

"How did he say it? What were you guys talking about when he said it?"

"We spent a lot of time together. A deployment is like a marriage in that you can drive each other crazy and still look out for and take care of each other. We came across a copy of *Boston Magazine* and there was an article about the North End in the off-season. He talked about how much he enjoyed being there with you. Then he said, 'Des, I can't stop thinking about her. I can't wait to see her.' I said, 'Sounds like you love her.' And he said, 'I do. I love her.'"

"It makes me a little less sad to hear that."

"Where are you staying? I'd like to meet Keith Jr."

"We're in Bart's room."

"I didn't know you were in the house."

"Savanna woke me up and said I should come out here and sit with you. She's watching the baby. She loves kids and she's so good with him. I feel like I don't know what I'm doing half the time, and the other half of the time I think what I'm doing is wrong. Then she calls and we talk, and I guess I'm doing the right things."

"You and little Keith are welcome here anytime. If you want, you can live here. There's always room for more."

"Thank you. Savanna already made the offer, but my family in Phoenix is great and they're already very involved with little Keith. My mother and father are here to pay respects to Keith and to the girl, sorry, Corporal Hamblin."

"I want to meet them."

"You've seen them. They were in the crowd out front when you got home. They knew Keith years ago."

"Back when you two dated in high school?"

"Yeah. But I want to ask about something else. Will you and Savanna be Keith's godparents? I want him to have a connection to you. If he knows you, you can help him know the kind of man his father was."

"It would be our honor. Thank you."

"So how will tomorrow go?"

"I'm not sure. The CO is going to call or come by in the morning and brief me. I think there will be a lot of guests."

"What do I do?"

"You stay close to Savanna and me. We're going to need each other."

The fire was dying down. Allison kissed Desmond on the cheek and said good night.

At two o'clock in the morning Des called Savanna. Minutes later, four men arrived and carried him into the house and helped him into the temporary bed set up in the living room. Savanna joined him and fell asleep. Des lay awake the rest of the night.

Funeral Honors

October 2010
Weymouth, Hingham, and Cape Cod

The same day Desmond arrived back in Weymouth, the coffins holding the remains of Keith and Christine were unceremoniously and quietly transported to the 1058th armory. Twenty-four soldiers, four noncommissioned officers, and four officers constituted the honor detail that would guard the coffins throughout the solemn night in the armory. Carefully, they removed the coffins from the hearse and carried them to a bier set up in the drill hall. Four soldiers, one noncommissioned officer, and one officer stood as guard at all times throughout the night. An officer stood at the head, the noncommissioned officer stood at the foot, and four soldiers stood at each point of each coffin. Every two hours, after standing at rigid attention, the honor guard was relieved and another detail took over the watch. They would do this until the coffins were loaded onto one of the unit's trucks for transport to Camp Edwards and ultimately the Massachusetts National Cemetery at Bourne. The final rotation of the funeral honors detail would be harnessed and secured in the bed of the truck and stay at attention with the coffins until the truck and accompanying convoy arrived at the National Cemetery on Cape Cod.

Throughout the night, quietly and without guests, family members, or media, past and present members of the 1058th and other Massachusetts National Guard soldiers silently entered the solemn drill hall, paid their respects, and noiselessly disappeared back into the night.

At seven in the morning, the soldiers returned and started

preparing the property for the unit's memorial service. Members of the unit, plus family, friends, and guests, were all welcome to the memorial in Hingham. Another, much larger memorial gathering was expected on the base. The governor of Massachusetts, the adjutant general, senators, Congress members, other members of the Massachusetts National Guard, members of other armed services, and the public were invited. The gates securing the base were open to all who wanted to attend. The guards were to wave everyone through without an ID check.

The town of Hingham and the surrounding communities had always been supportive of their soldiers. Residents turned out by the thousands each time the unit deployed and returned. For its most recent deployment, three thousand residents had turned out at five in the morning in ten-degree weather to wish the unit well. Even more turned out and welcomed the unit when they returned, before the news of Keith and Christine's death settled over the unit. Today would be no different. Thousands of mourners would line the streets of Hingham and Weymouth as the convoy wound its way to Route 3.

The doors of the armory opened to the public at nine in the morning. By nine forty-five, almost four hundred guests and soldiers filled the armory, the parking lot, and the street surrounding the building. Desmond, Savanna, their children, Allison, and Keith Jr. entered. The commanding officer greeted them. She took Keith Jr. in her arms and promised Allison that she and the baby would forever have a place in the heart of the unit. She then offered Allison an open-door invitation to call on the unit whenever she was in the area. She mentioned that Keith had not named a beneficiary for his serviceman's life insurance, but the legal officer had been in touch with Keith's mother and the money would be going to Allison and the baby. She kissed the baby, hugged Allison, and gave the baby back. She then gave a double-handed shake to Master Sergeant Jarvis's good hand and said she hoped he would be returning to the unit soon.

Wallace Hodges greeted Desmond outside the door to the drill hall. He expressed his great sorrow for the loss of Keith and Christine. Des asked about Pearl. Wallace replied that she was in an assisted living community.

The service began promptly at ten. The commanding officer of the 1058th spoke. She welcomed everyone and noted the tragic circumstance for which they were gathered. She spoke about the mission of the unit, the uncertainties of being in the service, and the difficulty of the day and weeks ahead. She concluded her remarks and introduced the chaplain. He covered similar themes and then spoke more eloquently about the beauty of the individual soldiers and the sometimes harsh realities and abruptness of life.

Keith had not stated a religious affiliation anywhere in his mobilization papers. However, Christine had stated a preference for Episcopalian. The chaplain introduced the minister from her church in Weymouth. He spoke about Christine and the verve she brought to everything. He quoted a simple poem and ended with a brief prayer.

The senior enlisted member of the unit spoke, sharing a couple of personal stories about Keith and Christine. He invited any guest who wished to say anything to come forward. A few did. They talked mostly about Keith and his patient way of developing soldiers. One of the younger female soldiers talked about how much fun Christine was, how kind she was, and the fact that she had just decided to go to school to become a teacher.

The last person to speak was a sergeant major no one recognized.

He introduced himself. "I'm Sergeant Major Anthony Steele, US Army retired. I met Sergeant Morris on his first deployment to Iraq. I'm saddened by the loss of both Keith and Corporal Hamblin.

"I've been to too many of these kinds of memorials over the years. This is my first journey to a memorial for a guard soldier, and it's the same and yet different. When there's a death of a soldier connected to a unit on post, it's no easier. The whole post grieves. Here, the post is smaller, but the greater community grieves too.

"Because this is an armory and not a base, I was curious about the last time a soldier from this place had died in action. With the help of the Massachusetts National Guard Museum, I discovered it was Corporal Alexander Borland. Like Sergeant Morris and Corporal Hamblin, Corporal Borland was killed near the end of his war, World War One. He died October 23, 1918, in Verdun, France, less than a month before the armistice.

"There certainly have been others from this town who died in service to America and others who were augments to units that originated from this armory. Corporal Borland, though, until two weeks ago, was the last soldier killed in action directly linked to this armory.

"I'm certain that on that sad day two weeks ago, Corporal Borland was filled with great sorrow for the death of these two soldiers.

"It took me a while, but I found my way to Jesus. I am a Christian. Believing as I do, I like to think that Keith, Christine, and Alexander are together with other comrades in heaven and that it is a peaceful place.

"I want to close with a quote from the French writer Antoine de Saint-Exupéry. Perhaps it throws a little light on the experience these two fine Americans shared. Exupéry said, 'One can be a brother only in something. Where there is not a tie that binds men, men are not united but merely lined up.' Perhaps it speaks to all of us who choose to serve and to those who support us. We are united.

"Sergeant First Class Morris and Corporal Hamblin are bound together forever. Thank you."

The memorial ended promptly at eleven o'clock. The soldiers opened a path through the crowd. The honors detail stepped aside, and the twelve pallbearers stepped up to the caskets. Slowly and stately, the remains were transported to a waiting army truck. Carefully, each coffin was set in the bed and secured. A bungee cord held the flags in place. The honor guards were harnessed into place and resumed standing at attention. A motorcycle escort from the state police was in the lead. All the vehicles in the convoy rumbled to life, and slowly the convoy moved forward. It moved down Central Street to Main Street and then turned onto Commercial Street in Weymouth. The Hingham and Weymouth police departments set up numerous traffic control points so the convoy could move unobstructed. The convoy turned onto Middle Street, where every vehicle stopped except the one carrying Keith and Christine. It continued by itself and turned onto Academy Avenue and slowly made its way to its namesake elementary school. The street was crowded with residents waving American flags. The solitary truck slowly turned into the school driveway.

The driveway, parking lot, and circular drop-off were lined with all the children, teachers, parents, and administrators from the school and throughout the school system. Dr. Monroe, Sharon Wells, Shawna, and high school students who had previously been in Mr. Morris's classes were there. Slowly the truck traversed the pavement. The students tossed flowers onto the truck and into its bed. Many were crying. Some of the smaller children did not understand the significance of what had happened; they waved at the parade. The honor detail soldiers wept, but they did not relax or wilt in their sacred post.

The truck departed the school and returned to Middle Street, where it slid back into its place in the convoy. The convoy wound its way through Weymouth to the Route 3 South on-ramp and completed its journey to Cape Cod, Camp Edwards, and the national cemetery.

Throughout the procession, there were hundreds of residents standing along the side of the route, most with their hands over their hearts. Many veterans wore their old uniforms. On the highway to the Cape, the bridges were lined with citizens and banners honoring Keith and Christine.

The convoy crossed over the Cape Cod Canal and exited Route 6 at Route 130. The base commander ordered a usually closed entrance to be opened. The convoy rolled to a large recently groomed parade ground. There, already present, were hundreds of soldiers, guests, and dignitaries. Attention was called as the convoy broke apart to it assigned spots. The truck carrying the fallen soldiers rolled to a stop next to the reviewing stand. Brief and sincere words were spoken, the muster was called, and a report of all present or accounted for was given to the commander. The commander read the citation for Sergeant First Class Morris's second Purple Heart and Corporal Hamblin's first. The crowd knew she was being considered for a Silver Star for her efforts to reach Keith and help him following the explosion.

The muster ended, but the soldiers stayed. Only family—Keith's father and mother, Sergeant First Class Jarvis and his family, Allison and her family, and Corporal Hamblin's family—would go on to the shelter in the Bourne National Cemetery for final military honors.

There, the funeral honors rifle team fired three volleys each for Keith and Christine. "Taps" was played once, and two flags were folded and presented to the families.

One by one, everyone left. The cemetery workers took the caskets to be interred.

Two weekends later, the guardsmen of the 1058th were back at the armory for the drill weekend.

He who has gone, so we but cherish his memory,
abided us, more potent,
nay, more present than the living man.
—Antoine de Saint-Exupéry

With respect to, and in memoriam of, former 1058th soldier and fallen Weymouth police officer Michael Davey, and Corporal Alexander Borland, the last soldier killed in action directly connected to a National Guard militia unit at the Hingham armory.

This story is fiction. It is not an accurate documentary of the 1058th's role in Iraq or in any other way. The characters and events in this story are fictitious and are in no way representative of any member, or any activity, of the 1058th.

Glossary of Military Jargon

556: bullet size

9-Line: a series of steps/instructions to initiate a medical evacuation

15-6 investigation: an informal army process involving detailed fact gathering, analysis, and recommendations based on those facts

activated: when a reservist or National Guard member's status changes from reserve component to active component

ACU: army combat uniform

ADSEP: administrative separation (discharge) from the service

AGR: active army duty guard and reserve members

AOR: area of responsibility

Article 134: charge of adultery under the Uniform Code of Military Justice

bag farm: bags of fuel at isolated spots throughout Iraq that served as fuel stops for convoys

Camp Edwards: Massachusetts National Guard training site on Cape Cod

CASH: combat army support hospital

challenge coin: a unit coin given for appreciation and respect; also, used to initiate a drinking challenge

charlie-foxtrot: phonetic alphabet *CF*, for "clusterfuck"; something poorly planned or poorly executed, and/or a lousy outcome

CHU: containerized housing unit

COB: contingency operating base

COMREL: community relations

DFAC: dining facility, chow hall, mess, galley

E4, E5, E6, etc.: enlisted pay grades E1–E9

FOB: forward operating base

frag: the murder of a military member by other members of the same military, often disguised as an accident or friendly-fire incident

FUBAR: fucked up beyond all recognition

Guns or gunner: nickname for a soldier manning a high-caliber machine gun

Hajji: term to describe Iraqi people regardless of sex or ethnic background

HEMTT: heavy expanded-mobility tactical truck

HET: heavy equipment transport

Humvee: high-mobility multipurpose vehicle

IBA: body armor

IED: improvised explosive device

JAG: Judge Advocate General's Corps—military lawyers

KBR: Kellogg, Brown, and Root, a contractor providing a variety of services to overseas military bases

KIA: killed in action

LT: lieutenant

LZ: landing zone

mob: when a unit or an individual is mobilized; usually refers to reserve and National Guard members

MP: military police

MRE: meals ready to eat

NCO: noncommissioned officer

NVG: night vision goggles

OIF: Operation Iraqi Freedom

PA: public affairs

PM: preventative maintenance

POS: piece of shit

PT: physical training; working out

PTSD: post-traumatic stress disorder

PW or POW: prisoner of war

redeploy: a deployed unit or soldier going home

RPG: rocket-propelled grenade

S2: intelligence / security / information operations

S4: logistics operations

SA: situational awareness

SF: Special Forces

stop-loss order: an order preventing service members from leaving the service at the end of their enlistment

TBI: traumatic brain injury

UCMJ: Uniform Code of Military Justice

VA: Veterans Administration

volun-told: told to volunteer for something

WARNO: a preliminary notice of an order or action that is to follow

𝕷𝖎𝖓𝖊𝖆𝖌𝖊 𝖆𝖓𝖉 𝕳𝖔𝖓𝖔𝖗𝖘

1058th TRANSPORTATION COMPANY
(LINCOLN LIGHT INFANTRY)

Parent unit organized 26 January 1903 in the Massachusetts Volunteer Militia at Hingham as Company K, 5th Infantry

(Massachusetts Volunteer Militia redesignated 15 November 1907 as the Massachusetts National Guard)

Mustered into Federal service 19 June 1916 at Framingham; mustered out of Federal service 9 November 1916 at Hingham and reverted to state control

Called into Federal service 25 July 1917; drafted into Federal service 5 August 1917

Reorganized and redesignated 12 February 1918 as Company K, 3d Pioneer Infantry

Demobilized 4 August 1919 at Camp Devens, Massachusetts

Reorganized and Federally recognized 23 August 1920 in the Massachusetts National Guard at Hingham as the 9th Company, 1st Coast Defense Command, Coast Artillery Corps

Reorganized and redesignated 1 January 1922 as the 329th Company, 1st Coast Defense Command, Coast Artillery Corps

Converted, reorganized, and redesignated 7 June 1923 as Company K, 101st Infantry, an element of the 26th Division (later redesignated as the 26th Infantry Division)

Inducted into Federal service 16 January 1941 at Hingham

1058th TRANSPORTATION COMPANY
(LINCOLN LIGHT INFANTRY)

Inactivated 29 December 1945 at Camp Patrick Henry, Virginia

Reorganized and Federally recognized 15 March 1948 in the Massachusetts Army National Guard at Hingham as Battery D, 704th Antiaircraft Artillery Battalion, and relieved from assignment to the 26th Infantry Division

Ordered into active Federal service 15 March 1951 at Hingham; released from active Federal service 15 March 1953 and reverted to state control

Reorganized and redesigned 1 October 1953 as Battery D, 704th Antiaircraft Artillery Battalion

Reorganized and redesignated 1 February 1958 as Battery D, 704th Missile Battalion

Reorganized and redesignated 1 May 1959 as Battery D, 1st Missile Battalion, 241st Artillery

Reorganized and redesignated 15 April 1962 as Battery D, 2d Missile Battalion, 241st Artillery

Converted, reorganized, and redesignated 1 March 1963 as the 1058th Transportation Company

Consolidated 1 April 1975 with Headquarters Detachment, 164th Transportation Battalion (see ANNEX) and the 393d Medical Detachment (organized 2 December 1972 at Hingham) and consolidated unit designated as the 1058th Transportation Company

Ordered into active Federal service 20 September 1990 at Hingham; released from active Federal service 4 June 1991 and reverted to state control

Ordered into active Federal service 3 February 2003 at Hingham; released from active Federal service 15 June 2004 and reverted to state control

Expanded 1 September 2006 to form Headquarters and Headquarters

1058th TRANSPORTATION COMPANY
(LINCOLN LIGHT INFANTRY)

Detachment, 164th Transportation Battalion at Dorchester and the 1058th Transportation Company at Hingham (hereafter separate lineage)

Ordered into active Federal service 8 January 2010 at Dorchester; released from active Federal service 11 February 2011 and reverted to state control

ANNEX

Organized and Federally recognized 28 June 1940 in the Massachusetts National Guard at Chelsea as Headquarters Battery, 2d Battalion, 241st Coast Artillery

Inducted into active Federal service 16 September 1940 at Chelsea

Reorganized and redesignated 7 October 1944 as Headquarters Detachment, 187th Coast Artillery Battalion

Inactivated 1 April 1945 at Fort Ruckman, Massachusetts

Redesignated 8 July 1946 as Headquarters Battery, 772d Antiaircraft Artillery Gun Battalion

Reorganized and Federally recognized 29 January 1948 in the Massachusetts Army National Guard at Hingham as Headquarters Battery, 772d Antiaircraft Artillery Gun Battalion

Reorganized and redesignated 1 October 1949 as Headquarters Battery, 772d Antiaircraft Artillery Automatic Weapons Battalion

Reorganized and redesignated 1 July 1951 as Headquarters Battery, 772d Antiaircraft Artillery Gun Battalion

Location changed 13 May 1952 to Boston

Reorganized and redesignated 1 October 1953 as Headquarters Battery, 772d Antiaircraft Artillery Battalion

1058th TRANSPORTATION COMPANY
(LINCOLN LIGHT INFANTRY)

Location changed 4 November 1957 to Chelsea

Reorganized and redesignated 1 February 1958 as Headquarters Battery, 772d Missile Battalion

Reorganized and redesignated 1 May 1959 as Headquarters Battery, 2d Missile Battalion, 241st Artillery

Converted, reorganized, and redesignated 1 March 1963 as Headquarters Detachment, 164th Transportation Battalion; location concurrently changed to Hingham

HOME STATION: HIngham

CAMPAIGN PARTICIPATION CREDIT

World War I
Meuse-Argonne

World War II
Northern France
Rhineland
Ardennes-Alsace
Central Europe

Southwest Asia
Defense of Saudi Arabia
Liberation and Defense of Kuwait
Cease-Fire

War on Terrorism
Campaigns to be determined

1058th TRANSPORTATION COMPANY
(LINCOLN LIGHT INFANTRY)

DECORATIONS

Presidential Unit Citation (Army), Streamer embroidered LORRAINE

Meritorious Unit Commendation (Army), Streamer embroidered SOUTHWEST ASIA 1990-1991

Meritorious Unit Commendation (Army), Streamer embroidered SOUTHWEST ASIA 2003-2004

Cited in the Order of the Day of the Belgian Army for the action in the Ardennes

BY ORDER OF THE SECRETARY OF THE ARMY:

ROBERT J. DALESSANDRO
Director, Center of Military History

1058th TRANSPORTATION COMPANY (LINCOLN LIGHT INFANTRY)

Design approved November 30, 1951

Shield: The shield is the coat of arms of the 241st Coast Artillery Regiment within a border, indicating descent from that unit. The shield is blue and red, indicating service of the parent organization as both infantry and artillery. (In the center is the device of the old Roxbury Artillery.) The white diamond is the badge of the Third Corps of the Army of the Potomac in the Civil War, and the falcon on the green hill represents Mont Falcon in World War II.

Crest: The crest is that for the regiments of the Massachusetts Army National Guard on a wreath of the colors (argent and azure), a dexter arm clothed blue, and ruffled white proper grasping argent, the pummel and hilt.

Motto: *Posset* (Latin), "It will be able."

Made in the USA
Middletown, DE
04 April 2017